BIG Sl

Richard Copestake

I
Ormskirk
P
r
i
n
t

This is a work of fiction with a message of hope. Although some events are drawn from the author's own experience, the characters are fictional, some serving simply as devices with which to develop and convey the message. Any similarity or resemblance to real people, living or dead, is coincidental and unintended.

© Richard Copestake 2020
ISBN: 9781716705137

Cover painting 'Big Shoes To Fill' © Susan Hodgkins 2020

The Ormskirk Imprint is a small publishing enterprise based in West Lancashire. It works on a not-for-profit, commission-only basis with any funds from book sales going, wherever possible, to a nominated good cause.

For Yumi and Hana

Autumn 1969. I Wish I Was Normal

Graham Skinner is the only boy on our road who can play football in his wellies. He can sprint, dribble, nutmeg defenders and once, when he attempted to score with an overhead bicycle kick, his welly flew off and landed in Mr. Spooner's back garden. He had to go round and ask for it back.

He never wears a coat. Instead, he tucks his two jumpers into an old baggy pair of corduroy trousers which are held up with a length of old washing line, knotted tightly at the waist. He can do all sorts of amazing things; spit twenty feet, hold his breath for two and a half minutes, and just last week, he turned his eyelids inside out. He lives with his mum. His dad seems to come and go as he pleases, often disappearing for months on end. Graham says that this is because his dad works for MI6, and like James Bond, he must be ready at a moment's notice to be sent on a secret mission anywhere in the world.

When I ask him to tell us about his latest assignment, Graham says that he can't because the information is classified and both he and his mum have had to sign The Official Secrets Act.

I just happen to mention this to my dad later and he comments, "Official Secrets Act my arse. The only information that comes out of that boy's mouth can be summed up in two words; the second word begins with 'S' and the first word is BULL."

I'm not allowed out without a coat and I have my name sewn into the inside in bright red indelible ink: *Colin Sparrow.* The same label can be found in every jumper, shirt, vest, pair of trousers, socks and underpants that I own. I could never work in the field of espionage like Graham's dad. If I was caught by the KGB, my identity would soon be compromised.

Under the glare of a bright white interrogation lamp, they would laugh, "So mister British agent Sparrow, vee know all about you. Yes, Colin is your first name isn't it? How do vee know that? Beecuz vee haf read your underpants! Ha ha ha ha!"

007 Skinner and 008 Sparrow live about a mile from the Cadbury's chocolate factory in south west Birmingham. When the wind's in the right direction, we can smell the cocoa butter in the air. About two miles in the

other direction is the huge Austin car plant at Longbridge. Everyone's dad on our road, except Graham's, works at one or the other.

This area of Birmingham is where *Crossroads* is supposed to be set; in the village of King's Oak. There are actually real places nearby called King's Norton and Selly Oak. This soap opera is obviously made on a very low budget because the set wobbles when a door is opened or closed too quickly.

The acting is wobbly too. Amy Turtle, the Motel's cleaner, often forgets her lines, or says them before another actor has finished. Sometimes she even answers the telephone before it rings. Graham says there was once an episode when *she* was suspected of being a Russian spy, but I never saw it.

Our back gardens open out on to a meadow of long grass that stretches all the way down to the Merritt's Brook. It's our little slice of paradise, where we spend whole summers building dens in the fields and dams in the water. But the brook is becoming sick. Only last year, we used to catch sticklebacks and tadpoles in its crystal-clear water. But since the housing estate has been built, several overflow pipes have appeared, emptying their foul-smelling contents into the brook, killing all vegetation, weed and fish life in its wake. The only things that live in it now are rats.

Mum is constantly shouting at us, "Don't go playing in that brook, you'll catch Weil's Disease!"

So of course we always go down there, and more often than not, end up falling in. After hours of thwacking our socks against the trunk of a tree to get the water out of them, I go home wearing socks that have stretched to about five feet long, thinking Mum won't notice. Of course, she always does and I get sent straight to bed, regardless of what time of day it is.

Jeremy Potts also lives on our road. He's the only kid who owns a proper leather case ball; the sort that if you head it when wet, will leave you with the imprint of its laces on your forehead for the rest of the day. But Jeremy's a selfish cry-baby. Every time one of his goals is disallowed, he takes his ball home with him. His mum doesn't approve of him mixing with us. She says when he gets into the grammar school he'll find new friends, then eventually, go to university and become a doctor. She says we are a bad influence and nothing will ever become of us.

My mum says the Potts are "all kippers and curtains."

We don't have enough players for a proper game of football. Instead of 4-4-2 we play 0-0-4 with rush-back goalies and jumpers for goalposts. I personally don't do much 'rushing back'. In fact, I don't do much running at all. I model myself on Birmingham City's local hero from Kings Heath, Bob Latchford, supreme goal hanger, who can score with both head and feet without breaking into a sweat.

There are two reasons why I don't run very much on the football pitch. Firstly, I have to play in my coat. I am sworn never to take this off, even in the 70-degree heat of mid-summer. Now let's be honest, how many professional sportsmen do you know who perform at their optimum, or break world records *in their coat?* Exactly.

Secondly, I sometimes struggle to get my breath. It's a long story. Apparently, when I was born, I 'failed to thrive' which is why I'm so small and thin. I had pneumonia and then for a while, they thought I had cystic fibrosis because I couldn't digest my food and I kept getting one chest infection after another. I'm now nine and thankfully, that diagnosis was wrong, but Mum is still terrified every time I get so much as a cold, so when I'm let out, I go everywhere in that coat.

My illness does have its advantages though. My poor digestion results in something called flatulence, which is a posh way of saying I fart a lot. My nickname at school is 'Methane' and the fact that I can fart at will earns me great respect amongst the boys in my class.

They are always urging me on, "Go on Methane, I dare you to do one in assembly, in front of the whole school!"

"Yeah, do an SBD (Silent But Deadly) during the Lord's Prayer, that would be hilarious! Ha ha ha!"

The girls however, are disgusted. This includes the lovely Doreen Drysdale, to whom I am invisible at the best of times. Doreen is the Form Captain and plays recorder in assemblies. Once, she stood very close behind me in the dinner queue. Her tray was pushing into my back and I was blushing from the neck up. I was so nervous, I put salad cream on my apple crumble by mistake. She didn't notice though. In fact I don't think she even knows I exist. But I know that will change some day because I believe she is 'the one'.

Everybody in the world has somebody out there who is their exact match, their perfect partner, and we all have to just go out there and find them. For some, it may be difficult; their match may be living on the other side of the world. But fate will provide them with at least one opportunity when their paths will cross.

For others it may be a whole lot easier. *Their* match could be right under their very noses; in the same town as them, on the same street or, as in my case, in the same class at school as them. How will you know they are the right one? You just will. You will see stars and hear bells ringing, just as I did that day in Reception class, when Doreen bounced a wooden cupcake off my head for daring to try and come into the Wendy house with the girls instead of playing in the sandpit with the boys.

My coat and general appearance however only emphasise my invisibility. On those days when I don't have a chesty cough and Mum allows me to go to school, it takes an age before I am allowed out of the door to face the chill of the autumn wind. Graham has always gone on ahead of me, while I am dressed as if for an expedition with Captain Scott to the South Pole.

"But Mum, I'm late. I haven't got time for all of this palaver."

I start to perspire with all the layers; two jumpers, long trousers over shorts, double socks inside wellies, shoes wrapped up in newspaper and carried separately. Duffel coat, gloves and scarf. Pack-a-Mac over the top of the duffel coat, balaclava and then a leather, fur-lined skull cap or helmet with adjustable chin strap that makes me look like a cross between Biggles and a Russian cosmonaut.

"Hold still will you and stop yer mythering!" she says as she pulls the strap tightly.

"Oww, you're strangling me!"

The skull cap goes over my balaclava and underneath the duffel coat hood, which is also fastened at the neck. The result? Total deafness and absence of any peripheral vision. Last week I was nearly killed by a fire engine with sirens going and lights flashing.

By the time I get to school, I'm pouring with sweat and late for registration. The corridor is deserted. Coats are already on their pegs and everyone is in their classroom. I panic at my peg, trying to get this lot off. The leather helmet amplifies the sound of my own heavy breathing as I battle with the buttons of the Pack-a-Mac. These macks have stiff, welded-on plastic buttons, impossible to undo when your hands are cold.

I try to pull it off over my head like a jumper, but I have a head the size of the Mekon's, due to the balaclava, hood and helmet.

"Come on! Come on!" I shout.

I force the two top buttons undone and squeeze out of it like a straitjacket, dropping it to my ankles. Duffel coat next, which has easy buttons. Then I kick off wellies, looking for the sock that's come off inside. Long trousers off, shoes on, leave the whole mess in a pile on the floor, then I sprint down the corridor until – wallop – I run into Mrs. King, my teacher, coming round the corner, leading my class down to assembly. I didn't hear them coming because I'm still wearing my leather skull cap and balaclava. I lip-read her telling me off and see all the other members of my class laughing with no sound coming from their mouths as they pass.

I have to go back to the cloakroom to take this sound-proof headwear off.

When I open the squeaky hall door, with my hair all plastered down flat with sweat, everyone looks round. I mouth the word "sorry" as I close the door behind me. There are no chairs left, so I have to stand at the back. Doreen is just about to start playing 'Morning Has Broken' on the recorder.

After her performance, before the Lord's Prayer, Graham and some of the boys look round at me for The Fart. But I daren't do it. Mr. George is standing right next to me. I only know up to "Give us this day, our daily bread". I am hopeless at the line about trespassing. I just know it's got lots of Ss in it, so I just say, "Pssst. … pssst … psst."

At this point in the prayer, I open one eye and look at Doreen sitting on the floor at the front. With palms together, eyes clenched shut, she looks like an angel. I calculate that one of her thighs is about the same girth as my chest. I wish I had the slightest sign of a muscle anywhere on my body.

I often read the advert in the Sunday Express for the 'Bullworker' device which guarantees that after just two weeks' use, no one will ever kick sand in your face again. I wish I could get the money to buy one. Instead, I have to make do with weights I borrow from the kitchen. My favourites are Mum's old-fashioned metal smoothing irons that I use like dumbbells. I also tie a shopping bag of books to each end of a broom handle and try to lift it above my head. I lock myself in the bathroom to do this.

After ten minutes of pumping iron, I get the tape measure and record the thickness of my arms. The measurement is always the same. Biceps: six inches.

Meanwhile, the mumbling chant of the Lord's Prayer is almost lost at certain points, but ends strongly on the words we all know.

"For thine is the kingdom, the power and the glory, Forever and ever, amen."

We have to keep our eyes closed at the end while Mr. Brown's voice asks us to pray to God to help those painfully thin children in Africa.

I also say a quiet prayer for myself. I ask from the bottom of my heart to be normal. To not spend half my life in bed or on the toilet. I wish I could just buy a bag of chips or an ice cream, without having to take a whole load of tablets. I wish I could go swimming or go on school trips. I wish my new teeth weren't brown, discoloured by the tetracycline they gave me as a baby before they knew the side effects; the staining of second teeth. I wish I had a chest or even just the slightest hint of a developing muscle anywhere on my body. Most of all, I wish Doreen could see past my skeleton frame and brown teeth and realise that I *am* the one for her.

Please God, I pray, I'll never ever ask for anything again. Let me be normal. Let me be well. Let me grow and put on weight. If you do that, I'll never forget and I'll never ask for a single thing again. Forever and ever, Amen.

Mr. Brown's voice jolts me, "Colin Sparrow, at the back."

I open my eyes to see two hundred heads turning round in unison towards me.

"Master Sparrow, while I'm sure your devotion to prayer is admirable, you *can* open your eyes with the rest of us, unless that is, you were asleep standing up?"

The whole assembly hall erupts into laughter.

When I get to the classroom afterwards, my face still glowing, I give Mrs King my absence note for yesterday. Mrs King has a massive collection of my notes in her bottom drawer. When I hand it to her, she doesn't even bother to read it but just drops it in with the rest. I think she hates me because of the mess I've made of her register. In the column beneath my name is a mass of red circles, like drops of blood dripping or a nasty rash spreading down a page of otherwise uniform, neat blue ticks.

Graham and I have been split up. He has to sit at the front, next to the teacher's desk, within reach of her wooden yard stick. I sit at the back, next to the radiator, by the window. I love the window. I spend hours looking out of it, watching the orange sky in the afternoon, the games lessons on the playing fields and the horse chestnut tree which sheds its polished conkers on to the path below.

I make a mental note where each one lands, so I can find them at play-time. Mrs. King is constantly telling me to stop looking out of the window but she can't move me because the headmaster has given strict instructions that due to my health, I am to sit next to the radiator.

Above me on the back wall, is a huge picture of Apollo 11 landing on the moon. The whole class did it together last summer term to mark the occasion.

My particular part, which I am very proud of, is the mother ship in orbit around the moon, piloted by Michael Collins. No one else wanted to do this bit, they all wanted to paint Neil Armstrong and Buzz Aldrin getting all the glory, planting the stars and stripes on the moon's surface. Neil and Buzz have smiles on their faces because the surface of the moon seems like quite a jolly place with the flag and that beach ball they throw. They bounce around having fun.

But I deliberately drew Michael looking out of his small porthole with a serious, worried look on his face, because he has the much harder job. He is all alone in space in that spooky, cold, empty metal ship, thousands of miles away from the earth, with infinity stretching out before him. If there is a malfunction, the ship might break free from the moon's orbit and start drifting away from the earth and out of the solar system into a black never-ending nothingness.

Eventually his air will run out. And because there is no gravity and he is in a vacuum; his dead body will float forever. It will never decompose. He will be just floating in space for eternity, with a pencil, a screwdriver and a paper cup, all similarly floating.

Yet he doesn't get any of the credit from NASA. The newspaper front pages are all of Buzz and Neil. There might be a tiny head shot of Michael tucked away somewhere on page six. Yes, I can definitely relate to Michael Collins. Another Colin, even if it is his surname.

I have a second picture on the wall, in the 'Work Of The Week' corner. It's an annotated picture (with arrows and labels) of Timothy

Winters, the tough little kid with the dirty face, ragged clothes and toothless smile.

I had to take it to show Mr. Brown in his office. He was full of praise and said Timothy's appearance was uncannily accurate, yet also reminded him of someone he knew but couldn't quite place.

Eventually, I owned up, "Well, actually I based it on Graham Skinner."

"Really?" he replied. "Ahh yes, I can see the resemblance now."

On a Friday afternoon, everyone in my class goes swimming at Northfield public baths. I'm not allowed to go in case I catch cold. I am the only kid in our class who can't swim. Instead, I have to stay in and help Mrs. King sharpen pencils and collect in all the books.

I take a sneaky look in Doreen Drysdale's English book. On the inside cover she's drawn a heart with an arrow through it, with TB 4 DD written underneath.

Later, as I walk home on my own, I try to work out who TB is. I'm sure it's an illness, one of the few I haven't had. Then a terrible thought crosses my mind. It can't be Tony 'toss-pot' Barton in 3B can it? No, don't be stupid, he's really ugly.

Then finally I realise. Of course, it's Tony Blackburn, the Radio One DJ. I've seen a picture of him on the inside lid of her desk. Tony frigging Blackburn.

Why do all the girls fancy *him?*

I spend the rest of the walk home dreaming about what *I* might become when I grow up. A disc jockey obviously gets all the girls. Or maybe an actor, like Roger Tonge: Sandy in *Crossroads*. He's very small and thin too, and he's done all right.

One thing's for sure, I won't be living round here, working at Cadbury's or Longbridge, or working as a teacher like Mrs King; bags under her eyes, permanent scowl on her face, wearing the same shapeless, chalk-dusty clothes every day and driving that Morris Minor Traveller. No way.

By the time I'm twenty, I'm going to be living in London, working in television, married to Doreen Drysdale, and driving one of those new Ford Capris.

My Left Hand. 2002

In the mirror in the bathroom, Colin Sparrow takes a good, long, hard look at himself. Aged forty-two. He looks older. His hair, which is thinning on top and going grey at the sides, is in need of a cut. The once frail frame is now supporting a bit of middle-aged spread. His shoulders have broadened and his previously puny chest has grown hair and is starting to sprout 'man-boobs'.

He never did get one of those Bullworkers. There is still that twinkle in the eyes, but the bags underneath are beginning to dominate and that worried expression has turned into a scowl.

I contemplate my reflection. I read somewhere once that the human body completely renews itself after seven years. In that time, every cell of the body will have died and regenerated. Skin, hair, fingernails, teeth, bones, blood, heart, brain, all will have grown new versions of themselves.

Of course, some cells are renewing at a faster rate than others. Some renew every day; some might take the full seven years. It's as if my body is slowly and continuously making a facsimile of itself. The new body is based on the old, so it's almost an exact copy.

But as we grow, or put on or lose weight, extra cells are added or taken away. And of course, some cells, after they have died, don't renew at all which is why we get old. Therefore, gradually over time, like a Chinese whisper, the next facsimile is slightly different to the last, and our appearance imperceptibly changes from day to day.

That all means that *this* Colin Sparrow who's looking back at me now is a completely different Colin Sparrow to the one who was nine years old in 1969. In fact I will be half way through my fifth different body since then. Another body, another person entirely. If I'd seen this now familiar face staring back at me in the mirror back then, it probably would have frightened the life out of me.

I can still just about see the boy's face, but it's like a garden that's become overgrown. You have to really look hard to see the original lines of the lawn and edges of the borders underneath. So, if this is a completely different body to the one I had seven years ago, I have to ask myself the logical question: "Is my body *me*?" If my body is changing all the time, which part of me is constant? While pondering this, I casually glance at my watch and the alarm bells suddenly go off.

What the hell am I doing? Philosophising at the sink like this! I'm going to be late!

After a shave and a shower, I dress hurriedly and give up on a half-sipped cup of tea. I put on my dusty jacket and notice the bulging pockets, overflowing with teaching paraphernalia: detention slips, sticks of chalk and whiteboard marker, Denise Payne's absence note for last Thursday, a circular from the head, a confiscated laser pen, masses upon masses of tissue paper and a bunch of keys so large they could belong to the jailer of the Tower of London.

I make a mental note: *Empty pockets when you get a minute.* I pick up my briefcase in the hallway and close the front door as gently as possible so as not to wake my wife Emm and daughter Lily who are still asleep upstairs. I leave the Astra on the drive for Emm to use, and I walk in, as the school is relatively close by.

I leave early enough so as not to have to mingle with the kids on the street going in to school. As I walk, I reflect on the achievements of Colin Sparrow aged forty-two, and become depressed. That's nothing to do with Emm and Lily. I love them both dearly. They *are* my two greatest achievements. But this job, it's not making me happy. It pays the mortgage and the bills, but I find myself more and more just living for the weekends and holidays.

I sometimes wish I could return to the past. Just climb into the Tardis and go back to my childhood, when life was so much simpler. When I didn't have a care in the world. Sure, I used to dread Monday mornings then too, but not like this.

It's during the last lesson of the day (English with Year 10, Set 5) when I first realise something is wrong with my left hand. We've just begun *Romeo and Juliet*. After finally getting them to settle down, and explaining what they have to do, work is set on the board and I have a quiet moment to myself.

I sit back in my chair, sigh and look out of the window.

Yes, forty-two years old and I'm still looking out of the window.

I watch the convoy of geese flying in from the arctic in V formation; honking silhouettes against the late afternoon orange sky. Further in the distance there is a huge, shape shifting flock of starlings gathering over the beech trees on Cooper's Hill, getting ready to roost for the night. Beneath are the stubble plains of Badgers' Field. It could almost be Keats' soft-dying day in 'To Autumn.'

"Sir."

I am summoned back to the real world by Gareth, class smart-arse, who is sitting with his hand up.

"Yes, Gareth. What is it?"

"Sir, I can't read your writing on the board. What does that word say on the end?"

"Capulet, Gareth. It says Capulet."

"Looks more like 'Copulate' to me."

There's a ripple of sniggering.

"It does not say that Gareth and you know it. So stop trying to be funny."

"It's not my fault I can't read your writing. Teachers are supposed to write clearly."

I go to the board, rub off the word and write in big letters: CAPULET.

"There. Can you read that? Good. OK, everybody, seeing as Gareth's disturbed us, put your pens down and look this way. Now, let's remind ourselves what we've learned so far. The Prologue tells us that there are two families, 'both alike in dignity'. Both powerful, respected families 'in fair Verona'.

"And where is Verona?"

"Italy, Sir."

"Good. Now Juliet, who is thirteen, is a Capulet. So what does that make Romeo?"

The giggles ripple out again. Someone asks, "Juliet is only *thirteen* Sir?"

"Yes, it was normal for girls of that age to be arranged to be married at that time."

"But Sir, that's younger than we are."

"Sir, is Romeo thirteen as well?"

"No, he's a bit older."

Silence.

"Now, where was I? Ah yes. So, if Juliet is a Capulet, what does that make Romeo?"

Gareth shouts out,

"A paedophile!"

The class explodes into laughter.

Someone asks, "Sir, shall we write that down? How do you spell paedophile?"

"No, *don't* write that down." I try to restore order.

"Now let's not be silly. As I said, it was quite normal for girls to get married at thirteen in Italy in the middle ages. Now what I'm asking is, what is Romeo's surname? I'll give you a clue, it starts with an M."

They continue to giggle.

"Come on, surely someone can remember. It's got eight letters."

A sea of lost faces stares back at me.

"OK, the second letter is O. What word has got eight letters and begins with M O?"

I prompt: "Romeo is a M…a MO…."

Gareth puts up his hand, so I give him a chance.

"Yes Gareth?"

"A molester Sir?"

"OK, now that's your final warning…"

"But Sir, it's got eight letters…M…O...L…"

"Yes, yes very funny. The word I was *actually* looking for is *Montague*. Remember? That's Romeo's family name. And the Capulets hate the Montagues."

"I'm not surprised Sir, if one of them is shagging their thirteen year old daughter."

"Sir, how do you spell 'molester'?"

"Sir, has 'paedophile' got an F in it?"

Thankfully, at that precise moment the bell goes.

"Right, we'll continue this discussion *sensibly* on Wednesday. I want you to read the Prologue again for your homework and answer the questions on the sheet. Put the chairs up please."

There's a stampede for the door, during which, only half the chairs go up.

"Walk! Walk!" I shout hopelessly as they thunder down the stairs at the end of the day.

After they've gone, I survey the wreck that is my classroom after an hour with them; the screwed-up paper on the floor, the pencil sharpenings on the carpet, the tipped-over chairs and the sweet wrappers carefully stuffed and concealed behind the radiators.

I put up the rest of the chairs then go round with the bin and pick up the worst of the litter so as not to annoy the cleaner, who I can hear bumping up the stairs with her vacuum.

I stand at the back of the classroom and look at the blackboard. My attention is drawn to my handwriting. Maybe Gareth's got a point. What's happened to it lately? I can hardly read it myself. The words seem to get progressively smaller and sort of spidery towards the end of the line and each line arcs downwards. Really messy.

I extend the fingers of my left hand, my writing hand, and wiggle them about. It's then that I notice that my fingers seem locked. They don't seem to be moving in a free-flowing motion, like they do on my right. It's as if they're moving through treacle. That's funny, I've not noticed that before.

I flex my fingers once more over and over, and this time notice a slight tremor. A moment of panic grips me that something's amiss with my left hand and fingers.

The cleaner's voice makes me jump. "Shall I clean the board Mr. Sparrow?"

"Yes, please, I'm done with it."

As she cleans off the mess, my fears go with it and I start marking homework.

I get home at about 7 p.m., just in time to play with Lily for half an hour before she goes to bed. She's two and should be sleeping right through by now, but she still wakes up every three hours and Emm and I are at our wit's end. She's also hit the 'terrible-twos', throwing tantrums in the daytime.

By the time I walk through the front door, Emm's face is pale and drained and she literally hands Lily over to me saying, "Your turn."

Tired as I am, I try to play the father's role dutifully. Her favourite song is 'I Am The Music Man' with me doing all the actions which she tries to copy. I start the first line:

> I am the music man
> and I come from down your way,
> and I can play.

17

What can you play?
I play piano…

She giggles in recognition and moves her fingers, "Pia…pia…piano, piano, piano, pia…pia…piano, pia…pia..no."

She runs in circles and squeals hysterically. While I'm doing the actions, I realise once more that the fingers on my left hand are not keeping up. They are not playing the imaginary keys of the piano as fluently as those on my right hand. Again, it's like they are moving through treacle and now my hand is starting to tremble. By the time we get to the trombone and umpah umpah umpapah umpapah umpapah, I stop the song and shake and flex my hand repeatedly. Lily is waiting for me to continue, but I'm seriously worried now and so decide to put her to bed, despite her protestations.

"LISTEN sausage, it's time to go up the wooden hill to Bedfordshire. No arguments."

I scoop her up and take her upstairs and get her settled. I read *The Gingerbread Man* to her. She dozes off and I turn off her Teletubbies bedside lamp.

In the gloom, I flex my fingers open again and wonder what it is, before I finally go downstairs.

Emm's at the sink tackling a mountain of washing up. Without looking round she asks, "How did it go today?"

"Trying to teach the finer points of Shakespeare to set five. Not easy."

She pulls the plug on the dishwater and dries her hands.

I sit at the table and she gives me my dinner. She usually eats hers with Lily as my arrival time can be unpredictable. She gives me a quick kiss on the lips, then curls up in the armchair with her book. I watch her for a few seconds; tall, elegant, beautiful, her long legs tucked under her.

I say, "Thanks Emm."

She looks up, "What for?"

"For everything."

She gives me a big smile, then furrows her brow and says, "Just make sure I get some sleep tonight mister. No tossing and turning and getting out of bed in the middle of the night to go downstairs. No wonder Lily keeps waking up."

She returns to her book. I continue to watch her. It's something I never tire of doing: looking at my wife.

The beautiful Mrs. Sparrow.

January 1970. Mr. And Mrs. Sparrow

My dad, Eddie Sparrow, has been a chocolate mixer at Cadbury's for the twenty-five years since the end of the war. When I ask him what he did in the war, he says he was a gunner in the DEMS (Defensively Equipped Merchant Ships). I've never heard of them, so I tell Graham and Jeremy that he was in the parachute regiment. They'll never know.

Dad's a bit old-fashioned and is going bald, which makes him look a lot older than some of my friends' dads. But there is one thing he's good at. My dad *does* know his stuff when it comes to football.

Ask him any question about any player and he knows the answer. He sometimes takes my older brothers, Brian and Rob, down to St. Andrews to watch Birmingham City play. Mum won't let me go any more, not after the last time. I only asked Dad a simple question when we got home, about what the crowd had been chanting at the referee.

"Dad, what's a wanker?"

Mum overheard and that was that. She said she didn't want me exposed to such language and I wasn't allowed to go any more.

I didn't even get the answer to my question.

As I said before, Dad is looking a bit ancient, which isn't helped by the really out of date clothes from the 1940s that he wears: billowing trousers, belted high above the waist and double-breasted jackets, as worn by his hero Fred Astaire.

He listens to Alan Dell's 'The Big Band Sound' on the wireless in the kitchen every Monday night, while bottling up his home brewed beer. No one else is allowed in during this complicated procedure, as the sound of Tommy Dorsey and Glen Miller reverberates around the house. I accidentally blundered in once to find Dad jiving away to Joe Loss and his orchestra, with a tube in his mouth, reaching for the next empty bottle to fill.

On a Friday night at 7pm he watches *The Virginian* in the front room before going down the club. He sits in his favourite armchair and cups his ears in the direction of the TV so he can hear it above the racket going on around him.

He reads the Daily Express, votes Conservative and is always going on about those "lazy buggers" at Longbridge who are forever on strike and ruining the country.

He says a lot of funny things. His favourite phrase is: "This ship is carrying too many passengers." We are all included in this classification of "passengers", even the cat and the budgie.

He says the working class are thick, that the TUC stands for "Troublemaking Under Class," and that he "wouldn't wipe his arse with the Daily Mirror".

I asked him once, "But Dad, aren't *you* working class?"

"Yes Colin, but I'm a working-class *Conservative*. There's a difference."

My mum, Ruth Sparrow, is ten years younger than Dad and she is constantly trying to update him. Just last week, she suggested he buys one of those hair pieces to cover up his bald patch.

Dad replied, "Oh yeah, I can just see it. One day I go into work, balding and grey. The next morning I go in, I've got a full head of dark, thick, bushy hair. How am I going to explain that overnight miracle?"

They met at Cadbury's in 1953, over the 'wet-end' of a conveyor belt of chocolate fingers.

Mum likes to tell the story of their first meeting and subsequent courtship. She lined up the biscuits on the belt while he operated the enrober, the machine that coated them in liquid chocolate. He'd had his eye on her for a couple of weeks and he was just waiting for the right moment and the right chat up line.

Then one morning he took the plunge. He casually ambled over to her while she was on her break and said, "You look knackered."

He's got a way with words. Nevertheless, it must have worked, because they went on a date. He took her to The Pictures in Selly Oak to watch *Shane*. They sat at the back in the 1/9s[1] and he treated her to a tub of ice cream with a little wooden spoon.

Now many people think they know a lot about films. But they don't. You may assume the line, "You talkin' to me?" was first coined by some tough guy actor in a New York cop show or film. Well it wasn't. No

---

[1] One shilling and ninepence. About 9p.

indeed! It was actually spoken by Alan Ladd, in *Shane*, the first film my dad took my mum to see.

But Alan Ladd doesn't say, "You talkin' to me?" He says "You *speakin'* to me?" And he delivers it with such perfection, with just the right amount of menace, as if to say, "Because if you are, you'd better be tough enough to back it up."

Then, when his tormentor in Grafton's bar, Chris (played by the equally excellent Ben Jonson) throws a whisky over Shane's shirt, "to make him smell more like a man", Shane doesn't lower himself to such provocation, even though little Joey might later suspect him of being "yella" for letting him get away with such an insult.

But Shane bides his time because he's got nothing to prove to anyone, and waits till a week or so later when he goes back into town with Joey's dad. Between them, they mop up the whole of the Ryker gang with their bare fists. Little Joey watches from under a table and crunches on his stick of candy as Alan Ladd knocks out Ben Johnson's teeth.

Later, during little Torrey's funeral, Mum felt Dad getting restless beside her, shifting in his seat, looking at his watch. She was slightly irritated as he was ruining a very touching scene. Torrey's dog whimpered and pawed at the little improvised coffin of planks as it was lowered into the dirt, while a man played 'Look away…Dixie Land' on his harmonica.

And all this was beautifully shot with the mourners and gravestones all silhouetted against the magnificent backdrop of mountains. But Mum didn't see any of it.

She felt Ed's arm slip round her shoulders. Anticipating an impending amorous moment, she didn't pull away. She felt his breath on her neck. She was like jelly in his arms. As his mouth got close to her hot little ear, she detected the distinct smell of Players tobacco and M&B Bitter.

Then he whispered the immortal line, "Come on, we'll have to leave now or we'll miss last orders."

As I said, he's got a way with words.

Leaving early, half the row had to stand up to let them out, and Mum was so embarrassed by everyone shushing and tutting. She never got to see Shane sort out Jack Palance and by the time he was riding into the sunset with little Joey running after him shouting his name, calling him to come back, Ed was on his third pint of M&B.

Mum says in seventeen years, she can't recollect ever seeing the end of a film.

After that first date, they started to see each other on a regular basis. On Tuesday nights, she watched him play darts at The Castle. On Thursday nights, she watched him fix his motorbike in the kitchen.

His green BSA Bantam was his pride and joy, and at the weekends he took her out on it, up to the Clent or Lickey Hills. She never quite got the hang of leaning into the bends and on one occasion, on the B4096, they came off.

While Ruth was lying in a ditch fifty yards back with laddered stockings and sprained wrist, Ed's first priority was to check the bike for any damage.

Clearly besotted, he'd made up his mind that Ruth was the one for him and a few weeks later he popped the question in his own unmistakable style. "Well Ruth, I've been doing some calculations, and I reckon we'd be much better off if we took advantage of the new Married Tax Allowance."

She considered this romantic offer. He wasn't exactly Trevor Howard but he made her laugh and had a secure job as a chocolate mixer. And so it came to pass, as 1953 was drawing to a close, they were married at Birmingham Registry Office.

Seventeen years on and they've now got five children.

I'm the second youngest. Brian's the eldest. He's fifteen, six-foot-tall, seven and a half stone and is convinced everyone other than himself is a moron.

He says, "I'm the only one in this house who's normal," while reading my little sister's copy of *Tammy*, and drying his hair with the Ronson 2000, the hairdryer with a bag that inflates on your head.

My older sister Laura is thirteen. She's mad about the pop group The Monkees and reads *Jackie* magazine every week, cutting out any pictures of the group she can find.

She writes regularly to Cathy and Claire, asking for advice about her feelings for Davy Jones and asking if the rumours are true that he recently got married. Brian laughs and says her letters are probably going straight in the bin. Mum clips his ear and tells him not to talk with his mouth full.

Rob, who's two years older than me, can do press ups on his thumbs and can pick up a full bottle of water with his toes. This is all part of his martial arts training. Already at the tender age of twelve, Rob has a deep hatred of the female sex and gives free advice to men in general.

"All women are naggers. Whatever you do, don't get married."

When I ask Rob if he can ever see *himself* getting married in the future he says, after some consideration,

"Maybe. If I can find a good looking mute."

My little sister Katie may be an important, determining factor in Rob's theory on the opposite sex. Although only seven years old, she's got one hell of a gob on her.

Red in the face and foaming at the mouth, she often bellows at one or all of us, "I hate you! I hope you die and your eyes pop out and I wouldn't save you!"

Her entire collection of dolls has undergone surgical alteration. Hair pulled out in tufts or cut to skinhead length, eyes poked in or blacked out with felt tip pen. Many of them have selected limbs removed or fingers cut off with the scissors. Her dolls' house looks like it has suffered a direct hit from a 500 lb bomb.

Mum says she's going to grow up to be a "proper little madam".

Dad says, "At this very moment, there's a perfectly happy seven year old boy somewhere in Birmingham, unaware that in about twenty years' time his life will be over."

Apart from Cadbury's, Dad also has an extra job in the evenings, pulling pints at the Allen's Cross Working Man's Club. Every night except Mondays and Wednesdays, he gets home from the factory at about half five, eats his tea, has a quick cat-lick and a polish and by seven is gone again, not to return before midnight.

He also works there at Sunday lunchtime. The result? We hardly ever see him. Dad says he's making this enormous sacrifice to bring more money in for Christmas and summer holidays.

Mum remarks how convenient it is, that his 'sacrifice' gets him out of a house of screaming kids and that free pints, courtesy of the customers, are a perk of the job.

The club is a huge, smoky barn of a place. With Rob I sometimes look through the windows while standing on the pedals of our bikes. On a stage backed with red and silver tinsel strips hanging down, are drums and an

24

organ which accompany the warm up act: a bloke from Tipton in cowboy boots and long sideburns, singing a poor version of 'Runaway' by Del Shannon. After the chorus of "My little runaway, run-run-run-run-runaway" ... the organist closes his eyes in apparent ecstasy as he rips through the little solo on his Hammond Organ.

Men, hair slicked, two pint jugs in each hand, make their way back to their tables.

Their women sit, engulfed in smoke, in front of Snowballs or brandy and Babychams, shouting into each other's ears, screeching with laughter at the 'medallion-men' cruising the floor.

In contrast, the older married couples sit in silence, small talk exhausted years ago, waiting for bingo at the interval, then the main act, often a comedian.

Dad's shift usually ends at 11.30 and he gets home about midnight. Because I frequently have nightmares, I can only sleep with the bedroom door open and the landing light on. So his arrival often wakes me up.

I hear his key in the lock, then the closing of the front door in that careful, hushed way that's a sure sign he's had one too many. I hear the squeak of a floorboard as he tries to climb the stairs two at a time so as not to wake Mum.

He goes into the bathroom without turning on the light and undresses quietly. I hear him cleaning his teeth and gargling loudly with water. Then he gets on his knees to go to the toilet.

He does it like this because Mum is always having a go at him for peeing on the carpet when he's drunk. If he's closer to the toilet, there's less chance of him missing. He stays in this position for several minutes while he gets rid of several pints of M&B Brew Eleven.

He whispers to himself, as if in prayer, "Oh God…..Jesus …Oh yes, I needed that!"

When he's finally finished, and he noisily gets to his feet, his knees cracking, I sometimes walk out into the light on the landing. I tell him I've had another bad dream. So he leads me back to my room, tucks me into bed and sits with me until I fall asleep.

Often he'll smoke a last cigarette while he does this. Mum is always telling him not to because of my chest but he forgets after a few pints and I like the smell of the tobacco.

I whisper to him, "Dad, what happens after we die?"

"Well, what a funny question. What's brought all this on?"

"I keep having nightmares about being dead."

"Well, you don't have to worry about that Colin. We don't float on clouds playing harps or go to hell, burning in fires, poked with pitchforks or other silly nonsense like that. When you're dead you're dead. It's actually very peaceful. There's just nothing. And that nothing lasts forever. Now you go to sleep."

I remember a passage from Jane Eyre that Mrs. King read to us one afternoon, all about hell and fire.

Mr. Brocklehurst, the head of Lowood school was quizzing Jane:

"Do you know where the wicked go after death?"

"They go to hell."

"And what is hell? Can you tell me that?"

"A pit full of fire."

"What must you do to avoid it?"

"I must keep in good health, and not die."

Yes, I think to myself over and over, I too must keep in good health and not die. I then think about Dad's answer, "a nothing that lasts forever" and wonder if that's not *scarier* than being poked with pitchforks.

I look at the orange, glowing end of his cigarette in the darkness, which suddenly burns brighter when he takes another drag on it. I can just make him out in the glow, sitting there round shouldered in his string vest and Y-fronts, most definitely not Alan Ladd or a member of the Parachute Regiment, but still my dad; solid, reliable, always there. The orange light comforts me and eventually I fall asleep.

Worrier. 2002

I suppose I've always had a bit of a nervous disposition. Emm says I'm a 'worrier'. I'm never happy unless I've got something to fret about. Well, that certainly seems to be the case at the moment. Apart from the problem with my hand (which I haven't told her about yet) there is an even greater concern just around the corner: the dreaded OFSTED are coming to inspect the school next week.

There's a saying in school staff rooms: *if you can't do; teach; if you can't teach; teach teachers. And if you can't teach teachers; then become an OFSTED inspector.*

On the Monday morning when they arrive there is a queue of teachers waiting to use the photocopier at 7.30 a.m. Everyone is nervous, waiting their turn to get lesson plans and 'schemes of work' ready for the inspectors. My turn arrives.

"You haven't got much have you Colin? We're all in a rush this morning. Briefing soon."

"Just be a minute folks, bear with me."

I try to do a set of 30 double-sided sheets. As I press start, the first sheet feeds in, then there's the familiar sound of crunching paper from somewhere deep in the machine.

Then a groaning noise, and the red-light flashing indicating a paper jam.

"Oh typical, Colin!! It's *always* you isn't it? Why do you have to do double-sided?"

"Don't panic, I think I can fix it."

I open up the machine to try and locate the jammed paper.

"Don't touch it Colin, if you don't know what you're doing, you'll make it worse."

"Stop panicking, I know how to fix it."

More teachers from every department arrive with work to photocopy.

"Oh my God, why such a long queue?"

"Sparrow's knackered the machine again."

Groans all round, verging on desperate panic.

"It's *always* the English Department isn't it?"

"COME ON COLIN, I'VE BEEN PLANNING THIS LESSON ALL WEEKEND!"

"Sorry, sorry, nearly there."

Suddenly all the lights on the console light up like a Christmas tree.

"What the hell are you doing Colin? It's ten to eight. Come on!!!"

There is a loud clunk, then all the lights go out and the warning light says:

Machine fault. Please contact engineer.

There's a loud collective groan. They all shout in unison: "OH COLIN!!!"

"You idiot Colin, now what are we going to do? You've dropped us all in it!"

I bang it with my fist. They all shout, "DON'T DO THAT!!"

It's 8 o'clock and everyone gives me a filthy look as they file out for the briefing.

As I walk across the playground to the staff room, I see the caretaker has been given a new machine; a giant hoover on four wheels, like the Noo Noo in Teletubbies, and is sucking up litter from the school grounds.

As I pass him, he gives me a wry smile and says, "Operation Bullshit."

OFSTED are waiting for us in the staff-room. They are on one side, all the teachers on the other. The headmaster introduces them and everyone's face is stuck in a frozen smile. All teachers will be observed three times during the week. We will not know in advance which lessons they'll be coming to, they'll just 'drop in.'

After the briefing, the head of English comes over to me.

"Colin, I don't want to worry you, but word on the grapevine is that you're first up. They're observing your Year 10 GCSE Drama, period one."

"Oh dear God! That's with Warren Newman."

Warren is the school fruit and nut case, who lives on a diet of e-numbers and artificial colourings. His attention span is virtually zero and it's quite normal for him to enter my class while walking on his hands.

No other department will enter him for an exam, as he can't sit in a seat long enough. Drama is the only subject he is taking. Being an 'active' lesson, it was decided by the powers that be, that Drama would help him and be a realistic GCSE target. While in theory I agree with all of that, it is nevertheless very difficult keeping him pinned down. He also swears like a trooper.

After I register my form, I sprint across the playground to get there before the inspector does. When I walk into the hall, the class are not sitting on chairs and are running screaming around the room.

The inspector is already there and she is in deep conversation with…. Warren.

Oh my God... "OK everyone, get a chair and make a circle, please. You too Warren…thank you."

I go straight over to the inspector, who's a sort of middle-aged, matronly woman and say to her, "I see you've already met Warren. Now you mustn't take too seriously what he was saying, or that he swears every other word…he's Special Needs."

She replies, "Oh that's quite OK. I think he thinks I'm his new teaching assistant. He was just telling me that 'If Sir didn't arrive soon, there would be trouble because this week is an OFSTED inspection week, and these inspectors can be real bastards.'"

I accidentally let slip a silent fart and reply, "Really? I wonder where he gets such notions."

Then I give her my lesson plan and learning objectives to read through, while I take the register. They are rehearsing scenes from Willy Russell's 'Our Day Out.' in small groups, which they'll showcase to the rest of the class in the second half of the lesson.

I've deliberately put Warren with the most responsible, trustworthy girls in the class who are themselves no little angels. I pull him to one side.

"Now, Warren, listen to me. Are you listening to me? Put that down, and look at me. Good. Now are you listening? No, not over there, look at *me*. Good. Now do you know who that lady is?"

"She's my new teaching assistant Sir."

"No she isn't. She's an Inspector."

"Really?"

Then he laughs,

"Oh shit Sir, I said…"

"Yes I know what you said and we'll forget about that for now. The point is Warren, I want you to be on your best behaviour from now on, OK? No swearing, all right?"

"Sir, don't worry, I'd never let you down...I fucking love Drama."

I look at him with the sternest face I've got, but can't disguise the faintest trace of a smile. Warren smiles too.

"OK, get into your group."

The inspector starts wandering from group to group, listening to their work. Everything seems to be going well. Then it starts. Warren's voice booms across the hall. He's having a disagreement with a girl in his group.

"No way, I'm not doing that. *You* do it. No, *you* say it! I'm not doing that, *you* do it, you prostitute."

"Warren, can I see you outside for a minute please? Thank you."

I get him outside in the corridor, behind the double swing doors...that are not sound proof, and hiss, "Warren, what did I say? No inappropriate language please."

"What have I said? I didn't swear. What have I said?"

"You can't go round calling members of the group prostitutes."

"Yeah, but Sir, she *is* one."

I lose it for a moment. "I DON'T CARE IF SHE *IS* ONE OR NOT...JUST DON'T *CALL* HER ONE IN MY LESSON,...OK?"

"OK Sir. Sorry Sir.......... but she is..."

"ENOUGH! Now go back inside."

The Inspector calls over.

"Everything all right Mr. Sparrow?"

"Yes, everything's under control, no problems. I think you'll find that group over there particularly interesting."

At the end of the lesson, I am summoned to sit with her while she gives me some instant feedback. I half expect the worst. She finishes taking notes, looks up at me with a serious face which suddenly broadens into a beaming grin and says, "Well, that's certainly a challenging group isn't it?"

I don't get another inspection for the rest of the day, and when I've finished teaching, in order to be ahead of myself, I write tomorrow's English lessons on the blackboard and whiteboard in readiness for a possible inspection.

As I do so, I periodically stop, stand at the back of the room and survey my effort. If anything my handwriting is getting worse, letters becoming small and cramped towards the end of each line. Terrible. I'd never have passed teacher training with board work like that. Goodness knows what the OFSTED inspector will think.

I rub it all off and start again, painstakingly gripping the board marker and trying to keep the words big. My hand starts to tremble and I can't grip the pen. By the time I've finished, my whole left arm is shaking with the effort. This shocks me. What on earth is wrong with me?

I sit down and look out of the window. Perhaps I should go and see the doctor. No, if I do that, he'll probably refer me to see a specialist, and I've had enough of hospitals to last me a life time.

1970. Birmingham Children's Hospital

This afternoon we take the long way home from school. We have Mrs. King's summer term reports in our hands.

Mine starts:

Colin would have a much better chance of achieving his potential, if he spent more time listening in class, instead of looking out of the window.

Graham asks me what *his* says. He hands it to me and I read it to him:

Graham is never going to learn anything unless he stays in his seat and stops wandering around the classroom. He must try and lower his voice, not throw objects and not use inappropriate language in front of the others. Please ensure that he washes his hands and brings a clean handkerchief every day.

Graham asks, "What does 'in a pro pry ate language' mean?"
"Swear words I think."
Graham concludes that Mrs. King is a first class, stuck-up bitch.

When I show my report to Mum, she's strangely unconcerned. She doesn't tell me off but speaks softly to me and tells me to sit down. She has a letter in her hand and I can read the words on the top. Three words that send a shiver down my spine:

Birmingham Children's Hospital.

I have to go in for more tests. The doctors at the hospital still don't really know what's wrong with me. It's been nearly a year since I had a major chest infection but I still can't digest my food. The last time I stayed on the ward, I had to have endless needles, tubes and X Rays, which quite honestly, terrify me. Especially when the man hides behind a metal screen when he zaps me for the umpteenth time.

Jeremy Potts says that X Rays eat your bones. But I put up with it because one day, as a result of all these tests, I may get better and become 'normal.'

Birmingham's Children's Hospital is a tall, red bricked, dark, spooky place. I dread every visit I make here. The transparent, bendy, plastic doors that the ambulance trolleys bash through are like something out of a horror movie, put there to stop the splatter of blood as they chop up bodies with an electric saw on the other side. There are failed attempts to make the place less threatening, such as the framed nursery rhymes on the walls, ending on lines like "So I took him by the left leg and threw him down the stairs." And there are huge standing teddy bears, strategically positioned to prevent any attempts at escape.

The sound of crying is everywhere.

Finally, up a newly mopped, disinfectant-smelling stairwell that echoes with our footsteps and heavy breathing as we near the top, we find the ward.

We're shown to my bed at the end of a long line next to someone with the curtains drawn around. I unpack my things into the bedside cabinet. Mum tells me not to worry, then leaves me to get the bus home to start cooking the tea.

I'm standing on tiptoes looking out of the window to see if I can see her when a voice behind me makes me jump.

"Right young man, what are you doing out of bed?"

I get into my pyjamas. The nurse takes my temperature, pulse and blood pressure, puffs up my pillows, then tucks me in so tightly, I can't move.

"What's for tea?"

"Oh, not for you I'm afraid, you're nil-by-mouth for tomorrow."

She sticks her head through the curtains that are drawn around the next bed, "Gary, what have we told you? When you've filled it up, you've got to call us."

She leaves his curtains open, then waddles off, her shiny black shoes squeaking on the lino floor.

Gary is connected by a mass of tubes to a machine that whirs and clicks. He gives me a pale, sickly smile.

"All right?"

"Yeah."

"What's your name?"

"Colin."

"And how old are you Colin?"

"Ten."

His smile gets broader.

"I'm Gary, and I'm nearly twelve. Don't worry, the nurses aren't that bad. Just ask me if you want to know anything, I've been here loads of times. I come three days a week for ten hour overnight sessions on this machine.

I look at all his tubes.

"Doesn't that hurt?"

"No, it's nothing, just a bit annoying that's all."

"What are all those tubes for?"

"I'm having my blood washed."

"Having your blood *washed*? How did it get dirty in the first place?"

"Well, your blood is cleaned by your kidneys. But mine don't work, so this machine does it for me. It's called Dialysis."

I can see his blood going round in tubes, like a giant racetrack.

"You mean your blood is *outside* your body at the moment?"

"Some of it, yeah, but not all of it all the time, obviously, or I'd be dead."

We both laugh.

"What are you in for?"

"Oh, just some tests. I don't think they know exactly what I've got… so, won't your kidneys get better?"

"No. I need some new ones."

"New ones? Well, where do you get them from? Are they expensive?"

"I need a transplant."

"What's that?"

"It's when they take the kidneys from someone else's body, and put them into mine."

"Someone else's? But won't *they* need them?"

"No, they take them from someone who's just died."

"*Died*? I wouldn't want some dead person's parts in me."

"They still work perfectly well."

"But won't the kidneys be dead too?"

"No. They can keep them alive for a few hours by keeping them cold."

"What, like in the fridge?"

"Sort of. Then they rush them over to me, usually by motorbike with flashing lights to get through the traffic jams...."

"Motorbike?"

"Yeah, and once they're inside me, they start working again."

"On a motorbike with flashing lights. Great, I'd like to see that. Well, loads of people die every day, so what are they waiting for?"

"Not everyone who dies gives their permission. And I have to have the right sort, that are a match with mine."

"How long have you been waiting?"

"Five years."

"Five years!? God, that's so unfair."

"It's OK. I'm used to it. If I ever get a new pair, I'll be the happiest person alive."

The nurse comes back with an empty bottle for him.

I sit there, thinking about taking an organ from someone who's died and the organ is still alive even though the host body is dead. How can that be? Do the various parts of our bodies die at different times?

At school once, someone told me that even after you're dead, your hair and fingernails continue to grow. Creepy. I wonder if your brain is still working after you're dead.

Just imagine, you'd still be able to think while they screwed your coffin lid shut and lowered you down into the hole. You'd hear the earth being shovelled on top of you, getting heavier and heavier. But you wouldn't be able to tell anyone because you couldn't speak or move your arms.

Before lights out, the doctor comes to see me. He's Australian. He treats me like a grown up by shaking me by the hand when he introduces himself.

"Hello Colin, I'm Doctor Cant," he smiles.

I double check the spelling on his badge as he leans forward to listen to my chest.

Definitely C-A-N-T. His Australian accent makes it sound like something else. He then explains what they are going to do to me tomorrow. I'll be awake throughout and it will just involve them passing a small tube into me and feeding it down into my gut.

He notices my pale, nervous look.

"Don't worry little fellah, I haven't killed anyone yet."

I feel a bowel movement coming on.

When he's gone, in an outrageous display of independence, I walk up the ward in my bare feet to use the toilet. The lino on the floor is warm and polished.

The nurse at the station calls over to me, "What are you doing out of bed?"

"I need the toilet."

"You should have called us."

Everyone is in bed, except me. Most seem to be sleeping or maybe they've been drugged. The nurses are in complete control.

When I come out of the toilet, one of them gives me a funny shaped bottle and tells me that if I need to pee in the night, I should do it in that, but on no account am I to get out of bed and move around the ward without their permission.

The lights finally go out but it isn't dark at all like at home. I study the details of the ornate ceiling which has carvings in plaster of flowers and fruit. I can still see right up the ward to the nurses' station. The light is on inside Gary's curtains.

Out of the window, the blinking of the Birmingham Post Office Tower in the distance continues as if nothing is wrong. I think about the world outside, where everything is carrying on as normal. Dad going to the club, Mum watching 'News At Ten,' Brian putting out the rubbish and Mrs. Perks walking her dog.

Do they know what goes on in this laboratory? Gary with his blood outside his body. Doesn't anyone care?

The nurses come to check on Gary every twenty minutes, to make sure there are no clots in his blood. They smile at me as they do so.

"You're all right aren't you Colin? Try to sleep love."

I resign myself to not getting any sleep at all and decide to count the number of clicks per minute his machine makes, using the second hand of the clock on the wall.

At 11.15, the nurses are back, this time round my bed.

36

"Colin, come on, wake up love."

I am being shaken quite roughly.

Doctor Cant suddenly appears. "How long has he been like this?"

"He was fine when we checked on Gary a while ago."

"You'd better phone home. But don't let them see him until I speak with them."

I ask him what's the matter. He ignores me, as though I'm not there. He shines a light into my eyes, puts his ear to my chest, then shakes me, and swears. I overhear him tell the nurse that I've been dead for at least half an hour and why the hell didn't anyone check? "In all my career, this will be the first one I've killed."

Dead?

I look at my hands. Hands that don't belong to me anymore and I feel the terror of not being part of the living world. My thin little body lying here in its pyjamas, is not me anymore. What am I? Where am I? Why can I still think? Is my brain still alive? But why can't I move my arms, my lips?

Doctor Cant closes the curtains round me and tells the nurse to help him. "We've got to remove his kidneys while they're still alive and freeze them as soon as possible."

He takes a sharp scalpel from his pocket and lifts up my pyjama top. My heart is pumping like a drum and I scream at him to make him hear me, "I'm not dead, I'm not dead! Listen, I can talk. Listen to me!"

My bedside light is switched on and the nurse with squeaky shoes shushes me, telling me I'm frightening all the little ones.

I'm drenched with sweat. The ceiling is still there, reassuringly familiar. Gary is looking at me with a worried look on his face.

When the nurse has gone and I've calmed down, the giant panda bear on sentry duty eyes me threateningly, daring me to go back to sleep. On the wall, I can just make out the nursery rhyme with the line:

Here comes the chopper to chop off your head.

Gary is soon asleep again and I hear the sound of the nurses' laughter down the corridor. I hear my name mentioned. They're talking about me.

"What was he saying?"

"He was screaming 'I'm not dead, I'm not dead.' I tell you, it put the shivers up me. The look on his face. It was like he was possessed. And pouring with sweat he was."

"Don't worry, I'll go next time."

"Make sure you've got your crucifix on."

More laughter.

The shame of the nightmare and waking everybody up is worse than the fear. I worry myself to bits that everyone will talk about me in the morning, so I lie awake, miserable until the sky starts to brighten and the blink of the Post Office tower begins to fade. I finally drift off.

Just as I do, the fluorescent strip above me stutters into life and the medicine trolley trundles down the aisle and bangs into my bed.

"Wakey, wakey, Colin. You're still with us then? My, what a fright you gave us all last night with all that talk of dying."

At eight o'clock the breakfast trolley comes round - not for me of course - and even the ladies in pink are talking about it.

"Is that the one who was screaming? Keep him off the cheese at night then, ha ha ha!"

Then Doctor Cant arrives.

"Hello young man, sleep well?"

Oh get on with it Cant.

He is followed by a procession of young student doctors in white coats, notebooks in hand. They crowd around my bed.

Doctor Cant addresses them.

"Now here, ladies and gentlemen, is an interesting case. Indeed, I'd go so far as to say, a bit of an *enigma*."

A what? Isn't that what they stick up old people's bums if they can't go to the toilet?

"He was diagnosed with cystic fibrosis at eighteen months when he failed to thrive. But that turned out to be false. He has a pancreatic enzyme deficiency, resulting in bouts of chronic diarrhoea. This malabsorption is rather poorly controlled by Pancreatin. He is still frail, but he's now ten years old and remains fit and active, which is usually a necessary precursor to a growth spurt, and we are expecting such a spurt any time now.

"So we have a mystery. Why is the chest clear and yet the pancreas still performing so poorly? This is why we've called him in. We shall

38

draw up some of the fluid from his small intestine, to analyse his digestion contents. So, Colin, we'll be back to see you in about an hour."

They all file out.

I look down at my stomach and try to estimate where my pancreas is in relation to my other organs, how big it is and what it looks like. As the hour passes I get more and more worried and they give me some syrup which is supposed to relax me.

How on earth are they going to get a tube down into my small intestine? When the trolley arrives with two burly looking nurses and the doctor, it begins to dawn on me that there's going to be a bit of a struggle.

While Nurse One starts to uncoil the tube, Nurse Two pins me expertly to the bed in a sort of half-nelson. The flesh on her arms is soft and cold, and her uniform crisp and stiff against my face as she leans over me.

Before I get the chance to react, the tube is being forced down my throat. I start to retch and thrash about. The doctor becomes annoyed and tells me off.

"Oh come on now, don't be such a baby, just swallow. It's only a little tube."

Look, Cant, I can swallow anything, so long as it's got a beginning and an end.

At this point I wriggle free and pull the tube out. They try again. This time with two nurses holding me down. But I am wiser now and clamp my mouth shut.

"Look Colin, this isn't helping the situation is it?"

It may not be helping the <u>situation</u> mate, but it's certainly helping <u>me</u>.

They hold my nose until I open up for air, then I gag and choke as it is literally forced down my throat. Past the point of no return, the urge to vomit passes and I become aware that I am shaking and soaked with sweat.

"Now, that wasn't too bad was it?"

Cant!

It then takes hours trying to get the tube in to the right position, while my mouth gets drier and my throat gets sorer. Then they draw up quantities of ghastly looking greenish, black fluid, which is sealed in test tubes and sent off to the lab. Finally at 6.30 p.m., nearly nine hours later, they decide they have enough and it can come out, which is much easier than going in.

By the time I'm sitting up in bed eating a meal of cold rice pudding, it's 'Visiting'. No one comes to see me. All the chairs at the side of my bed are being used by the hordes of concerned relatives surrounding a new, very sickly-looking boy on the other side from Gary.

Finally, with fifteen minutes to go, Dad saunters in through the doors at the top of the ward. Mum must have persuaded him to take a night off from the club. He hasn't seen me and he walks down the aisle, smoking a cigarette and carrying the Evening Mail under his arm.

A nurse rushes up to him and shouts at him to put that cigarette out. I cringe with embarrassment. The whole ward is looking. He extinguishes it and puts the stub behind his ear. Then he carries on walking, trying to find me. By now, everyone's eyes are following him and eventually settle on me as he spots me and gives a little wave.

He sits on the bed, despite the sign asking him not to.

"Sorry I'm a bit late. Whoever signposted this place ought to be shot. No wonder the country's in the state that it's in."

He takes a long look at my surroundings, scrutinising the very sick boy. Looking back at me and not bothering to keep his voice down, he smiles as he motions towards the boy saying, "Well Colin, things could be worse, at least you haven't got what *he's* got."

Then he spends the rest of visiting time testing all the gadgets around my bed, raising the feet end, switching the light on and off and pressing the nurse call button.

Each time she arrives, he apologises and says it was an accident, and each time she gives him a withering stare.

Using the clip-board at the bottom of my bed to lean on, he starts to fill in his Football Pools coupon.

"Dad, I don't think you should be using that. It's for my notes, for the doctor."

"Don't you worry yourself about it Colin, no harm is there? Here, tell you what, you can put one of my crosses down if you like. What do you think of Dunfermline versus Queen of the South?"

The bell rings for the end of visiting and he hasn't finished. Matron, who's taken a disliking to him for pressing the call button, is hovering around the bed.

"Mr. Sparrow, I must insist, the children are tired. You can come again tomorrow. I'm expecting the doctor at any minute."

He marks his last cross, hands the clip-board back to her and says, "It's not a doctor you need love, it's a plastic surgeon."

He says goodbye to me then he ambles back up the aisle, inspecting the stub that he takes from behind his ear.

After he's gone, Matron takes it out on me. She manhandles me roughly as she tucks me in, trying to get the bed back to its regulation height, cursing under her breath as the metal frame clunks and shudders.

Next day, to my enormous relief, Mum visits. She wears the brightest smile and tells me she has good news. The doctors say I may have something called 'Entero Kinase Deficiency'. She writes it down for me. She says it's very rare, so I must be very special. I still have to keep taking the tablets when I eat but it shouldn't be too long before I start to put on weight and grow. I can go home tomorrow.

Tonight, lying in bed, I think about it. Maybe God listened to me that morning in assembly. I suddenly feel drowsy and start to drift off into a deep sleep.

I have the strangest dream.

I find myself walking along a deserted beach. I am still in my pyjamas and bare feet. I am following a trail of footsteps in the wet sand. These footprints are very large. I can nearly fit two of my own feet into one of those in the sand. I can see the trail is leading to some cliffs in the distance. As I get nearer, I can see there is a large crowd of people gathered outside a cave at the base of one of the cliffs.

When I get there, I ask some of the people what it's all about. They tell me that a wise man has moved into the cave. He apparently has the power to grant wishes and heal people. The entrance to the cave is guarded by a huge giant panda bear. Everyone is jostling for position to be the next allowed in to ask for a blessing. I think I'd like to see him too.

No sooner have I thought this thought than I find myself inside and alone with the old man. His head is shaven and he is wrapped up in a plain robe, sitting warming himself in front of a small fire. He has the kindest, most loving face I have ever seen. I'm sure I know him, but can't remember from where or when. He has an air about him of sheer happiness and contentment. The more I look at him, the more his whole body seems to glow and vibrate, with joy, almost like a mirage in a desert. He smiles broadly at me when I appear before him and he asks me,

"Where have you been all this time? I've been waiting for you."

I reply, "Waiting for *me?* Why?"

"Because you are nearly ready," he says simply.

"Ready for what?" I ask.

"You will soon understand," he says. "In the meantime, you must stop worrying! I don't want you to worry about *anything* anymore. OK? Just think of me at all times. Whenever you're in danger, or afraid, just think of me, and I will protect you."

He fixes me with his smiley eyes and repeats, "Remember, just think of me. You don't need to do anything else."

I feel such love for the little man, I want to stay with him forever. He seems to be able to read my mind because he smiles brightly again when I think this.

"You *can* stay with me Colin, now we are friends. Be assured, we will never be without each other again. Now it's time for you to go."

Reluctantly, I stand up, say goodbye and go outside.

All of the people outside crowd around me, asking, "Did you see him?" "What's he like?" "What did he say?"

"Oh, he's wonderful!" I reply, and I run off, until I am running so fast, I am leaping high into the air. I am flying over houses, over tree tops.

I land on a railway track just as a train is coming. I can't get out of the way in time, so I close my eyes and think of him, and the train passes right through me. I thank him. When I do, I feel he's pleased with me, so I thank him for being pleased with me. This pleases him even more, so I thank him some more. And so it goes on, like a competition that I can never win because he is always more pleased than I can thank him for.

This is the sweetest, most indescribable feeling, and I wish it could last forever.

At that moment, I wake up. I am still on the hospital ward and my pillow is soaked with tears and sweat. I have the most terrible sense of loss. I think my heart will break if I don't see him again. I call the nurse and ask if she saw a little old man come to visit me in the night.

"You've been dreaming again darling. Try to go back to sleep, there's a good boy."

Post-OFSTED. 2002

Already awake. I look at the alarm clock, three minutes before it's due to go off at six. As usual, I press the alarm button down before it sounds. But this morning, I allow myself an extra ten minutes in bed to indulge in the realisation that OFSTED is over.

I roll over to face my wife Emm. She too is already awake and is looking at me bleary-eyed. She smiles. For a change, Lily is still asleep in her cot. Emm puts her finger to her lips, then cuddles up.

She whispers into my ear, teasing her teacher husband: "Morning 'Sir'. No need to rush today is there? Those horrible inspectors have gone haven't they? Now, let's see. Need any jobs doing Sir? Can I sharpen your pencil for you?"

She giggles, pulls the sheet up and over us and I smile and think, *Sod it, I'll take an extra twenty minutes.*

When I arrive at school, the sense of relief about the place is palpable. *Their* cars are gone from the car park and teachers are walking across the playground with a spring in their step saying "Good morning!" to everyone they pass, even to the most difficult kids.

During the day, the headmaster seeks out all members of staff, personally to thank them for their efforts last week. He finds me on playground duty at break-time.

"Colin my man, just wanted to express my gratitude for all the hard work you put in last week. The drama inspector was full of praise for you."

"Thanks. Pity they couldn't see the school play. It's really coming on."

"Can't wait Colin. Keep up the good work!"

Then he strides off across the playground. As he goes, a signet-ringed, tattooed hand is poked through a hole in the wooden school perimeter fence and gives him a V sign.

The other teacher on duty with me notices, nods towards the gesturing hand and remarks, "Probably his wife…" which reduces us both into a fit of giggles.

At the end of the day, I am in the hall working on the lights and scenery for the play. I am on my own on top of a high ladder replacing some coloured lighting gels, when suddenly I feel very giddy. It's a sort of light-headedness and I feel like I'm going to black out.

I hug the sides of the ladder for safety until it passes. Then, for what seems like an eternity, I inch my way down, one rung at a time. I almost embrace the floor when I get there and sit for several minutes really shaken.

What on earth was that? Strangest thing. I'm just grateful that I was on my own and no one saw.

The thought of going back up the ladder again terrifies me, so I lower the two extensions and stack it on the floor. I decide to set up the tower tomorrow, so for the time being I go back to my classroom to do some marking.

When I get there, someone is waiting outside my door. It's Warren Newman.

"Hello Warren. What are you doing here at this hour? I'd have thought you'd have gone home hours ago."

"Just come out of detention Sir."

"Oh, I see. Well, what can I do for you?"

"Well…I wanted to ask you a question…if you promise not to tell anyone."

"OK, so long as it's not anything that could get you into trouble."

"No, it's nothing like that Sir. I just wanted to ask…err… you know Reilly in *Our Day Out*?

"Yes."

"Well, does he end up going out with Linda Croxley proper like?"

"I think so Warren. It's all in that last scene on the bus isn't it?"

"And do you think things like that really happen?"

"Of course, every day Warren. It's what makes the world go round, what we're all looking for."

"What's that Sir?"

"You know, finding 'the one,' that special person to fall in love with."

"Yeah. But it's always like that in books and films isn't it? It doesn't really happen like that. I mean, what if the girl doesn't want to know?"

He bites his nail avoiding eye contact. Suddenly I realise what this is all about.

"Who's the girl Warren?"

He blushes.

"Promise you won't tell anyone Sir?"

"Promise."

"Kelly Mulligan. I asked her out at lunchtime."

"What did she say?"

"She just laughed at me and said 'In your dreams.'"

"Well, I wouldn't worry too much about that. Are you sure Kelly Mulligan is the right girl for you? I mean, half the boys in the school want to go out with Kelly Mulligan. Why don't you set your sights a little lower?"

"So, you don't think it's because I'm thick or anything like that?"

I laugh.

"Warren, I think Hugh Grant would have his work cut out, asking Kelly Mulligan for a date. You know there are probably loads of girls just right for a good-looking lad like you. You've just got to look a bit further than Kelly Mulligan."

"But it's all right for you Sir. Bet you never had these problems, being clever, when you were at school."

"Warren, you have no idea. *Everybody* has these problems, I can assure you. If you only knew the agonies I went through over a particular girl..."

He laughs, "Were you in love with her Sir?"

"I thought I was. Trust me Warren, there's a girl out there, somewhere, who will make you much happier than Kelly Mulligan."

"Yeah? Well, how will I know when I meet her?"

"Well it's like in the play isn't it Warren? I mean take Linda for example. She thinks she's in love with Sir, but that's never really going to happen is it? Then suddenly, right in front of her very nose, she notices Reilly. You never know Warren. There may be a girl, right under *your* very nose, perhaps in the same class as you, who you've never even thought about before, and suddenly she says or does something, you see her in a different light and bang, you're in Big Ben City."

"What's Big Ben City?"

"You know...BONG ... BONG ...in love!"

"Oh, right. You don't half talk weird Sir. So, someone right under my nose you say?"

"Could be. Could be not."

"And you think I should forget about Kelly Mulligan?"

"I think that would be wise."

"Right, OK. Well anyway, thanks Sir. I knew I could ask you. But just between us, yes?"

"Of course Warren. Now it's getting late."

And off he walks, deep in thought. Who said teaching wasn't a rewarding job?

I sit at my desk and get my things together, ready to go home. I yawn and stretch and move the fingers on my left hand again. It's definitely getting worse.

Before I turn my laptop off, I try a little experiment. I type my symptoms into the search engine:

Losing balance, trembling hand, poor handwriting.

I stare at the results on the screen:

Early symptoms of Parkinson's Disease.

That can't be right. Parkinson's is an old man's disease isn't it? Nevertheless, a cold chill blows over me. Best be on the safe side. I'll make an appointment with the GP tomorrow evening.

I look out of the window and see Warren kicking a can across the playground towards the gate, and chuckle to myself. Warren Newman. A bit like Graham Skinner in my day. Both cheerful in the face of adversity, with the gift of the gab and the skin of a rhinoceros.

Summer 1970. Fishing and Fires

Graham shows me the three R. White's lemonade bottles he's found in the stingers behind the pub. We take them to the out door and line them up on the counter. There's a 2d[1] deposit on each.

The assistant looks at us and at the bottles with suspicion. They are smeared with mud with labels torn or missing, no tops and there is a slug in the bottom of one that we couldn't shake out.

"Are you sure you purchased these here?"

We give her a look of sincere offence. I let Graham do the talking.

"Are you calling me a liar? Me mum sent me for the deposit. She bought them here last week. I can go and get her if you like."

"No, that won't be necessary. I believe you. Thousands wouldn't."

She rings up no sale, and careful to avoid any bodily contact, she counts the pennies into filthy hands. Together with the money we got from the Corona man, we now have enough to buy half a pint of mixed maggots to go fishing.

Next morning, I'm up at four to make my sarnies. I let Graham in by the back door. This doesn't please Dad when he gets up for work at ten to five. He had a skin-full last night and likes the kitchen to himself in the mornings to get his head together.

"What the hell is going on down here? How early do you have to get up in this house for a bit of peace and quiet? And what are you doing with your head in my fridge Graham Skinner, haven't you got a kitchen in your own house?"

"Sorry Mr. Sparrow, I was only looking at what you keep in here. We haven't got a fridge. I haven't used anything honest. I've already made my sarnies; HP sauce. I made them when I got up at two this morning."

We do our best to tiptoe around Dad until he leaves for work, in between explosions. The cat gets kicked up its arse for rubbing up Dad's leg for food and is called a "passenger".

---

[1] Tuppence. About 1p

Eventually, he goes into the outhouse to get his bike ready, when without warning, he throws one of his shoes in to the kitchen like a missile.

"I don't bloody well believe it, they've had them again! This must be the only house in Britain where you can't leave your shoes off for a minute without the laces being nicked."

He bangs about opening and slamming shut drawers and cupboards, looking for some string to tie his shoes with.

After a couple of minutes cursing while he threads them, he finally opens the outhouse door to the street to cycle off. Mrs. Perks' aggressive little Jack Russell is waiting for him in the road, as it is every morning. It growls when it sees him, wagging its tail furiously, as it waits to play its favourite game.

Dad shouts at it, "And you can bugger off too!"

He curses as it runs after him down the road, yapping and snapping at his rapidly pedalling feet.

We hear him in the distance as he disappears round the corner, trying to outpace it while kicking out at the snarling beast.

"Get out of it you little passenger!"

We fish in the reservoir at Lifford Lane industrial estate in Stirchley, next to the public tip. Behind us is a chemical works that pumps out noxious fumes all day long.

Clouds of orange and yellow smoke drift across the surface of the water, and there is the distinct smell of chlorine in the air. The water is skimmed with frothy scum, gathering at the edges where all the dead fish lie, belly up.

Not the sort of place featured in the Angling Times, but we like it because the Parkie doesn't always turn up to charge you for a day ticket, and even when he does, we just move our stuff till he's gone.

We know there are some big fish in the reservoir such as pike and tench, but usually we catch nothing more than the odd gudgeon or stickleback.

Today however, on my first cast, I catch a molly. This is a sort of exotic goldfish, usually kept as a pet in an aquarium. I can't believe it. Bright orange with large wavy fins, swimming in my keep-net. Jeremy says it won't last long in these waters, it will be attacked by other fish, jealous of its colour. Someone probably released it when they didn't want it any more. Sad really. Picked on and persecuted for being colourful by the majority who are grey and dull.

By seven a.m. we're starving and so start on our packed-lunch. Seeing this, a big kid sitting a bit further down the bank, saunters over. He's much older than us and we know there's going to be trouble.

"Give us some of your sarnies or I'll chuck you in."

With no adults around for protection, we reluctantly oblige. He takes half of everybody's, except Graham's.

He looks inside one of his and says, "Brown sauce? Disgusting. Give us some of yer drink."

Graham hands him his bottle.

"Help yourself. Have as much as you like. It's only Corporation Pop[1]."

So he leaves him alone. Instead, he picks on Jeremy who's got tinned salmon and a flask of tea. When he eats them all and drinks a full steaming cup, Jeremy starts blartin'[2].

At nine o'clock, one other angler arrives and sets up on the opposite bank. We've nearly run out of maggots, so I walk round to try and scrounge some from this new arrival.

"Excuse me mister, could you spare a few maggits?"

He has three bait boxes full to the brim. Mixed, white and casters. He's chucking handfuls in before brushing the sawdust off his fat, greedy fingers, on his trousers.

"Sorry, I can't spare any."

When I get back with the bad news, Graham says *he'll* try. He makes the long walk, empty bait box in hand.

"Spare a few maggits mista?"

"Look, I've just told your mate a minute ago, I can't spare any."

Graham looks across the water to where we are.

"Oh, I'm not with them, they're nothing to do with me."

"Look, just piss off, will you."

---

[1] tap water
[2] crying

An hour later, more anglers arrive, and we manage to scrounge some bait. Ten yards to our left is someone who looks like he knows what he's doing. He's got all the best gear: two rods, electronic bite-detectors, ground-bait, extendable rod-rests, umbrella, with night shelter attachment, reclining chair, waders, micromesh landing and keep-nets and, to top it all, Foster Grant sunglasses which, according to the advert on the telly, are worn by Peter Wyngarde in Department S and are also ideal for fishermen because they eliminate glare and "*they float*".

Why he's fishing here in this reservoir is a mystery. Perhaps it's for a bet. Within an hour, he's caught three tench, and a small gallery has formed behind him. The spectators watch his every move.

"Yeah, look, he's fishing a bit deeper. See how he baits the hook. What size is that? A number ten? Really? Well, he must know what he's doing, he's got Foster Grants."

Graham starts to cast diagonally, to get closer to his swim and when he isn't looking, he moves his stuff a yard nearer down the bank.

After one audacious cast, when his float ends up two inches from the expert's, the latter looks over and says sarcastically, "Are you sure you wouldn't like to come and fish next to me?"

He underestimates the thickness of Graham's skin.

"Really mister? Thanks. Hey lads, he said it's OK to fish next to him."

We all stay where we are but Graham moves all his stuff and sits right next to him for the rest of the day, even getting the benefit of his umbrella when it rains.

When we pack up for the day, I fill my bait-box with water and put the molly in. I can't bring myself to put it back into the reservoir where it faces certain death. Back home, I put it in a bowl and it immediately looks bigger and happier.

In the evening, after tea, we plan to light a fire in the fields on the other side of the brook. I wait until *Crossroads* has started before I sneak out. Mum is glued to the set, fascinated by the new black character, Melanie Harper, Meg's foster daughter, who has caused such a stir in the papers.

Personally, I don't know what all the fuss is about. I steal a potato from the larder and some old copies of the Evening Mail. Graham brings a Zip firelighter to get the wet wood going and Neil Walker brings a few loose matches that won't be missed out of the box. We once trusted

Jeremy Potts with this important job, and the knob-head brought safety matches. He still acts like a nerd tonight, bringing his potato wrapped in foil.

Inside the hawthorn den we have created, we make several attempts to light the fire. The smoke is choking and we spend the first half hour coughing our guts up outside the den, as fifteen editions of the Evening Mail still won't persuade the wet wood to catch fire.

Graham is the only one with a strong enough constitution to stay inside, blowing on it for all he's worth. He finally emerges with a black face and a huge grin as he announces the fire is lit and his potato is already in.

He can never wait for his to cook properly, so after thirty minutes, he rolls it out of the ashes with a stick. Then juggling it between hands, he takes a huge bite, getting black ash all around his mouth.

The undercooked potato crunches like an apple and Graham says, "Mmmm, bostin[1], cooked just right."

Jeremy butts in, "You'll get food poisoning if you don't let it cook properly."

We all tell him to shut his face and send him out to look for more wood.

After an hour, the crackling apology of a fire has turned into a raging inferno. The sap and knots in the wood pop and explode sending sparks showering over us and up into the night sky. We're all packed in tight inside the hawthorn den, no more than inches from the flames. At the point when Graham's Wellingtons start to smoke, he issues the instruction to retreat outside.

"Kin Aida!" exclaims Graham, outside in the cool air and examining his face.

"I've got no eyebrows left. How am I going to explain that when I get in?"

We all pick a stalk of dried long grass. Graham brings out the end of a burning stick and we all 'light up' pretending we're smoking a Hamlet, 'the mild cigar from Benson and Hedges.' Lying back in the grass, with hot faces, we look up at the stars and the bobowlers[2].

---

[1] brilliant
[2] particularly large, hairy moths

Doreen Drysdale is lying next to me. She's madly in love with me after I saved her outside the chip shop on Thursday night. She had been getting some unwanted attention from some big lads from The Bell[1]. She had asked them to leave her alone.

They just laughed and one of them grabbed her, so I went over. I didn't say anything, just put all five of them on the floor with my black belt in karate.

Anyway, it just so happened that a journalist from The Birmingham Evening Mail was in the shop at the time, buying some chips and a pickled egg and he took some pictures, which ended up on the front page of the next day's first edition, under the headline:

10 year old black belt cleans up Northfield scum.

The article went on to say how, like the monks of the Shaolin temple, I am essentially a peace-loving person, and don't like violence but, if you push me too far or back me into a corner, watch out! You will be picking up your teeth for a week.

Doreen was so grateful, I walked her home, sharing a bag of chips and we kissed under every lamp-post. We've been going out ever since.

Graham shines his torch on my face, kicks my foot and tells me to stop daydreaming: "Wake up dopey. Stop looking at the stars. It's gone ten and you'll cop it when you get in if you don't get a move on."

---

[1] Northfield pub demolished in the early 1980s

Warren. 2002

The doctor screws up his face as he shines the little light into my eye and he looks into his instrument.

"Hmmm … Aha … Good!"

He turns the light out, swivels round on his chair and scribbles a few notes.

"Well Colin, that seems to be quite normal, I can't see anything. I think we can safely say you haven't had a stroke or got a brain tumour. Any other theories you'd like to put to me? You really shouldn't self-diagnose Colin, you'll drive yourself mad with worry. A lot of what you read on the internet, you can take with a pinch of salt."

"Well actually, there was one other thing that kept cropping up, that seemed to match my symptoms; the early stages of Parkinson's Disease."

"Oh Colin, come on now. How old are you? Forty-two? Three? No, no, no, highly unlikely. You're far too young for that. No, my guess is that it's something far more straightforward like a trapped nerve in your left arm. There is something called Carpal Tunnel Syndrome…"

I stop him in mid-sentence.

"With respect, I'm sorry, but this is more than just a trapped nerve. It's spreading all down my left side, even into my leg which I'm starting to drag when I walk."

"Really? Show me."

I walk up and down his room.

"Yes, I see. There *is* a slight drag isn't there?"

He scribbles a few more notes.

"OK, I'll tell you what I'll do. As this isn't really my field, I'll refer you to see a neurologist at the hospital. They are the experts in these matters. If anyone can tell you if you've got Parkinson's, he can. You should get a letter with an appointment within three months."

"Three months!?"

"Sorry, it's the best I can do."

In the meantime, I compensate by burying myself in work and concentrating on a little pet project of mine.

A couple of days after we'd had our little chat, I see Warren in the playground. He is standing on his own, looking over at Kelly Mulligan and her group. I think, *don't make it so obvious, you idiot, you'll just drive her even further away*. But then again, I suppose he's got to learn the hard way. He sees me and trots over.

"Sir, you won't say anything about the other day will you?"

"About what Warren? I've forgotten already. Anything else I can help you with"

He smiles, scratching his head, as if trying to remember something.

"Oh yeah, and I've been meaning to ask you. Any chance of me being in the school play?"

"Sorry Warren, we're well into rehearsals and it's fully cast. Why didn't you come to the auditions?"

"Didn't think about it then."

"This hasn't got anything to do with the fact that Kelly's got the lead role has it?"

"Course not Sir…..erm … what about if someone drops out?"

"That's hardly likely to happen at this stage Warren. And we already have understudies."

"Oh go on Sir, just for me. You can write an extra part for me. I don't care how small it is. I don't even have to have any words. Just so long as I walk on stage and can be part of rehearsals."

Later, in the staff-room, I tell Neil in the English Department what I am thinking about Warren. He can't believe it.

"You must be mad Colin. I wouldn't let him have anything to do with the School Play. He's a psycho. He'll be a nightmare in rehearsals."

I spend all evening chewing over Warren's request. Something in my conscience tells me I should let him in. Something to do with Graham I suppose and how badly I felt he was treated at school and how no one tried to help him. This is my chance to do something that will really make a difference.

After dinner, I ask Emm what she thinks.

"Well, of course I don't know him but it could be that he's the way he is because the door's always shut in his face before he's even given a chance. It must be hard dealing with rejection all the time."

Next day, in the staff-room, I say to Neil, "Is it any wonder he's the way he is, if no one ever trusts him or shows any interest in him?"

"The words of an idealist Colin. And dangerous words. If you're not careful, he'll ruin the whole play and all that work will go down the drain."

"But what are we supposed to do, as teachers? Isn't this our job?"

"The damage was done long before he came to this school Colin. A result of poor parenting, lack of good male role models and holes in the social care system. We are teachers not social workers Colin. It isn't our job. You can't be expected to save him now."

"Well, at least I can give him a taste. It may be a real formative experience for him."

"Look Colin, be realistic. Being on stage in your play for five minutes is not going to change anything. His way is already set. Stop beating yourself up about someone who himself, doesn't give a toss about anyone else."

"Why should his way already be set? I think it's wrong to write someone off at such a young age. I'm going to let him have a go."

"Well that's your funeral Colin. Don't say I didn't warn you."

Back at my classroom, Warren's waiting for me.

"Did you want me Sir?"

"Ah yes, Warren. I've been thinking. I may be able to find something for you in the play after all."

"Really Sir? Do you mean it?"

"Well, don't get your hopes too high just yet. It'll be a non-speaking part."

"I don't care Sir. That's enough. That's brilliant."

"I'll try and work it so that you'll get a bit of a laugh from the audience."

"That's brilliant Sir. Thank you."

"But it's on one condition Warren. You've got to be on your best behaviour. No disrupting rehearsals."

"I won't Sir, I swear."

"Because I'm putting a lot of trust in you Warren, and I don't want you to let me down. Is that clear?"

"Yes Sir. I promise I won't let you down. I'm going to show you. I'm going to show everyone. I've just never had the chance before."

I reflect on Warren after he's gone. I hope I haven't made a mistake. Neil's words replay in my head,

"Well, that's your funeral, Colin."

Maybe. But you've got to give Warren some credit for persistence. I asked around amongst the staff about him. Seems he's got an older brother with drink and drug problems that has involved the police at their house on more than one occasion. Warren regularly misses sleep.

Yes, I see a lot of similarities between Graham and Warren Newman. They could almost be the same person forty years apart. I chuckle when I remember our last Christmas at junior school. Pantomime and Flatulence: a lethal combination!

Christmas 1970

It's been months since I was told I would start to put on weight. I just don't understand it; I'm still as thin as ever. My chances with Doreen Drysdale seem doomed. As Christmas draws near, everything seems to be working against me.

On the morning of our Eleven Plus exam, she sits in the aisle next to me in the hall. She finishes with loads of time to spare, yawns, looks at her watch and doodles on the edge of the question paper. It puts me into a bit of a panic. Why is it taking me so long?

At the end when Mr. Brown tells us to put down our pens, I look up and see he is looking directly at me.

Then I realise: so is everybody else. It seems *everyone* in the room has finished early and they are all watching me. I scribble my final sentence on the last question, put my pen down and there's a loud collective sigh of relief.

I glance over at Doreen and she's looking straight at me with this bored expression on her face that says *you're keeping us all waiting.*

As we walk out of the hall, everyone is talking about the exam.

"Yeah, it was easy..."

"Don't know what all the fuss was about..."

"Did you see Methane? I thought his pen was going to catch fire."

They all laugh.

Someone shouts, "Yeah, I thought he was writing War and Peace."

There's a silence, and Toss pot Barton who said it, blushes. Everyone stares at him and someone says, "What the hell is War and Peace when it's out?"

Toss-pot just mumbles, "Oh it's this really fat book that takes ages to read."

"How do you know? You read it?"

They all laugh at this and I'm just glad that the attention is now on someone else rather than me.

When I get home I run through the exam in my head. I thought it was quite hard. If they all thought it was easy, that must mean that I've failed.

Anyway, as a means of distraction from all this serious swotting, Mr. George and Mrs. King get the 4th years to put on a School Christmas Pantomime *Jack and the Beanstalk* for all the little ones and the parents.

Graham and I are cast as the cow that Jack takes to the market to be sold. I am the front end, controlling the head, Graham is the rear end, controlling the tail and the udders. Although you can't see our faces, this is actually a really good part as we get lots of laughs.

Mr. George has created loads of comedy by telling Graham to keep cocking his back leg as if going for a wee whenever we pass a tree. The udders also squirt water, which Graham constantly directs into the audience, who scream with delight when they get wet.

Jack is played by Doreen. My dream has come true. She leads me round the stage by a rope around my neck. Through my eye holes, I can see her hand on the rope and the back of her head as she walks in front of me.

On the night of the public performance, everything starts off well. Jack is told to sell the cow at market for as much as he can get. There's a touching scene when Jack cuddles the head (me) in an emotional farewell before we set off. I am in heaven.

Graham is so obsessed with the udders and cocking his back leg, to get more laughs, that Doreen has to really drag us with the rope.

"Come *on* Daisy!" she shouts at us constantly.

I keep whispering to Graham to stop messing around and to walk properly because Doreen is getting annoyed.

He whispers back, "Who cares? Listen to the laughs we're getting!"

Eventually, Doreen gives an almighty tug on the rope and some of the join between head and body of the cow rips apart. There's a bit of a gasp, then a laugh from the audience.

Then, because of the panic as I try to keep the head on, the worst thing imaginable happens: I let out a fart. I can't help it. It always happens when I'm stressed. Graham's hands are on my hips and his face is right up against my backside.

His reaction is loud and violent. He starts shouting, "Oh, no way man. I can't stand that. Oh God, I can taste it, get me out of here!"

He starts to walk in a different direction to me and the material rips further. Doreen is grappling with the rope, trying to control us, with her own fingers on her nose, because she too can now smell the awful fart that is starting to filter out. I am so ashamed.

Graham continues, "Argh, get me out of here man, it's killing me! I can't breathe."

Finally he pulls his section free from the front end. The audience are roaring with laughter. Mr. George runs on to the stage and tries to put Graham back with me.

Graham resists, "No way, I'm not going back down there, he's farted."

The audience are in hysterics. The back end of the cow walks off stage. Doreen leads my half into the wings on the other side.

When we get off she shouts at me. She says she's never been so embarrassed in all her life and that it's all my fault.

I take off my cow's head, my face all red and sweaty from the exertion and say sorry.

"My whole family's in the audience Methane, you freak, I hate you!"

I wish my life could end at this moment and the floor would swallow me up.

Doreen has to do the scene where she sells the cow, with just my end sticking out from the wings while she's holding on to the rope. Graham is being told off by Mrs. King, saying that he will not be allowed to come to the Christmas party or see Santa on Friday.

"Oh Miss, that is *so* unfair. It wasn't my fault. I bet you couldn't have kept your head down there. No one could. And I hold the record for holding your breath."

"I don't care Graham Skinner. Everything you touch, you destroy. Now get out of my sight."

As she walks off, he mutters under his breath, "Bitch."

He sulks backstage for the rest of the show. Towards the end, Mr. George speaks the Giant's voice in deep tones into the off-stage microphone. "FFEE FOH FAH FUM…" When he puts it back on its stand to go and attend to something else, Graham, with nothing left to lose now, picks up the microphone and switches it on.

There's a loud screech of feedback before he says in a loud voice while laughing, "Villa are shit and King's a bitch!"

Again the audience roar with laughter. Graham hastily puts the microphone back, then runs away. He isn't allowed back for the rest of term. But there *is* one consolation for Graham; his dad is back, looking leaner and paler. Graham says he's been on Her Majesty's Secret Service again, while 'Toss Pot' jokes that it's more likely he's been detained at Her Majesty's Pleasure. Sometimes I don't understand a word that weird kid says.

Christmas ends early in our house, on Boxing Day to be precise. Sick of the constant squabbling and screaming, Mum takes a large pin and bursts all the balloons, then proceeds to take down the decorations, cursing us all under her breath, saying that Christmas is cancelled, and there won't *be* a Christmas next year at all, if we can't stop arguing. We watch her do this in mournful silence.

Katie, sobbing, promises she'll behave better if Mum will just leave the tree up. Mum shouts, demanding total silence. The budgie doesn't understand this enforced silence and chirrups away, until Mum throws her slipper at his cage, and he falls off his perch in a cloud of feathers.

She then sends us all to bed at 7 p.m., without any tea. Dad tries to reason with her on our behalf, before he too is sent to bed. He does as he's told. He knows hell has no fury like his wife when she's in this mood.

When we go up, we are warned not to make a sound, but Rob keeps picking on me, flicking my ear, until I shout at him. This is a mistake considering Mum's unpredictable temper.

We hear the kitchen door fly open with a crash, then the stomping of her feet on the stairs as she shouts, "Are you *still at* it? Wait till I get up there, you're gonna cop it!"

She bursts into our bedroom armed with a big wooden spoon from the kitchen. She chases Rob and me out of the bedroom and down the stairs, into the living room and round and round the sofa. After a couple of minutes, Rob gives up, takes his beating, then sits on the sofa that I am still running around. It's like he's watching a live Tom and Jerry cartoon, playing out before his very eyes.

As I continue to run round the sofa, he is laughing and shouts, "Colin, just give in! She'll get you in the end!" Eventually, she *does get* me and delivers a few extra swipes for making her work so hard.

Not another sound is heard for the rest of the night.

Easter 2003

The hospital takes forever to get in touch with me, so that it's the end of the spring term before I get my appointment. Just before I'm due to go, it's the performance of the School Play.

On the whole, Warren keeps his word and doesn't let me down. At rehearsals, he isn't absent once, except when he has a detention. Sometimes he is mildly annoying, but in such a way that I can't help smiling. He likes to upstage scenes, particularly difficult ones, while they're being rehearsed. It is because he is bored.

At moments of high tension and emotion, Warren will suddenly stick his head round the edge of the curtains and pull a face. All of the other actors who are watching the rehearsal from the auditorium will suddenly crease up laughing.

This includes Kelly Mulligan. It is his way of getting attention and making her laugh. He is also just captivated by being on stage and with people looking at him. Warren has no conception of live performance. The 'fourth wall' doesn't exist for him. He feels he can just wander on stage and interact with the players any time he wants.

He's never been to the theatre before, so he doesn't understand the rules.

As part of their GCSE Drama, I take the class to the local theatre to see a performance of *Fame*. We are in the front row, so close we can actually touch the acting area. Warren watches open-mouthed as the female dancers writhe in front of him.

Turning to me, not bothering to keep his voice down he says things like, "Sir, she's looking at me," and, "Which one do you fancy then Sir?" or, "Sir, look, she's got a mole on her tit."

It doesn't occur to him that they might be able to hear him and that it is distracting for them. During one scene in the Fame canteen, one of the actors accidentally drops an apple and it rolls all the way to the front of the stage. The actors try to ignore it and carry on with the scene. The whole auditorium watches the apple's progress, rolling in a sort of lop-sided way across the boards down the rake of the stage. It comes to a halt just inches from Warren. He can't help himself. He reaches out, picks it up and takes a huge bite out of it. The whole audience erupts in laughter and I shrink down into my seat.

On the night of the School Play this evening, Warren gets a huge roar from the audience, this time for the right reason.

A few weeks ago, I inadvertently stumbled across a secret talent he has. He can *juggle*! I saw him in the canteen juggling with three oranges, to everyone's amusement, before getting his ear clipped by the dinner lady who told him he would have to pay for any fruit that he has bruised. Something I can definitely harness I thought.

So, near the end, during the fairground scene, we dress him up as a circus performer, and he walks across the stage juggling three coloured balls. As he goes, he can't resist looking at the audience and grinning. They roar their approval, at which point he fumbles the balls and drops them, which gets an even bigger laugh.

He bends down, picks them up and takes a deep bow, grinning all the time, and gets a spontaneous, thunderous round of applause. People can't believe this is actually Warren Newman. Even Kelly, who is watching from the wings is laughing. But she still won't entertain the thought of going out with him. Well, certain realities have to be faced up to.

At the end of the show, the head asks me, as the director, to come up on stage and say a few words. I address the audience.

"I'm sure there are lots of you here tonight, not just parents but members of staff too, who are a little taken aback, perhaps pleasantly surprised with what some of these very 'familiar' faces can actually do. I am immensely proud of them. Six months ago, I couldn't get them to stand still for ten seconds. I couldn't hear them when I was supposed to, and always could when I wasn't. They missed their cues, they stood in front of one another, they were terrified of singing out loud.

"Well look at them now. I wish those OFSTED inspectors were here tonight because this is a good school, with tremendous potential and opportunity. You saw the results for yourself tonight, these young people are capable of anything if we show enough trust in them. I think they deserve another round of applause!"

Everyone cheers. I see the headmaster standing and clapping, and smiling broadly. At moments like this, I think, it's all worthwhile, and I cheer and applaud them too.

It's gone midnight by the time I get home. I don't mention my appointment at the hospital to Emm, and instead show her the card that the cast presented to me, after the show, thanking me for all the work I'd put in.

Amongst the lovely tributes is a touching message from Warren Newman:

Sir, thay wer all rong about me wernt thay?
from warren newman.
ps your a grate teecher.
pps pittee abowt yoor focking bold hed and fulse teeth!!!

Emm laughs. "Yes," she says, "I suppose you are going a bit thin on top aren't you? Old man, we'll have to get you a walking stick soon!"

I laugh. "Old man? I'm only forty-three you know! Same age as you. But I suppose we can't all have a portrait locked away in an attic somewhere.

She laughs at this, then puts the card on the mantelshelf. It's then that I notice Lily standing in the doorway in her pyjamas, rubbing her eyes. "What are you doing out of bed poppet? You should have been asleep hours ago."

"I could hear talking and laughing, Daddy and I wanted to see you."

I get down on one knee, hold out my arms and she walks to me. I envelop her and stand up with her in my arms.

"I heard what you were saying. Are you really very old Daddy?"

I laugh. "No, of course not darling! At least I hope not!"

"You're not going to die are you Daddy?"

"Oh what a silly thing to think poppet. Nothing's going to happen to me, I promise."

I give her a tight squeeze. Lily then says, "You cuddle too mummy."

So Emm joins us, and we all hold each other for a minute, pinching and tickling each other and giggling.

I lie in bed later when Emm's fallen asleep and look up at the ceiling, worrying. What if it really *is* Parkinson's? I really *will turn* into an old man. What am I going to do? When am I going to tell Emm?

Decisions. Decisions.

1971. The Golden Shot

"What do you mean, you don't want to go to the grammar school?"

"I want to go where Laura and Rob go, and where Graham will go."

"What a waste Colin. Don't you realise this is your big chance? You are the only one to have passed it in this house. You could end up getting a really good job, wearing a suit and tie, working behind the counter in a bank. I'll bet Mrs. Potts isn't letting her Jeremy go to the comprehensive."

Mum turns on Dad, demanding some support for her argument. He is dozing in his chair. She throws a cushion at him. He wakes with a start.

"What?"

"Will you have a word please? This is your own son's future we're talking about, and you don't take any interest."

"What?"

"The grammar school, his Eleven Plus. Are you even listening?"

"His eleven what?"

"God, you are totally useless. If World War Three broke out tomorrow, you wouldn't notice, unless the Traveller's Rest was bombed. Do you even know that he's passed his Eleven Plus?"

"What's his eleven plus?"

"Oh forget it. I'll get Vera to have a word."

Her staunchest ally, Aunty Vera will be arriving in a minute, to put me straight.

Vera is Dad's sister. She cleans the public toilets in Weoley Castle, Northfield and Selly Oak. She's like a cross between Lady Docker and Elsie Tanner. She clips up the road in stilettos and mink coat, smelling of Rive Gauche. Her hair is back-combed into an indestructible beehive, held in place by half a can of Bristow's. Eyebrows are plucked to invisibility and redrawn with pencil and pearly white dentures are smudged with the bright red lipstick which she likes so much.

Her emerald green handbag with brass clasp matches her emerald green shoes with brass buckles, green gloves and green silk scarf. Her permanent smile belongs to someone who enjoys life to the max. She is the life and soul of the Barnes Hill Working Man's Club, even though she's teetotal.

We have a picture of Vera on our mantelshelf, dancing on a table, hoisting her skirts. She laughs like a drain, particularly at her own jokes, and today, when she walks through the front door, she shrieks at the top of her voice, "Where is he then? Where's Bamber Gascoigne? Come over here and give your Aunty Vera a kiss."

She smothers me in her fur coat, and gives me a wet, red kiss on my lips, which I wipe off with the sleeve of my jumper. Then she gives me a pound note for doing so well.

"Now what's this your mother tells me about not wanting to go to King Edward's? You don't want to end up like me do you? Cleaning up other people's mess for a pittance. You know, I even had to work this morning? On a Sunday. And I don't get double time for it neither. Not even time and a half. No. I just get time and a turd."

She erupts at her own joke.

"Oh Jesus wept, time and a turd. I'm gonna wet myself."

Her laugh is totally infectious, and we all join in.

"Do you know how hard I've had to work all my life to get all the nice things I've got?"

Aunty Vera's terraced house is a shrine to hard work. Garden gnomes on the lawn, stone cladding, bay windows with fake lead latticing, displays of cut crystal and polished brass, flame effect gas fire, and leather settee, which you can spill as much orange squash over as you like, because, as she tells us, "It'll wipe clean my dear, it's *leather.*"

She also owns the only colour television in Weoley Castle, which is positioned in a prominent place facing the window, so that it can be seen from outside. All paid for by the fruits of cleaning toilets or as Vera would say, 'the shit business.'

She has seen shit in the most unexpected of places; on the walls, on the ceiling. Once, in a man's sock, nailed to the cubicle door. This morning, she found a hole drilled through the wall in the Ladies' cubicle. Ever the detective for foul play, she suspects it's been drilled from the Gents' side. But she wants to make sure before she makes an official report, and a request for the maintenance department to come and fill the hole.

So she asks Dad to go up with her to verify her suspicions that someone is spying on the Ladies' toilet from the Gents' side.

Dad's reluctant. "Oh come on Vera, do you really need me? I mean, what do you expect me to do?"

"Just see if you can see anything from your end, when I shine a torch from my side."

Eventually he agrees. He's on all fours in the Gents' public lavatory, with his eye up close to the hole drilled in the wall. It's just unfortunate that at that exact moment, four blokes on the way back from The Stone pub, come in to spend a penny. As they walk in, Dad stands quickly and pretends to wash his hands in the basin.

They all give him a filthy look, one muttering under his breath, "Bloody perverts, should be locked up, the lot of 'em."

Dad continues to wash his hands, clearing his throat and avoiding their stares.

Eventually, they leave. Dad gets back down on his knees and shouts through the hole, "Vera will you please hurry up, this is embarrassing!!"

Vera's muffled voice can just be heard on the other side, "Hang on a minute Ed, I've just got to clear the hole!"

At which point, she blows into the hole just as Dad has his eye up close to it. A cloud of dust nearly blinds him.

"Argggh!! What are you doing? You could at least have given me some warning!!"

Vera's suspicions are confirmed. Dad exits the toilets rubbing his eye, while the four blokes who have been hanging around outside waiting for him, shout things like, "Pervert…. Paedophile… We know all about you."

When they get home, Vera rants, "There are some dirty buggers about. Now what kind of a person takes off his sock, has a shit in it, then nails it to the door? Or takes a power drill into the cubicle with them. Education is lacking. There are too many people idling their life away, so that moral standards have slipped. Now I'm telling you Colin, you go to grammar school, go off to university and better yourself. Lift yourself out of Northfield and Weoley Castle and aim for the stars. The world is your lobster."

After an hour of gossip and putting the world to rights, it's time for Vera to go. I collect all the empty tea cups and put them in the kitchen sink. Aunty Vera's has red lipstick on the rim. She puts on her mink coat reapplies lipstick in the mirror, delivers her usual farewell, "Tararabit." before tottering back down the road in her high heels.

When she's gone, after dinner, the Sunday blues start to set in. I've always hated Sunday afternoons. They are so depressing. Between four and five, there's nothing on the telly except *The Golden Shot* with Bob Monkhouse and his assistant, Anne Aston, who can't add up.

The climax of the show is when this week's winner goes for the jackpot by shooting an almost invisible cotton thread that's holding closed the strongbox full of gold coins. Not only do you have to achieve this near impossible feat with a tele-bow (a crossbow tied to the camera from about 50 feet) but you don't actually get to fire it yourself.

The contestant has to give instructions to a blindfolded cameraman … over the phone. I can't help thinking that this is a little dangerous. This week, the combination of a contestant with a stutter and a bad phone line and a cameraman with a hearing aid and a nervous twitch, results in a bolt being fired into the studio ceiling.

By the time *The Onedin Line* starts, full blown depression has set in about unfinished homework. Oh for Friday night again and the music of *Hawaii Five O.*

Cold Sunday roast meat sandwiches for tea followed by jelly and custard, then a bath in Rob's lukewarm water and I'm allowed to watch a bit of *Doctor at Large before* I go up.

Lying in bed, looking up at the ceiling, I wonder if I've made the right decision to go to the comprehensive.

Vera's words go round in my head. "You go to the grammar school Colin, better yourself, and aim for the stars."

She's right. I don't want to end up like Malcolm Pryor, in his forties, who still lives at home and works at Longbridge with his dad. I'm going to be different. I'll train to be an actor. Then I'll slowly make a name for myself.

At first, just a walk on part on *Crossroads*. David Hunter will be in deep conversation with Sandy at reception about some dire crisis like the motel going bust, and I will interrupt them to hand back the keys to Chalet 43, then walk off.

Then gradually, as I get more famous, I'll progress to appear on shows like *Doctor Who* and *Star Trek*. In the words of William Shatner, I'm going to boldly go where no man has gone before.

Yes, Birmingham is not the centre of the universe. In twenty years' time, I'll be a thousand warp factor miles from this town.

Q.E. Hospital, Birmingham. 2003

"Colin Sparrow."

I raise my hand like a schoolboy.

"Will you come this way please?"

Flushing with self-consciousness, I get out of my chair and excuse myself squeezing around and past others in wheelchairs, who have been waiting longer than me. Feeling like a fraud, I gallop after the nurse down the corridor.

In the examination room, the consultant neurologist's face is inscrutable as he reads my letter of referral.

"You're forty-three and a teacher, is that right?"

"Yes."

"And what do you teach?"

"English and Drama."

"Oh, that sounds interesting."

"Yes, it can be."

He looks up and studies my face intently.

"Would you say that your face has changed recently? Have people who know you, said you look different?"

"No."

"It's difficult for me you see, because I don't know you. It's the first time I've seen you."

I think to myself, what on earth is he going on about?

"Can you take off your shirt and trousers and pop yourself up on to the bed please?"

He starts manipulating my left arm and shoulder, winding them in a circular motion.

He does the same with my right side, before moving on to my legs, while nodding and saying "Aha …" or "Yes!" to himself occasionally. He then asks me to tap forefinger on to thumb very quickly, first right, then left. He nods again.

"Have you been feeling very stiff and aching in your joints and muscles lately?"

"Yes."

"Do you get tired easily?"

"Yes, and I find myself nodding off, even in public."

"Do you think you are moving more slowly lately?"

"Yes and my left leg seems to drag as I walk."

He then asks me to close my eyes, hold my right arm out to my side, then with my right forefinger, touch the tip of my nose.

Then he asks me to do it with my left. Easy.

After the examination, in between making notes, he watches me as I button my shirt.

"Do you have difficulty doing that?"

"Well, it's just this shirt, it's new and stiff."

"I see."

He reads the letter again.

"Your doctor tells me here that you have your own suspicions and have given yourself a diagnosis of Parkinson's Disease."

He suggests an arrogance in me with this simple statement.

"Well, I just looked up my symptoms on the internet, I know I'm no expert."

"It's not a criticism Mr. Sparrow. It's only natural to conduct your own research. Your doctor says that he thinks it highly unlikely, because of your age."

Inside, I wish I'd never come, wasting their time like this.

"I'm sorry, I've been presumptuous."

The neurologist smiles again and looks me straight in the eye.

"Mr. Sparrow, what I'm trying to say is; I agree with *your* diagnosis not *his*."

After the consultation, I sit on the station platform. My train's been delayed and I'm half glad as it gives me time to think. A cleaner is changing the plastic bin liners and is sweeping the concourse.

Lucky sod. Not a care in the world.

I sit on and watch the numbers flip over inside the large split-flap display station clock hanging from the roof. Every five minutes, its steady tick is drowned out by the next train arriving, disgorging hundreds of commuters, students, doctors and patients for Birmingham University and The Queen Elizabeth Medical Centre. They all hurry on their way, late for lectures, meetings or appointments, where many will be given the news they've been dreading.

70

Then, for a couple of minutes, after their heels have click-clacked up the staircase and over the bridge, silence returns and I am alone again with my thoughts.

I always assumed Parkinson's was an old man's disease, or something that ex-boxers like Mohammed Ali got, after a lifetime of blows to the head.

The neurologist told me an area of my brain is dying. He told me it has been dying for up to ten years and had lost maybe eighty percent of its function, by the time I'd even noticed any of the symptoms that led me to make an appointment with my GP. He said it's the area that produces dopamine, the chemical neurotransmitter that sends the signals from your brain all around your body.

When there is a shortage of dopamine, those signals only get through intermittently, resulting in movement that is slow and jerky. Fine motor control of the fingers is lost, so that simple tasks such as writing, doing up buttons, cleaning your teeth, or holding a knife and fork become increasingly difficult.

There's also a lack of facial expression, a sort of 'mask like' quality, hence his question about my face. It's progressive and degenerative.

In other words, there is no cure and it just keeps getting worse.

I'd asked the neurologist if he could be making a mistake.

He said it was unlikely, but that he'd refer me to a colleague of his for a second opinion. He'd see me as soon as possible, but it could be towards the end of summer now.

I also asked him, "Why me?' He said he didn't know. The cause of Parkinson's remains a mystery. Some articles have been written claiming that it's genetic, others that it could be a result of exposure to pesticides or head trauma in the past. (Could I remember an incident when I was knocked unconscious? Yes I can, actually). But most probably, he said, it's just a case of bad luck. Bad luck? That doesn't sound very scientific.

What am I going to tell them at school? What am I going to tell Emm? And what about Lily? She's three years old and her dad is already like this. Children need their dad. They need a dad who is active, who does stuff with them, who takes them on holidays and swims in the sea with them. A dad who is their hero.

Like I wanted mine to be over thirty years ago.

Summer 1971. Withernsea

I climb up on to the board that he puts across the arm rests to raise me up. I look at Rob in the mirror who is trying to make me laugh. The barber flicks the sheet, showering me with the previous customer's hair, then tucks it in tight, into my collar. "And how would you like it young man?"

"Well, I'd like this side left long, over my ears and the other side completely bald. At the back, I'd like random bald patches, and on top, a tuft sticking up like a pineapple. Comb the hair on top forward with Brylcreem, cutting a fringe that's all wonky and uneven. Oh, and give me a large cut on my ear as well."

"I'm sorry, I can't do that."

"Why not, you did last time, NOBHEAD!"

But I haven't got the bottle, and instead I say what Mum told me to say, "Short back and sides with plenty off the top please."

When I get home, Mum says it's not short enough, and sends me back to ask for more off. With no extra money, the barber is not pleased.

Switching on his clippers, he says, "So, not short enough eh?"

It's a good job I won't be seeing Doreen Drysdale for another seven weeks.

Next morning, we're up at six a.m., along with everyone else on our road, at the start of the industrial fortnight, packing suitcases on to the roof rack.

Graham, who's not going on holiday because his dad is still away, gets up early anyway and comes across to our driveway.

He asks where we're going.

"Withernsea."

"Withered sea? Where's that?"

"Somewhere on the east coast."

"What's it like there?"

"It's OK, there's Amusements, but the sea's brown."

"What do you mean, the sea's brown?"

"It just is. It's green or blue everywhere else in the country, but brown at Withernsea. Dad says it's something to do with the silt from the Humber estuary."

"The what? The shit from the Humber estuary? Well, why are you going there?"

"My dad says there will be less traffic."

"Well, bring us a stick of rock when you come back."

I have to sit in the 'very very back' of our old Vauxhall Victor F-type Estate, which is overloaded to the hilt, including a roof rack full of suitcases, covered with an old tarpaulin. A little space is made for me behind all the luggage, next to two crates of Dad's homebrew. Then the hatchback door is slammed down and locked behind me, so I am in effect cut off from everyone else in the car. I am put here for a reason. Dad's home-made beer is potent. After being strained through an old pair of net curtains, then fermented for two weeks in the airing cupboard, the resulting concoction is every bit as volatile as nitro-glycerine. Every time we go over a bump in the road, the corks will pop and the beer foam down the sides of the bottles. So, it's my job in the 'very back' to replace the corks. I like this job. I can look out of the back window and put two fingers up to the cars behind without Mum ever knowing.

Before we leave, Mum tries to go to the toilet for one last time. She has a weak bladder, particularly in the mornings and the movement of the car will just make it worse.

As we start the engine, there's a clunk and horrendous vibration when Dad puts it into gear. Mum says she doesn't like the sound of that - and is it normal?

Dad replies, "Perfectly normal, I just have to put in a bit of oil at the first stop we make."

As we pull away, Graham is standing in the middle of the road and I feel sorry for him, stuck at home. I stick two fingers up and he laughs and chases us down the road. We wave at each other like mad until we turn the corner and he disappears from view.

It's been only forty-five minutes, and already Mum is desperate for a wee. Dad refuses to pull over.

"We're already behind schedule and this is a dual carriageway, so no stopping. You'll have to do it in the bucket. If you stoop down in front of your seat, no one will notice."

Her urgency forces her to agree to such humiliation. Everyone has to look away. It's just bad luck that there's a coach in the slow lane, doing about thirty miles an hour, belching out smoke. Dad says he has no choice but to overtake.

A minute into the manoeuvre, and we do seem to be passing them incredibly slowly.

Mum shouts at him from her stooping position. "For God's sake Ed, speed up, they can all see!"

"Look, my foot's on the floor, this is only a 1300 you know and we're carrying a lot of weight."

The coach is an old people's outing. No one seems to notice, until Mum decides to try and get off the bucket and flashes a large portion of her backside. One old guy nearly chokes on his Murray Mint, before directing everyone else's attention down to us, where Mum is hastily trying to pull up her knickers, and tuck herself in.

There's a row of old faces, mouths open, looking down. When we finally pull ahead of them, the coach driver tries to sneak a look too, and nearly veers off the road.

Getting rid of the contents is even trickier.

Dad insists, "We're not having this inside with us, sloshing around, for the next two hours."

Down goes the passenger seat window, out goes the bucket, then WHOOSH, as the contents of the bucket are jettisoned. Even at 50 mph, some of the spray comes back in on us at the back which is unfortunate for Katie, who's got her mouth open. The majority hits the car behind. A yellow torrent that thunders onto their windscreen with real force. His wipers are going ten to the dozen as they look on in stunned silence at this madman in front who's got a little kid in the back doing something with corks and sticking his two fingers up.

As it turns out, the biggest threat to Dad's military style planning and time schedule for the journey, is not Mum's weak bladder but our crap Vauxhall engine. Its complaining is getting louder and louder and more urgent with every mile we do. Eventually Dad is forced to pull into the next garage we come to. It limps on to the forecourt, clunking, before coming to a shuddering halt.

There's an old guy wiping his hands on an oily rag.

"Sounds like your universal joint has gone, mate."

"I only need a can of oil."

"It'll take more than a can of oil to solve that problem. You can't drive off with a worn joint like that, you'll cause even more damage in the long run. It'll have to be replaced or eventually you'll need a whole new crank shaft. On a model of this age, it wouldn't be worth your while by then. Best to sort it now."

Reluctantly, Dad lets him have a look at it. He drives the car over the pit and the old guy looks underneath with a torch.

He climbs out, shakes his head and says, "Yep, worn to nothing. That's why you're getting that clunking sound and vibration when you change gear and when you accelerate."

He says he's got the parts, but we'll have to wait until he finishes the job he's working on. Dad tells us we're going to be here for a while, so we may as well get out and stretch our legs. They all pile out, while I wait to be released from my den at the back. I jump out with pins and needles and trousers stuck to the back of my legs. We eat slightly warm corned beef sandwiches out of tin foil and share a cup of thermos flask tea. The roar of the passing juggernauts is deafening and we have to shout into each other's ears to be heard. The lorries create gusts of wind that snatch foil and napkins from our hands, and spin them into the air and into oncoming traffic.

The waiting becomes endless, hour after hour. It seems the mechanic doesn't have the part after all, not for our particular model. He has to send off for it from a service centre 50 miles away. Waiting for the part to be delivered, then having it fitted, takes the whole day. Mum is getting more and more anxious. We are in the middle of nowhere and the sun has gone down. Where are we all going to sleep? Even if we could afford it, which we can't, there isn't a Bed and Breakfast for miles.

It's dusk when we finally pull away, and I hear the old man saying to his partner, "Jesus, what a rough looking crew. Have you seen all the stuff piled up in the back? I wouldn't go on a long journey in an old banger like that, carrying such weight."

It's getting dark and Dad says we'll never find the site at this hour and that we should pull over for the night. It's a busy road, yet he decides to pitch the small two-man tent in front of the van on the narrow grass verge.

Everyone else will sleep in the van, except Dad and me. The inside of the tent is lit up by approaching headlights. Shadows race across the canvas and the whole flimsy structure shakes and flaps every time a lorry passes. Not the safest place to camp.

We've been lying in our sleeping bags for half an hour when Dad groans and says, "Christ, is that you?"

The corned beef has given me a serious bout of wind. Dad says he can't stand it much longer. He says it's making him feel sick. He unzips the tent doors and sees a clear moonlit sky. He puts on his cap, lights a cigarette, puts his pillow on the grass outside, then zips the doors down to his neck, so that his body is inside the tent but his head is outside.

During the night, I hear occasional sudden braking, as drivers' headlights pick out a head on the grass, outside a closed tent … smoking a cigarette.

Next day, when we finally arrive at the campsite, the weather has taken a turn for the worse and the rain is coming down in diagonal rods. We check in at the site office and I have to lie still in the back, with a coat over me, because we're only paying for a party of six.

The warden comes out in the rain, and I hear his voice from underneath the coat.

"Keep your vehicle to the tarmacked areas please, no driving on the grass. No open fires, no transistor radios. Everyone must be back on site by 11 p.m."

When he gets back into the car, Dad says the place is more like Stalag IV B. He drives to the far side of the field, as far away from the 'Camp Kommandant' as possible.

Mum says, "You'll have to put it up on your own, there's no way the kids are going out in this."

He puts on his gabardine mack and flat cap, then starts to empty poles and pegs and canvas on to the wet grass.

As if getting pleasure from someone else's misfortune, the rest of the campers, snug and dry under the awnings of their expensive looking trailer tents, look on and judge Dad's camping know-how as he begins his task.

An hour later, soaked to the skin, standing over an un-numbered, un-colour-coded tangle of poles, we can hear him cursing, "Camping? You can stick it."

It's an ex-army frame tent, with no instructions, bought cheap from the classifieds in the Evening Mail.

"This lot is all going down the tip as soon as we get home."

Poles don't fit together and need to be forced in with incredible strength. He strains, eyes bulging, veins standing out on the sides of this neck. "Christ! You need to be Garth to get this in."

He throws the pole on the floor, and we are informed that our tent is a useless pile of shit, probably made in Britain and put together by some left-wing arsehole who's on strike every other week.

He gets back into the car and asks for a bottle of homebrew to be passed forward. He pours it in one smooth movement into the teapot, to avoid upsetting the sediment at the bottom of the bottle, then drinks it in one go through the teapot spout. The fact that Mum hasn't washed it out and that there are still tea leaves in there doesn't bother him one bit.

Revived and in a better mood, he goes back out to finish the job. Two more bottles later and the tent is finally up, the rain has eased off and we start to unpack the car. The other campers watch us as we do so.

Our tent looks like something out of the Korean War, with bits flapping and hanging off here and there, and one pole left over. Dad says it must be a spare.

One smug nosey parker makes an observation as he passes. "I think you'll find you've got that inside out."

Dad replies, "Rubbish. This is a British army tent, seen service in the far east in monsoon conditions. 100 percent double-sided canvas, both sides waterproofed. None of yer modern nylon, polyester crap. Oh no, they don't make them like this anymore, nothing will blow this down."

We try to ignore the camper as we struggle past with the crates of beer. Mum in her shame, has draped bath towels over the crates to try and disguise them. The chinking of the bottles and popping of the corks underneath is giving us away.

The tent looks sort of lopsided. The main body of the canvas has been pegged too far back so that it doesn't join up properly with the front section. As a result, there's a gap between the roof and the top of the front section, that the zip won't close over.

Dad says that that is how it's supposed to look. He says the gap is meant to be there for ventilation. Later in the evening, Mum expresses her concern about this, but Dad, with one eye on the clock and closing time fast approaching, says it will be fine.

The suitcases on the roof rack have leaked and all his clothes are soaked. He has nothing dry to put on to go down the pub. He asks Mum to lend him something of hers. Dressed in a pink cardigan three sizes too small for him, with just his string vest underneath, he sets out across the fields, his change jingling in his pockets.

He will have to sleep in the porch section with me when he returns. I have a camp bed and his sleeping bag is on the floor. He's still out when I get into bed and the rain has started drumming on the canvas again. I begin to drop off with that warm cosy feeling that it's better to be inside than out there.

I wake at about five. Dawn is just breaking and I can hear a faint splashing sound and whispering very close. I'm still half asleep and can't quite make it out, but I distinctly hear, not particularly in this order, the words, "Bollocks!", "Stick it"! "My arse!" and "Camping!"

I turn over to see Dad on all fours, in his underpants and socks, with a toilet roll in one hand, trying to mop up rainwater from his sleeping bag.

I get up, trying to avoid the huge puddle that has collected on the centre of the groundsheet, and with a pile of wet towels, accompany him to the toilet block, our shoes getting soaked in the wet grass.

Despite the early hour, there's a queue at the Gents. The row of men's WCs is unfinished and only one cubicle of the eight has got a door on it. Naturally, this is the only one the campers are using and they're waiting in line. It flushes, the door opens and the occupant, aware that his every sound had been overheard by the queue outside, emerges with a sheepish look on his face as he tells the next in line, "I'd give it a minute if I were you mate."

On seeing this, Dad says, "Sod this, I haven't got all day. When you've got to go, you've got to go."

He goes to a cubicle with no door, drops his trousers, sits and calmly reads the Daily Express. Startled campers, passing with their toothbrushes, on seeing him blurt out words like, "Oh, I do beg your pardon."

As casual as you like, he replies from over the top of his paper, "Don't mind me mate, you're all right, just carry on."

When Mum hears about this later, there's an almighty row. She says she's sick of being a laughing stock. How could he do such a thing?

Everyone knows which tent he is from.

Dad is a constant embarrassment to Mum throughout the whole holiday. Apart from dressing like Humphrey Bogart or Fred Astaire, his navy blue swimming trunks are World War Two issue and are, unbelievably, made of wool. He carries a telescope around with him in an old sock and he wears a pair of 'Rommel-style' desert tank commander sunglasses. These are fixed to the head with a broad band of elastic. The eye pieces are like welding goggles, the glass so impenetrable, that you don't have to heed those warnings on Blue Peter when observing eclipses of the sun.

These sunglasses also double up as swimming goggles. When Dad starts to strip off to go for a swim, Mum takes herself off for a walk.

Dad's body is lily white, except for red face, forearms and V at the neck. With this bizarre suntan and in woollen trunks and Rommel goggles, he walks down the beach towards the water. As he does so, toddlers scream and run for their mothers and dogs go berserk.

When he gets to the water, his routine is always the same: painful, delayed entry, punctuated by sharp intakes of breath as the swell nears his crotch. Ten strokes front crawl, ten on his back, one surface dive, from which he bursts up, retching and heaving, having swallowed a bit of sea water.

Then he emerges in all his glory. Skin has now turned to an unhealthy shade of blue. Trunks, being made of wool, have absorbed ten times their volume in water, resulting in them stretching from a point just above the belly button, to just below the knee.

He is probably carrying an extra twenty pounds back up the beach, and it's all swinging between his legs. This is exaggerated all the more by him being forced on to all fours by the sharp pebbles, as he shivers and winces his way back to us.

"Where's your mother?"

"She went for a walk, said she'll be back in an hour."

"Well, did she say where she was going?"

"No. She said something about divorcing Johnny Weissmuller."

Mum has climbed the breakwater of giant rocks, up on to the road, trying to put as much distance between herself and Dad's spectacle as possible. I can see her as she walks along, occasionally looking back to where we are.

She sits on a bench in the late afternoon sun, looking out to the North Sea. I wonder what she's thinking. She had argued with Dad last night before he went down the pub. Even though they were only whispering, you can hear everything in that tent.

This is part of what I heard.

"I don't know, I sometimes wonder how I got here. People once told me I had good prospects. I could have married anybody. How did I end up here? I mean, do you call this a holiday?"

"What's the matter with it?"

"Well, it's OK for you, but it's just nonstop work for me."

"We can't afford anything else."

"And why is that? Three times they've offered you promotion at work and three times you've refused, stuck to your precious chocolate mixer."

"I'm not going into management, wearing a suit, telling people what to do. I'd hate it."

"And so we have to stay stuck in this rut, coming on holiday in this tent, paying dead money in rent on that house, when we could put a deposit on a place of our own."

"There's nothing wrong with that house, it's perfectly good for us."

"But it's not *ours* is it? You have absolutely no ambition, and can't see further than where the next pint's coming from."

There was a silence.

"I'm going out."

"Yes that's right, run away. It's 10 o'clock, closing time soon. You prove my point exactly."

Another silence.

"I won't be late."

"Well, I may not be here when you come back."

Silence again.

"Did you hear what I said?"

After busying himself with the zipper on his jacket, which was caught in the material, he eventually said, "Don't be silly. We'll talk about it when I get back."

"Oh yes, and you'll be in a fit state to talk."

Then there was the sound of the tent being unzipped, then zipped up again.

In the black silence, I could hear Mum talking to herself and cursing under her breath before sighing deeply.

Today, on the bench, she feels the tightening on her shoulders that tells her she should have covered up hours ago. Her delicate skin is an angry pink across her shoulders, sliced painfully by costume straps that reveal two lilywhite tramlines where she has tried to adjust them.

She carefully clambers back down and over the big rocks to the beach in the late afternoon. She crunches over dried seaweed, and nearly steps on a dead herring gull, wrapped in oil and infested with flies. She trudges back past the wooden groyne stretching into the sea and casts a long shadow.

When we get back to the campsite, there's trouble on the horizon. A group of bikers from Hull have pitched their tents next to ours. They're very rowdy, revving their bikes, swigging cans of Special Brew and lobbing their empties dangerously close to our tent. Dad's fuse is short and he is simmering, eyeballing them as he takes long drags on his Number Six.

A football is kicked against our tent and one of them comes over to collect it.

"All right, Grandad? Enjoying your holiday?"

Dad mutters under his breath,

"Get your hair cut, you Commie layabout."

That night, they come back late from the pub, shouting and falling over. Someone tries to unzip our tent before being pulled away in a fit of giggles. Near to my head, I hear footsteps, then the trickle of someone urinating on the grass, occasionally splashing our canvas.

This is the last straw and Dad says he's going out. Mum pleads with him not to, but he insists on asserting himself. Unzipping the tent in a really aggressive manner, he strides out purposefully in his underpants, getting his foot caught on the guy rope.

"Do you know what the time is? There are kids on this campsite you know."

"Ah go back to bed Grandad."

81

"You cheeky bugger, I'm reporting you lot to the warden, first thing in the morning."

As he turns to come back in, he stubs his toe on a tent peg, and this causes an uproar of hilarity.

When we get up in the morning, there's a chorus of, "Shhhh … here he comes …" followed by the chanting, in mocking high pitched voices of, "Gonna tell the warden, gonna tell the warden."

Mum says she wants to change campsites, but Dad says you can't give in to these sorts of people. The warden is spineless and does nothing. Dad tries to build some solidarity with the family opposite, but the bloke says he doesn't want his tyres slashed.

Dad, to his credit, doesn't hide from them and gives as good as he gets. They think he's a bit of a nutter, especially by the way he uses the toilet with no door.

One evening, he makes an observation about one of their bikes, a subject on which he is quite knowledgeable. One of the bikes is a Triumph Bonneville and Dad just makes a passing remark that it would be left for dead by a BSA Lightning.

"Think you know about bikes, do you Grandad?"

"Well, if you want to waste your money on that. The Lightning is a 650 Parallel Twin, same as your Triumph, but the BSA can generate more power. It's not called a 'power egg' engine for nothing."

"And how do you work that out Grandad?"

"The BSA's single camshaft is mounted behind the crankshaft and operates the overhead valves through tunnels cast in the cylinder block. That gives it more power."

There's a roar of laughter.

"Blimey, listen to Harley Davidson!"

As they get into it, he brings out some of his homebrew, which they sample, exclaiming that it's "lethal stuff."

Within an hour, they are the best of friends, he is referred to as "Mad Eddie" and they roar with laughter again when, agreeing to let him ride the Bonneville, he tears up the grass at breakneck speeds without a helmet, in his shirtsleeves. He lifts both hands off the handlebars for a brief second, which is greeted by howls of admiration.   Mum tells him off when he comes back in, for behaving like a big kid, but we have no more trouble for the rest of the holiday.

Dad's mood lifts considerably, and one night he even takes us to the pub. Mum has been having a go at him for deserting us every night.

"You're their father. You should be spending as much time with them as possible, not swanning off down the pub every night."

"It's my only pleasure, are you going to deny me that too?"

"Well, take us with you."

"You can't take kids into a pub."

"There's a beer garden isn't there? Or do you not want us to come because you're meeting someone in secret?"

"Don't be ridiculous, woman."

So, while we all sit in the beer garden outside with Mum, drinking lemonade through straws and eating salt and vinegar crisps, Dad makes several trips into the bar, asking who wants a top up every five minutes. Mum's head is constantly craned behind her, trying to see if he's talking to the barmaid.

Sometimes, I go in to help him carry them back. The barmaid is not the reason he keeps returning. Every time he buys himself a pint, he drinks another one at the bar down in one, when Mum isn't looking. Each time he does so, he gives me a little wink, puts his finger to his lips
and I smile in understanding, happy in our little secret conspiracy.

On the way home, walking twenty feet behind us, they have an enormous row.

"Don't deny it. I saw you looking at her. You were in there more than you were out with us."

"I've got to get the drinks haven't I?"

"Any excuse to go back inside."

"Oh, now you're just being paranoid. I didn't ask you to come you know."

"Yes, and now I know why. I don't know what you see in her anyway, all cheap nail polish and vulgar neckline."

"I don't see *anything* in her. And anyway, barmaids have to dress like that to get the customers through the doors."

"Yes, dirty old men like you who should know better."

"Keep your voice down will you. They'll hear."

And so it goes on, all the way back to the tent. I think to myself, I'm the only one who knows the truth.

On the last day, we visit the lighthouse at Flamborough Head. Dad loves anything to do with ships and maritime history and brings along his telescope in the sock.

There's a force nine gale blowing and a large party is sheltering behind the massive base, waiting for the lighthouse keeper to open up. We all start to climb the winding stone staircase in single file. There are too many of us in the party and we all have to really squeeze together to get into the lamp room at the top.

The keeper begins his talk and I can't understand a word of it. We are really wedged in and my face is squashed into the back of the woman in front of me. I am beginning to feel a bit claustrophobic, when suddenly I shame us all. Christmas pantomime all over again: I accidentally release into the cramped atmosphere a particularly lethal SBD.

People say nothing but there is an uneasy shuffling of feet, like nervous horses in a horsebox. Mum has gone bright red. She recognises my distinctive smell and knows it's me. The bloke standing a step down behind me, has got a pretty good idea too, his face being level with my backside.

The keeper is rapidly winding up his speech. Some prat decides to ask him a question about the magnification of the lamp. He just ignores him and says, "OK ladies and gentlemen, that's all for today, can you calmly make your way to the exit please."

There's a bit of a stampede and people get in each other's way.

"Look mate, you can't get out until those in front have gone, can you? Wait your turn."

People start to surge for the stairs.

"Coming through, this woman's feeling sick."

After an eternity we finally reach the bottom. Outside in the fresh air, people are clearing their throats, and the woman is heaving.

Mum says, "I've never been so embarrassed in all my life."

Dad is more philosophical.

"Look, it's only natural. He can't help it. And anyway, how do they know it was one of us?"

Next day, before we get on our way, we go down to the Amusement Arcade to spend our last pennies. We love the Penny Falls where you have to roll your coin in and if it lands between the lines you win. Or Bingo, with those plastic shutters you slide across, and the prize for a single win token is a tin of baked beans.

Back at camp, the tent is taken down and everything is packed into the car in a much less organised way than on the way out. We stand for a few minutes round the yellow, dying square of grass where the tent stood. We are revolted by the woodlice and earwigs now scurrying for cover, who were probably sharing our sleeping bags and inner ear cavities as recently as last night.

A quick tramp along the prom for one mournful, last look at the brown sea, nip into the beach shop to buy Graham's rock and then we're gone.

Back at the house in Birmingham, everything looks different. The doors and door knobs look sort of old fashioned, as does the television with its tiny screen. In the garden the grass and hedges need cutting and Dad is marvelling at the size of his runner beans.

This evening, when I get ready for a bath, I take off my trousers and smile as the fine sand spills out of my pockets and turn ups, on to the carpet. There's a big shell in one of the pockets that I put to my ear to see if I can hear the sound of the sea.

Later, I get into bed, which feels enormous and comfortable, the sheets crisp and clean, luxurious on my legs after a fortnight in a sleeping bag.

I stare at the ceiling and have a feeling of loss. I get that churning in my stomach, that Sunday night feeling, that the summer holidays are now well into August and that school is looming in the distance.

And a big, new, scary school at that.

Summer 2003

"The next train to arrive on Platform Two will be the delayed 14.55 to Hereford."

I must have been dozing for a few minutes. The anaesthetic of that shingle beach and the brown lapping sea, shrouded in mist and low cloud, slowly wears off and I am suddenly aware of my diagnosis again, like a sore, open wound that's started to throb once more.

Reality rushes in: the multitude of hurrying feet jostling for position and the slowing thud of the engine's wheels on the sleepers as it pulls into the Queen Elizabeth Hospital station. It's like waking with a hangover, then suddenly realising with horror what you did the night before.

On the journey back, the neurologist's words keep going round and round in my head. As I get closer to home, I try to work out how I am going to break the news to Emm.

By the time I reach the front door, I've made the decision not to tell her yet. I'll wait for the second opinion. No point worrying her if it's a false alarm.

As soon as my key is in the lock, Lily is at the door.

"Daddy, Daddy, you're early!"

"Yes, I wanted to see my two favourite girls in the whole world!"

"Who's your other favourite girl Daddy?"

"Why, Mummy of course!"

"Oh yes, of course, of course!"

Emm takes my coat and bag while Lily starts to tell me all about her day.

Emm calls in from the kitchen, "Why haven't you eaten your sandwiches?"

"Oh yeah, sorry, I had a meeting all through lunch, didn't have time. Tell you what, leave them, I can eat them tomorrow, save you another job."

"You've got to *make time* for lunch Colin, or you'll make yourself ill."

"Yeah, I know, sorry. I won't do it again."

Make time for lunch? I wish that was all I had to worry about.

The whole summer passes between the two appointments. Finally it is upon me in September. Today is the day before I'm due to see the second neurologist, and I'm stuck again with bottom set GCSE English, who are now Year 11.

"Sir, will you tell Gareth to stop banging our table."

I stop looking out of the window and return to face them. This particular class is the last thing I could do with on today of all days. The kids are getting a bit suspicious about how much time I've been having off. Well, I'm not going to tell them am I?

Any sign of weakness and they'll eat you alive.

"OK, can I have a bit of quiet please? That means you too, Gareth. And stop tipping back on your chair, if you fall backwards, you'll crack your skull. Thank you.

"Now, I'm not going to be here tomorrow, so I need you to get on with your essays on *Lord of the Flies*. Has anybody *not* found all the quotations you need to show the importance of the conch and Piggy's glasses?"

"Where are you going Sir?"

"I have an appointment at the hospital, if you must know Gareth."

"Oh yeah, don't you mean the clinic? What you got then Sir, crabs or the clap?"

"Yes, very amusing Gareth. And can you please take your coat off, like everyone else. Surely you must be hot in all that. Wearing a scarf and hood, you look like a terrorist."

"I am Sir. I'm sweating. Can we open the window Sir?"

"Paul, open the window a crack please."

This is a mistake. My window is above the alleyway at the side of the school, where all the smokers, truants and recently expelled hang out trying to incite unrest in the present school population. With the window open, they can hear my lesson.

"Gareth, I'm not going to tell you again, take your coat off please. DO IT NOW BOY!"

There's a voice from the alleyway below. It belongs to Dean Richards, expelled two years ago.

"Sparrow, you're a wanker!"

There's a burst of laughter, which I have to be quick to quell.

"Paul, close the window again, please"

Groans of disapproval.

"But Sir, it's boiling in here. These radiators are on full blast."
"THEN TAKE YOUR COAT OFF!"

When everything has calmed down, Gareth starts up again.

"Does that mean we're going to have some crap supply teacher, tomorrow Sir?"

"Yes, Gareth, but I'm sure they won't be 'crap' as you put it."

"That's the second time this year Sir, and I think it's damaging my education. How would you like it Sir, if I sued you for failing to do your job properly?"

I think, 'How would you like it, if I bashed you over the head with a mallet, you annoying little twat?'

Instead, I say, "Go ahead Gareth, see you in court."

I know it isn't their fault. I shouldn't take it out on them. I never used to shout at the kids. What's wrong with me? When they all settle down to their work, I return to the window and the playing fields and mull things over in my mind.

I've got to tell Emm tonight. I can't keep going to the hospital and pretending I'm going to school. Each time, briefcase packed … lunchbox … set of books marked … kiss goodbye, then at the end of the road, cross back over and head for the train station instead of the school.

She's my wife for God's sake. This is supposed to be a partnership. How can you keep this from her? I am definitely telling her tonight. Well, tomorrow, after I've heard what the second neurologist has got to say.

On the playing fields, Mr. Eustace is organising a class of Year Sevens into two teams and a pale kid with thin legs and boots too big for him is being told to go in goal.

Remember, Colin? That was *you* thirty-two years ago in 1971. That old Colin Sparrow with baggy shorts and oversized rugby shirt is long dead and gone. Was it ever really me?

I look back out of the window at the boy in goal, wrapping his arms around his body to keep warm. The other team shoot and, after a feeble attempt at a dive, he trudges to the back of the net to retrieve the ball, with his own team's criticisms ringing in his ears.

Don't worry lad, I've been there. Everything will be fine.

September 1971. First Day

Monday morning, and as I walk up the road with Graham in oversized new uniform with rigid, leather smelling satchel (that contains just pen, pencil, rubber, ruler, and games kit), we see Jeremy Potts being bundled into his dad's Toyota before he gets the chance to say hello to us. He's on his way to King Edward's, complete with briefcase, violin and navy P.E. bag. His mum shouts at him as he tries to look back at us and they drive off, accelerating past the hordes of kids walking up towards the comprehensive, shirts hanging out, kicking footballs into the road.

Standing in the playground, waiting for the bell, we are joined by Simon Spinks, a boy more unlike Graham you'd be hard pressed to find anywhere. He's a very clever, very posh lad, whose dad believes "Education is a right not a privilege" and that everyone should go to the comprehensive, including his own son.

To break the ice, Graham says, "What I want to know is, when are we gonna get some bloody books?"

To which Simon replies, in that ludicrous upper-class accent of his, "Well, when we do get them, I doubt they'll have any blood on them."

(He's got a hard five years ahead of him).

When the bell finally goes, we are formally welcomed in assembly, then spend most of the morning with our Form Tutors filling in our timetables. One period before lunch, we have our first lesson, which for the girls is home economics and for the boys, it's woodwork. This is a mixed ability class, one of the few I will be having with Graham.

Mr. Jones finishes every sentence in his broad Welsh accent, with the words "Do we not lads?"

He is a small, fussy, pedantic man. In the top pocket of his brilliantly white, starched woodwork coat, is a row of perfectly sharpened pencils.

He takes the register, which sounds like a roll call from *The Flintstones.*

"Ben Blunt."

"Sir."

"Edward Box."

"Sir."

"Simon Cave."
"Sir."
"David Gunn."
"Sir."
"Daniel Oak."
"Sir."
"William Rock."
"Sir."
"Graham Skinner."
"Yes, Mr. Jones."
"Sir will do lad."
"Colin Sparrow."
"Sir ... "

When he's finished, Mr. Jones walks up and down the workshop, arms behind his back, eyes on the floor, delivering the lecture he must have delivered a thousand times before, warning us of the dangers and hidden perils of his workshop.

"We never cross this yellow line when a machine is working, do we not lads?"

"We wear our goggles at all times, do we not lads?"

"Place all sharp tools in the well of your bench, so they can't roll..."

"Wash your hands thoroughly after using this..."

"That will slice through bone like hot butter..."

"And never EVER press *this* button."

The viciousness of the equipment established, we are then instructed in the use of the file, one of which is called The Bastard File.

"Yes, go on, get it out of your system. Let's say it all together, shall we not lads?"

"BASTARD, BASTARD, BASTARD, BASTARD, BASTARD."

We chant in unison until it's not funny anymore.

Half way through the lesson, I ask to go to the toilet. There's a pause, Mr. Jones raises an eyebrow and the collective rasping suddenly stops.

He asks, "Is it for a number one or a number two?"

Apparently, he always asks this to humiliate you, so you'll never ask again.

Graham chips in to help me out of my embarrassed silence. "He needs a shit, Sir."

The class explodes into laughter. He roars at Graham, the veins standing out on his temples.

"Get out! And wait for me outside!"

"But Sir, it's true, he's got a problem."

"GET OUT!"

Turning back to me, he then asks if I still want to go.

"I can wait Sir."

"Good lad."

No one asks again for the rest of term, during which, Graham's life is made a misery. This culminates in the last lesson before Christmas, when Graham's salt and pepper pots will bounce off his head, after being thrown at him by Mr. Jones.

"Total crap, Skinner. A waste of fourteen weeks. God help Mr. Franks in metalwork."

At lunch on this first day, I head straight for the toilets. But it's not like junior school. I am stopped at the door by a fifth year blocking my way.

"Where do you think you're going, you little runt?"

"I need the toilet."

"Really? Are you sure you want to go in there?"

"Yes please."

He shouts in, "It's OK!" and stands aside for me. I regret it almost immediately.

There's a wall of smoke, and the scariest collection of individuals I've ever seen in my life.

"What the hell do you want? You ain't allowed in here."

"I need the toilet."

"Go somewhere else."

"I'm desperate."

They all burst out laughing. Someone impersonates Mr. Jones's Welsh accent.

"What is it for…a number one, or a number two, boyo?"

"A number two."

More laughter.

"Get lost, you ain't stinking out the place while we're in here."

The biggest kid says,

"Oh leave him alone, that's Rob and Brian Sparrow's little brother."

"Is it?"

More laughter.

"Go on then you cheeky little sod. No one else would have the nerve to come in here. But be quick. And it had better not smell."

I go into a cubicle right at the end, as far away from them as possible, and try to bolt the door, but there's no hole for the bolt, so I have to lean forward and keep the door shut with my hand. I can hear them laughing, but don't have any choice as I am desperate.

Just as I've started, the guard outside shouts in, "Holmes is coming!"

I can hear panic outside and several toilets flushing at once. Mr. Holmes opens the main door.

"Roberts, stay exactly where you are...don't move!"

I hear him walk in while I tremblingly keep my arm on the door.

"My, what a breath of fresh air it is in this little smoke factory. Right, every one of you, empty your pockets."

"Why Sir? We're not doing anything. The smoke was already here when we came in."

"Do me a favour Roberts and shut your mouth."

There is a lot of moaning and tutting, and the sound of pockets being emptied and then the sound of a slap.

"Oww! What do you do that for Sir?"

"Because I felt like it, and because you're lying to me."

"We're not Sir, honest, we weren't doing anything."

The sound of another slap.

"Right, who's in the cubicles?"

"Dunno Sir."

I've never been so terrified in all my life. It's a good job I'm sitting on a toilet. I hear Mr. Holmes walk to the other end of the line of cubicles, and kick the first door in.

Then, like a gunslinger in a cowboy film, he proceeds to kick in every door, all along the line, getting closer and closer to me. I am absolutely panic stricken and as he reaches my door, I release my hand, and the door is kicked in.

"What are you doing in there, boy?"

"A number two sir."

He inhales, pulls a face and says, "Yes...that's patently obvious. Jesus, laddie, I'm not an expert in these matters, but I think you should see a doctor about the state of your bowels."

"I already do Sir."

"All right then, be as quick as you can, then go outside. The rest of you clear off out of my sight."

I hear them all going out and then Mr. Holmes opening the windows.

Back on the playground, Ben Blunt attaches himself to me like a limpet. He's a weird kid who lives in fear of being bullied. He's thinner than me, incredibly ugly, looks permanently terrified, and might as well have the word 'victim' tattooed on his forehead.

He follows me everywhere. I wish he wouldn't, I've got enough problems of my own. He carries a note from his mom with him at all times, explaining how he has low muscle tone and can't do PE or games. I'd keep quiet about that if it were me.

Ben's already had his lunch money taken off him. Stupidly, his mother gave him a pound note. Devastated by the loss of such a large amount on his first day, he resorts to asking Matthew Chinn, school hard-knock, to get it back for him in return for 50 new pence payment. Matthew duly obliges, pinning the other kid to the wall.

Ben is delighted at having cut his losses by a half. But I wonder about the wisdom of entering into such a financial arrangement with the scariest kid in the school.

When the bell goes, Ben is stopped by Mr. Holmes, and told to take a note to the staffroom.

"But Sir, I don't know where that is."

"Don't be so pathetic boy, ask if you get lost."

Mr. Holmes then notices me.

"Oh, it's the boy with the bowel problem. Are you feeling better now lad?"

"Yes Sir. Thank you Sir."

He then sees a disturbance on the stairs. Someone is spitting from the top floor down the stairwell. Mr. Holmes looks up and a huge gob just misses him by inches.

"Every person on that top landing, stay exactly where you are, I'm coming up."

There's the sound of running and general panic on the landing.

Ben begs me to go with him to the staff room. As we go downstairs, we can hear Mr. Holmes' voice thundering from above.

"Don't lie to me boy, I saw it coming out of your mouth…it damn well nearly hit me in the eye…and stop smirking, do you think that's funny, do you?"

We get lost and find ourselves in the Science Corridor, which is a hell-hole during lesson changeovers. The corridor is narrow at normal times, but when there are classes queuing on both sides to get into the labs, it's almost impossible to make your way through. There's lots of pushing and shrieking and every now and then I get a slap across my head, an elbow in my back or someone deliberately twists my ear.

The pain is excruciating and we realise that a couple of first years are prime targets and we'll never come this way again.

When we reach the staffroom, there is a sign on the door saying:

UNDER NO CIRCUMSTANCES
ARE PUPILS TO KNOCK ON THIS DOOR
OR ENTER WITHOUT PERMISSION.

On the wall opposite, another sign reads:

NO LOITERING.
THIS AREA IS OUT OF BOUNDS TO PUPILS.
NO EXCEPTIONS.

Ben looks at me with a face even more filled with terror than before. They may as well have put a sign saying:

WE DON'T CARE WHO'S SENT YOU,
PISS OFF!

I knock the politest knock I've ever knocked. No reply.

I try a bit louder and still nothing. I can feel my palms starting to sweat. Ben is holding his groin and is about to shit his pants at any second. I tell him I'm going and that he'll have to do it on his own. He tries to slide it under the door, but the carpet inside makes it impossible.

We hear the sound of laughter, and a male voice booming from inside. We freeze in our crouching positions.

Then, in an act of supreme bravery, Ben decides to open the door a crack. Holding out the note, together with his own (believing low muscle tone will save him in times of danger) he waves them through the opening, like flags of surrender.

We can clearly hear the conversation through the door now. A male voice is in mid-flow, entertaining the other teachers.

"I mean, basically, it all comes down to the parents doesn't it? They are to blame at the end of the day. You only have to look at the mothers, in their slippers, pushing a pram with a fag end on their bottom lip. And where are the fathers, you may ask? Where indeed? Most of them are probably chained up to the kennel at home, chewing a bone."

There is a huge roar of laughter. They still haven't seen the door open, so Ben decides to stick his repellent head in.

A sudden hush descends as they notice the gargoyle at the door and wonder if he overheard the last comment.

This is replaced by a huge wall of laughter when they realise that he probably did, and the speaker says, "There, you see? I rest my case. Whoever fathered that must have fur and a tail."

More shrieks of outraged laughter.

"Oh don't worry, the Neanderthal can't understand, can you lad?"

"What Sir?"

"See what I mean? It certainly can't read, otherwise it would never have opened the door. GET OUT BOY. CAN'T YOU READ THE SIGN?"

A hardback copy of *Treasure Island* is thrown at Ben's head. He shrieks, drops the note with the message and closes the door, just as the book thuds into it.

We can hear their laughter all the way down the corridor as we sprint to English.

Because we're late, I have to sit next to Ben. The lesson is called 'Someone's Story'.

We're told to choose someone famous from history, preferably dead, and produce lots of snippets of documents like old letters, diary pages, newspaper cuttings, train tickets etc, which, when pieced together, will tell the story of their lives.

I choose Marilyn Monroe and Ben chooses Adolf Hitler. I write a letter from Marilyn's doctor, warning her to cut down on the number of painkillers she's taking.

I look over at Ben's. He's working on a love letter from Eva Braun. It begins:

Dear Hitler, I missed you last night...

Before I get the chance to make a suggestion, the bell goes. Ben checks his new timetable, and he turns white again. Last lesson of the day is games.

Lining up outside, Ben reads his own note "...has low muscle tone...", his lips moving as he reads the words that he hopes will save him.

It's rugby, with Mr. Stanton, former county player, and there's a buzz of excitement in the changing room. Everyone is showing off and comparing the latest pair of Puma or Adidas, discussing the relative merits of twelve studs over thirteen.

I am in the corner, lacing up 'Billy's Boots', antique hand-me-downs, two sizes too big for me with just six huge studs and rusty steel toe caps that serve to emphasise the thinness of my legs. Dad gave them to Brian years ago. He had to go through this ordeal and so did Rob, until they grew out of them.

Now it's my turn.

Dad says Stanley Matthews used to wear a pair just like them.

I ask, "Who's Stanley Matthews Dad?"

He answers me in disgust. "You what? You should be ashamed of yourself. Kids today, you don't know anything."

Someone in the changing room notices me. "Ha ha! Look at his boots man. You look a right wanker in those."

Dad's words echo in my head. "Listen son, these are a classic design, with proper leather and steel studs, much better than the plastic crap you get these days. If anyone says anything, just you tell them that."

But Dad doesn't understand what kids are like now. He doesn't understand that times have changed and that this is the age of Trevor Francis and not Stanley Matthews.

Ben is still in his uniform, waiting self-consciously. The teacher finally arrives, inspiring awe and respect amongst the boys.

Ben gives him his note, he reads it, screws it up, throws it in the bin and tells him to get changed. "If you want to be excused on medical grounds lad, you need an official letter from a doctor."

"But Sir, can I have the note back? I need it for other lessons."

He ignores him and tells the rest of the class to line up.

We are taken up to the top playing field, right on the summit and edge of the school grounds. Here the wind whistles and in the winter, snow falls a good five minutes before it reaches the ground in the valley below.

The strict PE department rules about not wearing a vest or underpants under your games kit, means that it's usual for your penis to shrink to the size of a cashew nut and your testicles to retreat to a position they haven't taken up since you were in the womb.

Before the game, the teacher likes to "toughen us up." We have to form two rows facing one another. Then we have to lower our heads and charge at the person opposite until we clash heads. When we are sufficiently "warmed up," we move on to the game and the degrading selection process, in which Ben, Michael Gadd (a fat kid) and me are last to be picked.

"Go on then, I suppose we'll *have* to have him."

I don't understand the rules and am banished to the position of winger at the end of the line, while the forwards hog the ball for the whole lesson. Two minutes from the end - and I get my chance; a hospital pass in front of the advancing Michael O'Rourke. Michael is a full-grown man at age 11, with muscles, body hair and beard. I throw the ball away but he tackles me any way. After the game, I limp back to the changing rooms, wondering if I'll need a skin graft.

I suffer the final shame of passing the girls coming back from hockey. Doreen Drysdale, currently light years out of my orbit, and now like a young grown woman, in grey PE skirt, white socks and fully developed bosom, bursts out laughing at the sight of my spindly legs.

For a while now, I've been getting the feeling that she may not be the one after all.

It's the end of the day and I'm last out of the changing rooms after Ben, who's dawdled and delayed getting changed, so that he could root around in the bin for his note after the teacher had gone.

Smoothing out the creases on the paper, he says he'll see me tomorrow and I struggle to get my trousers on over the open wound.

Outside in the corridor, most people have gone home but as I approach the main exit at reception, there's a bit of a commotion. It's a scene that makes me question whether I've come to the right school.

A very scary looking female parent has come in to confront the head of year, who has in turn, locked herself in her office and is phoning the police. The mother bangs on the door with her fist.

"Come on out you fucking bitch, I know you're in there!"

Second Appointment. 2003

The door opens and the consultant smiles warmly and welcomes me in. I enter like a condemned man. I've been clinging to the hope that they've made a mistake, but deep down, I know what he's going to say.

After a brief examination, this second neurologist tries to be upbeat. "Mr. Sparrow, I'm afraid I have to agree with my colleague. There is no definitive test for Parkinson's Disease. It's not like we can take a sample of blood or do a scan. The evidence is purely clinical and we have to see how it develops or how your symptoms respond to medication.

"You know, being diagnosed with Parkinson's at your age is really not the end of the world. Your youth is in your favour. It means the illness will develop much more slowly than in an older patient. There's absolutely no need to think about giving up your job yet. You should get on with your life and try to forget it."

"Could I conceivably work to my retirement age of sixty?"

He looks me straight in the eye.

"No."

"Ten years' time?"

"Maybe. Possibly between five and ten depending on how the illness develops and how much you can reduce stress at work and adapt your timetable around your limitations. A classroom on the ground floor for example. An inter-active whiteboard that will eliminate the need for holding a marker pen or chalk. You know, that sort of thing."

"Yes. A left-handed teacher whose left arm is becoming useless. Not the best combination is it?"

"Be positive Mr. Sparrow. You've got a lot going for you."

Outside, in the fresh air, I think things through. Be positive he says. I'm Head of Performing Arts, for goodness sake. What good is a classroom on the ground floor when I'm on my feet all day running workshops, dance classes, directing the school play, climbing ladders to fix the lighting rig and paint the back-drop scenery? He's no idea what my job entails. It's enough to exhaust someone half my age and in perfect health.

Back home, I bite the bullet and come clean to Emm. She is taken aback.

"Hospital? You've been to hospital today? I thought you were at school."

"I know. It's just that I didn't want to say anything until it was confirmed. I didn't want you worrying if it was nothing."

"Well, how long have you been feeling unwell? You never said anything to me."

"I know, I'm sorry, I should have. I didn't know what it was at first, just some stiffness and lack of movement in my left hand that wouldn't go away."

"Well, what did the doctor say?"

"Neurologist."

"Neurologist! What's wrong Colin?"

"They think it's Parkinson's"

"Parkinson's? At your age? Well, what about work? I mean, will you have to stop? What about the mortgage, what about Lily?"

"Slow down, slow down. It's OK, really. He said it's a very slow illness. I'll be able to keep working for many more years yet … maybe even up to my full retirement age in sixteen years' time. He said get on with your life. Forget about it."

"Forget about it? Lily needs her father. We both need you."

She comes over to me and hugs me and starts sobbing on to my chest.

"I knew there was something. Why didn't you tell me?"

"Really, I just didn't want to worry you. It's OK, it'll be fine. Lily probably won't even notice."

Later, lying in bed, I can't sleep. I think it was only a white lie, to soften the blow. I don't have to be so graphic immediately. It's better if I give Emm and Lily a chance to get used to the idea of me being ill.

Illness, sleepless nights. Things haven't changed much since I was a boy, except Dad isn't here to sit with me after a nightmare.

Dad made me feel safe. And not all kids can say that about their dads.

1972. First Taste Of Loss

Graham is always in our outhouse early on a school morning, waiting for me to finish my breakfast, but these days he is earlier than ever, sometimes sporting a bit of a black eye. He is sitting on our dustbin as Mum opens the front door to take the milk off the step.

"Blimey Graham, you're an early-bird, Colin's not out of bed yet. Well, I suppose you can wait in the outhouse, but he'll be at least half an hour."

"That's OK Mrs. Sparrow. I can wait. Can I count the shoes?"

Mum laughs. "If you want to."

Graham enjoys counting and matching up the Sparrows' multitude of shoes. We never throw anything away, and with a family the size of ours, there must be at least a hundred shoes out there, most discarded years ago.

As I eat my breakfast, I can hear him counting aloud. By the time I've finished and go out to join him, all the shoes are counted, paired up, and placed on the shelves, toes facing outwards. He reliably informs me and Mum that we have forty-nine pairs, including pumps, wellies and flip flops. There's only one green girl's shoe that he couldn't find a match for.

I'm looking at him as he speaks, and feel there's something not quite right, but I can't put my finger on what it is. Then suddenly I realise. He's wearing an old pair of Brian's shoes! Mum hasn't noticed, but he sees that I have, and winks at me then puts his finger to his lips. As soon as we are outside on the way to school, I say to him

"What the hell are you doing wearing Brian's old shoes? He'll kill me if he finds out."

He replies "Well, he doesn't need them any more and mine have got a hole in them."

"How do you know he doesn't need them? How do you know he won't start looking for them tonight?"

"Because I've had my eye on these for quite a while now. I've been checking. He hasn't worn them for over a year, so I don't think we've got anything to worry about. They probably don't fit him any more anyway. Mine leak every time it rains. I tried to fix them with a big bicycle repair patch, but they still let in water."

I am just about to ask why his mum doesn't buy him a new pair, when I think better of it and decide to drop the subject.

As we are approaching school, I ask him, "Have you done your Art homework?"

"Shit, I forgot about that."

"He'll kill you. That's the second week in a row."

"Can I hand in yours instead?"

"It's my sketchbook. And we're not allowed to tear out the pages. He's going to know it's not yours."

"Yeah, of course."

"You've had all week. Why didn't you do it? You're quite good at drawing."

He doesn't say anything, but is deep in thought as we reach the top of the hill. I ask, "How are things at home?"

"It's scary. Mum and Dad are always arguing. Then sometimes Dad will smash something."

"Can you sleep?"

"A bit, but not much. I'm too scared to go upstairs. I sometimes doze in the armchair downstairs but it's given me a terrible crick in my neck."

Mr. Jenkins is in a bad mood when we go in to the Art studio.

"Right, homework on my desk please, and I don't want to hear any excuses."

We all queue up and put our sketchbooks on his desk. Graham stays where he is, sliding down in his seat, to be as low as possible.

"Skinner, where's yours?"

"I've done it Sir, but I've left it at home because I was late this morning."

"I am sick and tired of your pathetic excuses Skinner! If it's not your grandma dying, it's your mother being taken to hospital. You're a liar and a lazy little cretin. You can spend an hour with me at four o'clock."

"But Sir, I'll be in trouble if I don't go straight home."

"I don't give a damn Skinner. You're not going home at four. Would you like me to phone home and explain why you'll be so late? I can then take the opportunity to ask your mother if she's recovered from her broken leg."

"No Sir. I'll be here."

"Too right you'll be here. And bear in mind that parents' evening is coming round."

Graham makes the mistake of yawning at this precise moment.

"Don't you dare yawn while I'm talking to you boy. Sit up straight you lazy, slovenly little devil. You should get to bed early instead of sitting up till all hours watching television. God knows what your parents are thinking of."

I look at Jenkins and think, this is so unfair and want to push him out of the window.

Graham just sits there fiddling with his chewed pencil.

"And that had better not be a school pencil you've been chewing, or you will pay for a new one."

I look at Graham, expecting him to be upset. Anyone else by now, would be in tears. But Graham's face is red and hardened. His eyes are burning with anger.

"You give me an attitude like that young man, and you'll spend two hours with me instead of one. So wipe that scowl off your face boy!"

He can't win and sits with the best impression of a neutral face as is possible.

"Moron!" spits Jenkins in a final passing shot, before he starts the lesson.

By five past five, I've been home, got changed and come back again to meet him outside the school gates. He doesn't want to go home because he knows what is waiting for him, so we walk the mile and a half into Northfield.

When we get there, most of the shops are closed, except for Woolworths, which is open till six. We go upstairs on the escalator to our favourite department, the fishing tackle section. We like to try out the rods and reels and sit on the brand new, squeaky creels.

While I'm looking at the green bait boxes, I see Graham out of the corner of my eye, putting a handful of floats into the inside pocket of his blazer. My heart starts racing and I look around the shop floor to see if anyone has noticed. I'm bright red and Graham tells me to act natural.

Act natural, I think, how do I do that? I walk a few paces then I yawn and stretch.

"No you idiot, I said act natural."

"I am."

"You couldn't draw more attention to yourself if you tried."

I am useless at it and absolutely terrified we'll be caught. We take the escalator back down. I head straight for the exit but Graham, as calm as you like, hangs around in the toy section at the back of the ground floor.

I'm waiting outside on the pavement for him, when he appears ice cool through the double doors, then says, "Leg it!"

We sprint all the way home. I keep looking round to see if anyone is following us.

"Calm down Colin. We were clear ages ago."

"You could at least have given me some warning you were going to do that!"

"Ahh, what's the matter yer big tittybabby? Too dangerous for you? I sometimes wonder why I hang around with you."

Do you ever get the feeling that certain relationships are never going to be quite the same again?

Later in the week, two significant events take place. The first is the death of our border collie Judy. She's been off her food for weeks now and is just a bag of bones.

Finally, Dad takes me with her to the vet who, after examining her, says there's nothing he can do and it would be kinder to put her to sleep. Dad agrees and I have to hold her in my arms as the vet prepares the lethal injection. She knows something is wrong and trembles in my arms, but she looks into my eyes in a trusting way.

I feel I am betraying her terribly when I stroke her and tell her everything is going to be all right. She gives a little yelp when the needle goes in, then her eyes glaze over and she is gone. She suddenly looks different. Her face is like a mask, her body just this lump of flesh and fur that bears no resemblance to her at all, like her clothes in a pile in my arms.

I think, what is it that's 'gone'? Something has gone. Her body is still here, just the same as it was a minute ago, but without that 'something' her body is nothing. For the first time in my life I've witnessed death first hand and I can't explain how the living body and the dead body are two completely different things, with only a second separating the two.

The second event is on *Crossroads*. Sandy's life has been changed forever. He's had a car crash and he's been in a coma for a week now. If he ever wakes up, they think he'll never walk again.

Declining Rapidly. 2004

I fell off the stage today during Period 2. I stood up quickly, became really light headed, staggered backwards and suddenly there was no floor beneath my feet.

At first, everyone laughed. Then all the class crowded round.

"Are you all right Sir?"

"Yes fine, fine thank you, don't fuss."

"Sir, you should have seen yourself. It was so funny, almost like you were drunk."

"Well, as you can quite clearly see, I am perfectly all right...and sober, I just lost my footing that's all. Now everyone get back to your groups and carry on with your work please."

It's a good job they were only Year 7s and well behaved at that. Still, I'm sure it's going to be the talk of the playground.

Nursing my arm in my classroom that lunchtime, I realise I'm going to have to tell the head about my illness.

Apart from anything else, it's now a health and safety issue.

When I get home in the evening, it affects my mood. Lily is there as usual, at the bay window, just the top of her head visible, watching and waiting for me to turn the corner of the road.

Then up goes her little hand in a wave and she's off, to tell Emm I'm back. I open the door and there she is, holding her ET doll, its finger glowing. She presses its head down and it calls out, "ET phone hooome!"

She repeats, "Phone home, phone home!" I pick her up and take her into the kitchen, where Emm is getting the dinner.

"Daddy, Daddy look at this, look at me." I put her down.

"Yes, yes, in a minute, give me a chance, I've just come through the door."

I put down my briefcase, kiss Emm and pour myself a drink.

"Bit early for you isn't it?"

"I need it. Bad day."

Lily's tugging at my jacket, screaming. "LOOK DADDY LOOK!" I raise my voice a little.

"All right! Just be patient will you?"

A cloud passes over her face and she goes to Emm.

"What's wrong with you Colin? She only wants to play. She's pleased to see you that's all."

"I know, I'm sorry poppet, come here."

She stays behind Emm.

"No. You shouted."

"Come on, come to grumpy Daddy."

"No!"

"Suit yourself."

There's an atmosphere all through dinner, after which I go upstairs and mark a set of Year 11 English essays.

After Lily's been put to bed, Emm comes in.

"I don't know what happened today at work and you don't have to tell me, but it's not fair taking it out on Lily. She only wanted a little time with you. I know you're busy Colin, and you're worrying about this other thing, but you've got to get your priorities right."

She doesn't wait for a reply, just closes the door on me and goes to bed herself. When she's gone, I wish the floor would open up and swallow me.

I mustn't shut them out. Lily needs her father.

1974. Outgrown

The pile of old shoes in our outhouse begins to take over as the years pass. Shoes that are outgrown, worn out, or simply out of fashion are gradually moved up a shelf, out of reach, to the graveyard at the top with the rest of the monstrosities from yesteryear. They form a chronicle of past trends, from winkle pickers to Clarke's Commandoes with compass in the heel, all now wrapped in cobwebs and full of dead bluebottles.

Occasionally, they are disturbed by the likes of Graham, who counts them, and occasionally helps himself to the odd pair, or Mark Harris, Brian's friend, who tries some of them on. He fancies himself as a comedian and while he and the rest of the football team are waiting in our outhouse for us to finish our dinner, he amuses everyone by tottering about in some of the more grotesque ones. He clumps up and down in them in an impromptu fashion parade, to squeals of delight from the others.

One week, a boy scout called for 'Bob-a-Job'[1] and Dad said there were a few shoes needed cleaning out the back. The poor sod was still there when it was dark.

I'm beginning to see less and less of Graham. Being separated at school, we've fallen in with different crowds, his being more dangerous to know. He's frequently up before the headmaster for the cane.

Last month, he was up before a magistrate at Youth Court for shooting Jeremy Potts in the head with an air rifle. The police wanted to let him off with a caution saying it was "accidental" but Mrs. Potts was determined to press charges. When Graham was asked by the magistrate why he did it, he replied casually, "I gave him ten to get away."

He got a suspended sentence, but they said, taking into account his previous appearances for shoplifting, if he got into trouble again, the court would take a dim view. A custodial sentence in a borstal would not be out of the question as he gets older.

Mrs Potts won't even speak to him anymore. If she sees him coming in her direction, she'll cross the road. And Jeremy is definitely not allowed to have anything to do with us, not that we care very much anyway,

---

[1] a fundraiser where cubs and scouts would knock on doors and volunteer to do jobs ...

certainly not Graham, who's found a new friend in the scary Wayne Brooks, who is quite a bit older than us.

Wayne has a Yamaha FS1E on which he tears up and down the road. Regularly, there is a police car outside the Brooks' house. The whole family seem to live in chaos. There are used mattresses and overflowing bin bags in the front garden where the grass has gone to seed and is waist high. Once, I saw a real live horse looking out of the ground floor living room window!

Wayne is sixteen and doesn't go to school any more, not that he ever did. I think the head was quite happy to turn a blind eye to his truanting.

Now he has Graham following in his footsteps. Considering Graham still can't read or write, that's not a good move for him and I seriously fear for his future.

When Wayne's mum has gone to work in the mornings, he opens up the house. Admission is a cheap bottle of Blackthorn cider. These impromptu daytime parties are a magnet for all the waggers in Northfield and Graham never misses out. He leaves for school in the morning with a change of clothes in his bag. By 11 a.m., he's drunk.

Sometimes, if Wayne's mum is on night shift, they hold a party in the evening. The Brooks' driveway and front lawn is packed with mopeds and small motorbikes, in between all the rubbish. There's never a shortage of giggling girls going in through the front door.

The house is three doors up, on the opposite side, and I hang out of my window to watch in envy, when I should be doing my homework. The music blasts from inside every time the front door is opened and I can hear shrieks and female voices, as I try to concentrate on The Rime Of The Ancient Mariner.

There's a particularly loud cheer when a pair of white knickers are thrown from an upstairs window. This is too much to bear. The thought that there's a girl sitting in there with no knickers on just drives me to distraction. *Don't think about it Colin*, I tell myself.

At this point, I hear a familiar shrieking voice and look out to see Doreen Drysdale being chased out of the front door by Wayne Brooks, who corners her by the hedge and proceeds to snog her. But most unbelievably of all … she snogs him back.

How can she do that? With Wayne Brooks? He's absolutely vile with stinking breath and yellowed teeth from all the fags he smokes.

I watch and feel sick. I'm consumed by jealousy. I can't think straight. Were those *her* knickers flying out of the window? Jealousy is quickly replaced by a feeling of revulsion. The sight of her literally chewing on his tongue is enough to finally confirm that she definitely is NOT the one after all.

Swearing a life of celibacy from this day forth, I return to Samuel Taylor Coleridge and close the window. Let them have their fun while it lasts. I'll get my head down and work for the future. I'll get out of this place of losers. I'll move to London and hit the big time. I'll even go abroad. And when I come back to visit, I'll be a changed man, but they'll still be doing the same thing: getting drunk on a Friday night with a bottle of Blackthorn cider and a grope in Doreen Drysdale's underwear.

Letting Things Slip. June 2004

Still feeling guilty from last night, and having resolved to be truthful about my condition from now on, I knock on the headmaster's door, open it a crack and put my head round.

"Ah, Colin. You wanted to see me. Come in. Come in."

"Not disturbing you am I?"

"Not at all. Always time for you Colin."

I sit down in the comfy chair on the other side of his tidy and spotless desk.

I take a deep breath and start, "I need to talk about something personal, but please don't jump to any conclusions."

"Well, this all sounds very mysterious Colin. Not been caught with your pants down in a brothel have you?"

He roars with laughter.

"No, no, of course not, nothing like that … I wish!"

The head laughs again.

"No, you see, the thing is, I'm not very well."

"Oh, sorry to hear that Colin."

"It's a long-term thing I'm afraid. I've got Parkinson's Disease."

"Really? Oh dear, I *am* sorry."

There's an awkward silence.

"Well, I'm afraid I don't know much about that, what does it mean for you Colin?"

I proceed to give him a brief summary of the illness and typical symptoms, then seek to reassure. "Firstly, I just wanted to promise you that it won't affect my ability to do my job. I've had it for a while now, but it's still in its early stages and shortly I'll be starting medication to keep it under control."

"Of course Colin. You're one of my best teachers. You have absolutely nothing to worry about on that score. The important thing is, what can *we* do to help *you*, to support you?"

"Well nothing really, maybe a classroom on the ground floor and perhaps one of those new-fangled interactive whiteboards, that I can write more clearly on. But really I just wanted to tell you, so that everything is above board, health and safety and all that."

"How do you mean?"

"You know, in case I fall over or something…not that I'm likely to of course."

"Of course. Of course. Look Colin, I don't want you to worry about anything. You carry on exactly as you are, and if there's anything you need, anything at all, my door is always open. I'll look into the change of classroom and the whiteboard. OK?"

"OK. Thanks."

As soon as I'm outside, I regret it. What the hell did I say that for? "In case I fall over". Are you soft in the head, Colin Sparrow?

I walk down the corridor with a gnawing suspicion that the head's never going to look at me in the same way again.

Damn it, I should have kept quiet.

Some lads are running down the corridor towards me and I shout, "WALK!"

They stop momentarily and walk until they are past me, then they giggle and run on. That's always been my problem as a teacher: too soft. Maybe I should go into the toilets at Break and kick in a whole row of doors, looking for smokers.

"Wow," they'd all say. "Sparrow has gone mental."

I can just imagine it: English, Period 5.

"Gareth, come here please."

"What Sir?"

Slap.

"Ow, what did you do that for Sir?"

"Because you're an annoying little twat. Now take your coat off and get your book out."

No, I suppose I could never do that. It just isn't my style. I think I do have a bit of a rapport with the kids. That's one of the benefits of being the drama teacher. Still, they do take advantage of my softer nature.

These days, by the time I get home from a full day at school, I'm completely exhausted. All I want to do is lie down and sleep. But there are essays to mark and reports to write. Inevitably, I continue to neglect Lily.

It's 7.30 and Emm confronts me. "Will you leave that for a minute and come and spend some time with your daughter, Colin! She's four years old, probably *the* most important time in her development. She needs some interaction with you before she goes to bed."

112

"Yep, give me five minutes to finish this and I'll be with you."

"No, Colin. *Now!*"

I look up and see real anger and upset in Emm's eyes and I suddenly realise how much I've let things slip. She is holding Lily and I go over and give them both a sort of 'group hug.'

Emm puts Lily down with her toys. When she stands up to face me, her lip is quivering and she starts to sob.

"You just don't know what it's like for me Colin, alone all day with her. You forget, I had a career as well you know, which I gave up so we could bring up Lily properly. You have no idea what it's like at home, stuck within these four walls all day. She has tantrums. She gets bored with me. She waits for you to come home, then you just go upstairs and start working. Can't you at least wait until she's gone to bed? That's only 7.30 you know. She doesn't see you at all. You're gone in the morning when she gets up. She needs her daddy. At least read to her or put her in the bath like other dads do."

I suddenly feel ashamed and so guilty. I remember Mum's words to Dad at Withernsea. "You're their father, you should be spending as much time with them as possible."

"Oh Emm, I'm really sorry. I'm just so ploughed under and didn't think. I'm sorry, I've been so selfish. I love you both, you know that don't you?"

"To be honest Colin, no, I really don't know any more. We're drifting apart. Can't you see it?"

"Look, let me put her to bed, then I'll come down and we'll talk."

Twenty minutes later, I'm back down and Emm is curled up on the sofa asleep, a tissue in her hands and her eyes all puffy. What have I done? She means more to me than anything in the world. Dear, sweet Emm. I make us both a drink, sit on the arm of the sofa and give her a gentle nudge.

"Hey ugly, drink this."

She takes the glass, has a huge swallow, then chokes.

"Christ Colin, it's so strong. Haven't you put anything in it?"

"I thought we both could do with a proper drink."

The whisky gives a warm glow as it goes down and slowly I start to relax.

"We break up for the summer holidays next month, then I promise I'm going to make it up to you. I'll take Lily out every day. We'll go on day trips. I'll book a holiday. We'll eat ice cream. And I swear I'll make you both happy."

"You say that now, but when the time comes, I know you'll just be too tired again with the illness."

"No, it's going to be different. I've made a decision. I'll start the medication as soon as I break up. I've been waiting because some people feel nauseous when they start and I don't want that while at school. But the consultant told me I'll have much more energy and will seem to have a whole new lease of life."

"I hope so Colin. I really do."

She sips her whisky and I scrunch down into the sofa and we sit quietly curled up with each other. I think about what she said, "You forget, I had a career as well you know." She's right. It's not fair. Her life now is just cooking and cleaning and looking after Lily. This is a bit of a wake-up call.

As I sit there with Emm in my arms, I can see how much I've taken her for granted. I've got to support her more. Emm's right: dads have an important role to play in their children's upbringing.

1974. St. Andrews

It's nearly eight o clock. Dad's favourite TV programme is about to start on ITV. *The World At War* narrated by Laurence Olivier. Dad's even changed his shift at the club so he can watch it. Tonight's episode is called 'Wolfpack: U Boats in the Atlantic.' It's about how Britain was nearly starved into submission by Hitler's submarines as they attacked the North Atlantic food convoys.

And guess who were the heroes of the day? The Merchant Navy. At least 35,000 Merchant seamen lost their lives in the war. By the end, I am genuinely shocked and immensely proud when I realise what Dad went through.

"Was it really like that Dad?"

He gets up to get a refill of homebrew and says, "Well, sometimes. But we weren't really heroes. Everyone had their job to do, and we just did it."

Just before the end of the year, three days before Christmas, Dad takes me to the football. (I'm allowed to go now I know what a wanker is).

Birmingham City versus the mighty Liverpool at St Andrews. There's nothing else on earth like walking up the steps of the Spion Kop, smelling the pies and tobacco smoke, hearing the roar of the crowd, then suddenly, as you reach the top, the ocean of heads stretching out below you down to the brilliant green of the pitch.

It never fails to take my breath away. We get our usual place, as it's not the biggest crowd I've ever been in, about 25,000. This is probably because it's only a month since the IRA pub bombings in the town centre at The Mulberry Bush and The Tavern in the Town. Indeed there is a bomb scare today, just before kick-off, and the announcer says the gates are being opened if anyone wants to leave. This is greeted by a chorus of jeering and whistles.

No one leaves, but another 800 get in without paying.

There are a lot of star names who play for England in the Liverpool line up. Emlyn Hughes fouls our Bob Hatton in the box, just fifteen minutes in, and there is a massive surge forward when I am literally lifted off my feet by the baying crowd as we are awarded a penalty.

But the England goalkeeper Ray Clemence saves Alan Campbell's spot kick and I think it's going to be one of those games. I'm also a little bit nervous about the bomb threat as the clock ticks on, but no one else seems to care.

At one point, I let slip a Silent Killer, and about a minute later, some wag behind us with the thickest Brummie accent says, "OK, own up, who's disgraced themselves?"

Half an hour in and we take the lead with a Gordon Taylor goal. I didn't see any of it, as I'm tossed around like a small boat in a storm.

Then we are awarded another penalty, this time taken and scored by the ever reliable Howard Kendall, who has been booed mercilessly throughout by the away fans because of his Everton connections. Liverpool instantly reply through John Toshack to make it 2-1 at half time.

There is a constant trickle of water down the steps of the terracing, and I ask Dad what it is. He replies that some lazy buggers further back from us, don't want to lose their place by struggling to the toilet, so they relieve themselves where they stand.

I am disgusted, "You mean we're standing in someone else's pee?"

"Yes son, but be sure not to tell your mother, or she'll never let you come again." He then recalls, "I remember one year, just after the war, a gap opened up in the crowd, to reveal a great steaming turd, dumped by someone desperate enough to do it. How he got down into a crouching position, I'll never know."

In the second half, Bob Hatton seals it for us in the 80th minute, the crowd go wild again and I hang on to Dad, so I don't fall into the puddles around my feet.

We win 3-1, not bad against a team that are fourth in the table and includes Kevin Keegan, Tommy Smith and the rest.

After the match, we're in the Spotted Dog in Digbeth having a drink. Dad says that as I'm now fourteen, I can have a shandy when I'm out with him. The pub is warm and smoky, and humming with the sound of post-match analysis. Dad is in no rush to leave, even though he's on his third pint.

I remind him what Mum said to us when we left home; that we were to come straight home after the match for our tea.

Dad says, "You let me worry about your mother. Women are funny creatures and you've got to learn how to handle them. If you always just do what they tell you, you will be miserable, and so will they."

He takes another long gulp of his beer and continues on his favourite subject; how to deal with a nagging wife.

"Let me give you a bit of advice, man to man. You see, all women try to change their man. It becomes their little project. For most of the time, don't let them get their way. The trick is, just occasionally give them a little victory. This gives them the false impression that they're winning and they're happy with that.

"If you just become a full-time doormat, you'll be miserable and ultimately, so will she, because you are no longer a challenge to her. Simple, see?"

He downs the remainder of his pint and wiping his mouth, says, "Do you understand?"

"Not really Dad."

"You will, as you get older, trust me. Another Shandy?"

"Just some crisps please, cheese and onion."

He goes back to the bar with his empty beer glass. He seems to be well known in here and the barman, as he pours Dad's pint, keeps looking over to me, making comments, to which Dad nods, glancing over to me every time he does so.

At one point, when I hear my name mentioned, there's a sudden burst of laughter from the crowd that Dad's with. They are all looking at me. I wish we could leave.

Dad gestures to me to come to the bar. I shake my head.

"Come on!" he shouts. "Don't be shy, they all want to meet you."

Reluctantly, I get up and go over to them, eating my crisps.

"Here he is: my little Einstein, my little thinker."

"Yes, I can see you in him Ed," says one of the barmaids,

"Shame he's so thin."

"Yes, he's had his problems, haven't you Colin?"

"Maybe he'll fill out when he gets older."

"So, got a girlfriend have you, Colin?" This from the bloke with the huge beer belly next to Dad.

I blush and wish this torture would end. They all laugh.

"Ah, we've touched a nerve there, look."

"What's her name, lad? Go on, tell us, we might be able to put a good word in."

More laughter. Dad says,

"It's Doreen, isn't it? I've heard you and Graham talking."

"Don't be stupid Dad, she's just a girl at school."

"Doreen who?"

"What's her surname again, Colin?"

"Look, I *don't* like Doreen Drysdale, all right Dad!"

They all laugh again. "Oooh, we've *definitely* touched a nerve there, haven't we?"

One of the barmaids says, "Oh leave the poor lad alone, can't you see you're embarrassing him."

The fat guy says, "And who's Graham?"

"Graham Skinner, his best friend who lives up the road."

One of them asks, "*Skinner?* Is he Michael Skinner's boy?"

"Yeah, a shame isn't it? He won't be seeing his dad for a while."

"Well, it runs in the family doesn't it?. Michael's father and uncle were the same. Always in trouble with the law. If the son, what's his name? Graham? If he's not careful, he'll end up the same way."

I can't just stand there and say nothing. "No he won't. What do you know? You don't know anything about him. You've never even met him!"

I go back to my table. Dad follows me over. "What's up?"

"Nothing. It's just that they don't know what they're talking about, that's all."

"What, about Graham?"

"Yeah, he's not as bad as all that. Just because Mrs. Potts hates him. He just does stupid things without thinking."

"I know. He's a good lad at heart isn't he?"

"It's just that no one understands what it's like for him. It's not his fault he's going the way he is. He has to practically fend for himself."

"Well that's not your concern Colin. That's down to the social workers or the teachers."

"You're joking aren't you? They all hate him. If you could see the way they treat him at school. It's hardly surprising that he truants so much."

"Well, I suppose it's none of our business is it Colin?"

118

"Yeah, exactly, it's nobody's business is it? If someone just spent some time with him, took an interest in him, he could turn out so differently."

"Like I said before Colin, it's probably best if you steered clear of Graham for a bit."

"I already do Dad."

He downs his pint.

"Right, let's get back and face the music, shall we? And remember, I've only had two pints, OK?"

"OK."

Later, back home, after our tea, and after Dad's gone down the club, Mum asks, "Did your dad really only have two pints?"

"I think so, I wasn't counting."

"And who did he meet?"

"I don't know, just some friends in the pub."

"Anyone I know?"

"I don't think so."

"And what did you talk about?"

"Oh, you know, the match …and some other stuff."

"Such as?"

"Graham, actually."

"Oh him. Listen Colin, maybe you should be seeing a little less of Graham after all that business with Jeremy Potts. Why don't you make friends with that Simon Spinks? He seems like a nice lad."

Lying in bed later, I think about the match and the pub and the 'grown up' conversation I was having with Dad, and feel there is a sort of bond developing between the two of us.

Summer Holidays. 2004

This summer I vow, will be all about spending more time with my wife and daughter. I start the medication. Just a little L-Dopa, (substitute dopamine,) combined with a dopamine agonist, Ropinirole, which is supposed to enhance the working of the L-Dopa. I'm a little averse to taking the L-Dopa because of its reported long-term side effects; namely 'Dyskinesias' or uncontrolled spasms and jerks that start appearing after five years into medication. Still, I think, that's a long way down the road.

The most important thing is the quality of my life *now,* and what I can give to Emm and Lily. But despite everything I've read on the internet about the magical effect of L-Dopa - patients transformed within thirty minutes of taking it, loose, fluid body movements etc. - it just doesn't seem to happen for me. My Parkinson's seems to be a little unusual. Firstly, I don't have a tremor at all. My problems lie more with stiffness and slowness of movement - 'Bradykinesia' - and poor balance. I walk like I'm drunk some days. The L-Dopa seems to do very little to ease these symptoms. And still I suffer with chronic fatigue.

Nevertheless, I vow to keep my word and make a superhuman effort to be a proper dad during the holidays. We go to the Zoo and Theme Parks like Drayton Manor, where Emm and Lily howl with laughter as they watch me catapulted along some roller-coaster ride, gripped in its G Forces, throwing up my lunch and probably most of my medication.

At West Midlands Safari Park, our car is surrounded by ostriches when I hold out handfuls of food. Emm and Lily scream as the birds stick their long necks through the partially wound down windows and go mad for the food. In a panic, Lily throws her food up in the air. Most of it goes down my neck and the beasts are pecking away in a frenzy as I slowly accelerate the car to get us out of there, the ostriches trying to keep pace with their heads still inside.

When we get clear and wind up the windows, we collapse into a heap of laughter, so much so that my stomach and head hurt. We've never had so much fun together.

We have a week's holiday in a caravan in north Wales. The sort of holiday that I enjoyed as a kid, with buckets and spades, spinning plastic windmills and brightly coloured stripy wind-breakers. Emm and Lily bury me up to my neck in sand then like the Incredible Hulk I burst my way out, covered in wet sand, I chase Lily up a sand dune while she squeals in terror. Emm is laughing hysterically.

"Oh Colin, stop I'm wetting myself. Don't you realise what you look like in those 'Speedos.' I mean look at you with all your bits on show. Don't you realise nobody wears those 'budgie smugglers' anymore? I'll have to get you a sensible pair of boxers."

We build a sandcastle on the beach surrounded by a moat and high walls and try desperately to keep it standing as the tide advances relentlessly before finally smashing its way through. I watch them both as they walk down the beach looking for shells and I can see so much of Emm in Lily.

We spend the evenings eating fish and chips and a pickled onion on the sea front before we take Lily back to the caravan where, exhausted and sun-tanned, she sleeps right through. Then Emm and I sit on the folding chairs on the grass in front of the caravan and watch the red sky as the sun goes down while drinking a well-earned glass of wine.

Things definitely get a little better between us. I feel closer to Emm and especially to Lily than I've ever been. But the holidays can't last forever, and by mid-August I'm again getting the churning in the pit of my stomach about having to go back to work.

At the end of the month, I have another appointment at the hospital. I talk to the consultant about the poor response to the meds and he agrees to increase the dosage for when I return to school.

My response again, is negligible. Curious, I start researching more and more on the internet. Again I type my symptoms into the search engine. No tremor. Poor response to L-Dopa. Autonomic dysfunction, which includes blood pressure problems, poor balance, staggering backwards, falling, inability to control body temperature, partial incontinence, gasping for breath, choking on food, and so the list goes on.

I keep coming up with the same common denominator – the difference between Parkinson's Disease (PD) and Parkinson's Plus disorders. The latter is an umbrella term for diseases that initially mimic PD symptoms. Two of these that seem most akin to my symptoms are MSA (Multiple System Atrophy) and PSP (Progressive Supranuclear Palsy). Now these are seriously scary diseases that make Parkinson's look like a walk in the park. The prognosis is much worse; death within eight to ten years of diagnosis, often not from the illness itself, but by choking or from bronchial pneumonia due to a compromised swallowing reflex. This puts the frighteners on me. Yes, I know it's my own fault; too much research, a little knowledge is a dangerous thing and all that. I keep imagining my next appointment:

Doctor: Well, Mr. Sparrow. We've got some good news and some bad news. Which would you like to hear first?

Me: The good news please.

Doctor: You've got twenty-four hours to live.

Me: That's the *good news*? What's the *bad*?

Doctor: We couldn't get hold of you yesterday.

Oh, I know, if you believe everything you read, you'll think you have got every disease known to man. The flow diagrams in *The Book Of Family Health* are the worst.

Have you experienced a rise in blood pressure lately?

YES

Has your vision become blurred recently?

YES

Do you find yourself going to the toilet more frequently?
.... oh my God, this is me.

YES

Do you feel tired all of the time?
Yes, definitely me!!!

YES

WARNING! DON'T DELAY!
CONSULT A DOCTOR IMMEDIATELY.
YOU MAY BE DIABETIC

Cue the alarm in your head, like the siren in the film 'Alien' when Ripley is running for the escape pod and 'Mother' is announcing over the loudspeakers that the ship will self-destruct in "T Minus two minutes."

A little knowledge *is* a dangerous thing. But Alexander Pope, who wrote those words of wisdom, also went on to say:

Drink deep, or taste not the Pierian spring:
There shallow draughts intoxicate the brain,
And drinking largely sobers us again.

So I determine to 'drink deep' and become an expert in this matter. By the time my next appointment comes round in the autumn, I am probably the world's leading medical brain on Parkinson's Plus disorders.

My neurologist is however, becoming a little irked by my self-research.

"You really must stop reading on the internet, Mr. Sparrow. Every individual case is different. It's true, some of your symptoms are indeed very atypical of straightforward Parkinson's disease. However, it's too soon to say whether you have one of these other conditions. There are no tests for them, we'll just have to see how your symptoms evolve."

"But if it is one of these others, then I've got to know. I need to make arrangements. I mean, the life expectancy is much lower isn't it?"

"Don't pay too much attention to those American websites, Mr. Sparrow. The figures quoted about life expectancy apply to patients much older than you, who would naturally be more likely to decline more rapidly. You are still a young man. Remember that."

On the way home, I catch sight of myself on a TV screen in the window of an electrical goods shop. It's one of those CCTV images recording the passers-by on the pavement in front of the shop, where you see yourself from an unusual angle and can't quite work out where the camera is.

It takes me by surprise. Apart from looking much older than I thought, it just doesn't look like 'me'. Is that really what I look like? Round shouldered, shuffling. Hordes of pedestrians brushing past me, nobody giving me a second glance. I really do look like an old man! The cells in my changing facsimile must have been dying at quite a rate recently without me noticing.

It reminds me of the time I saw my dad looking old for the first time back in 1975.

1975. Benidorm

Mum's made a decision. She's going on holiday with Aunty Vera and her friend Joyce. Now their children are reasonably grown up, they've decided it's their husbands' turn to do their bit and run the house for a week. They're going to Benidorm.

"And what am I supposed to do while you're swanning around Spain?"

"Well, you'll have to do what I've done for the last twenty years and roll up your sleeves."

"And what about the club?"

"You'll just have to miss it for a week. It won't kill you."

"So you expect me to come home from work at 5 o'clock and start all over again, cooking and cleaning?"

"Yes. Then perhaps you'll appreciate what I've gone through all these years."

"I should never have agreed to you going on those girls' nights out, they've put ideas into your head. And anyway, whoever heard of going away in April?"

"Spain's cheap out of season and it's already warm over there."

Mum and Vera have both never even been on a plane before, so this is quite a big thing for them. Vera is a bit more worried about it than Mum. For years, Mum has dreamed of the balmy Mediterranean, with moustached waiters fawning over her every whim.

Vera is having second thoughts. She's reluctant to leave her beloved Weoley Castle. She can't stand the heat and would much prefer crunching through the frost on the way to the Barnes Hill Club. They've got what you call a package deal, and Mum has been squirreling away a little bit of the housekeeping every month.

"If I'd have known you were saving, I wouldn't have given you so much every week."

"Well, you can moan till you're blue in the face, it's booked and I'm going, and that's that."

On the morning they leave, Vera comes round to our house with her bags packed. Dad helps her bring them over and is out of breath. He says he thinks he's pulled a muscle in his back. She has two huge suitcases.

"Blimey Vera, what have you got in there? We're only going away for a week you know."

"I've just bought a few essentials."

"Well let's see."

Vera unzips the largest case.

Inside, beneath a layer of towels, is a treasure trove consisting of Robinson's marmalade, HP sauce, Marmite, McVitie's chocolate digestives, Smiths' crisps, Glenryck pilchards, Heinz baked beans, Typhoo tea, Horlicks, a big bottle of R. White's lemonade, a shrink-wrapped pack of Danish bacon, a loaf of Sunblest bread, and, in their foil wrappers, two blocks of Anchor butter.

"Vera, are you mad? You can't take all this. You'll never get it past Customs."

"I don't care. I can't eat that foreign muck. It'll give me the shits."

"But look, the butter's not even sealed. Already it's starting to melt."

"I don't care. If I can't take this, I'm not going."

"Well have you packed your swimming costume?"

Vera lets out a roar of laughter.

"Jesus wept, you're joking aren't you? I'm not stripping off. I shall be keeping my tights on at all times."

"But what's the point of going to a sunny destination? And what's this? Oh come on Vera you can't take your mink stole."

"I have to look my best."

And with that, she slams her case shut.

"You're not looking at anything else. It's private. To tell you the truth, I'm dreading it. I'm a bag of nerves. I haven't slept all week, worrying about it."

"Well, what are you coming for?"

"I said I'll keep you company and that's what I'll do."

The taxi arrives and the colour drains out of Vera's face. As they drive off, Mum gives us an enthusiastic wave and Vera looks like she's going to the gallows.

The following Monday evening, we all watch *Crossroads* as normal. Benny Hawkins, the new handyman character, has got a bit of a crush on

126

'Miss Diane', but he's a bit simple and becomes all flustered when near her.

Dad is in the kitchen making his homebrew, listening to Alan Dell and the sound of the Big Bands. I can hear him muttering to himself. "Who the hell does she think she is? Jackie bloody Onassis? Well, you won't get me over there with all that garlic and those slimy waiters. French, Italian, Spanish, all the same. You couldn't trust them in the war. I just hope she knows what she's doing, that's all."

Dad spends the week getting everything ready for us before we get up. The coal fire is raked, the embers thrown away, the grate swept and a new fire built and lit before we're even awake. Breakfast cereals on the table, packed lunches made, all before he leaves for work at 5.30.

Brian, Rob and Laura look after themselves before going to work. But Katie and I have to live with Dad's sandwiches at lunch. They are not what you would call delicate. Huge, half inch-thick slices of cheese, equally thick slices of cucumber, between two doorsteps of bread. No mayonnaise, salad, dressing or salt and pepper. A Desperate Dan lunch, made by someone in a bad mood and in a hurry. Katie says she will be making her own from now on, as everyone laughed at her when she opened her lunch box.

By Thursday night, Dad knows he has to do some washing before Mum comes back at the weekend, so he decides to take it all to the laundrette. This will be easier than doing it himself in our old-fashioned top-loader and mangle. Keen to develop the new-found bond between us, I volunteer to help him.

We squash as much as we can into two big bin liners, then struggle up to Northfield High Street, each with a sack on our back.

"Why don't we take the car?"

"Because I want a pint while it's washing."

He checks all the machines, weighing up the various costs, then selects one big machine, instead of two smaller ones. We pack it all in so tight, we can barely close the door. The sign above the machine says:

Please Do Not Overload The Machines

"That's not overloaded, it's just making use of the machine's full capacity."

He tries to read the instructions on the machine and on the packet of powder, but he hasn't brought his glasses. "Here, Colin, read that, what does it say?"

"It says 'one cup of powder per average load.'"

"Well, what do they mean by a cup? Is that a plastic cup, a teacup, a mug, what? What's an average load? I don't know. This is obviously a large load, that's double average, that's two large mugs. How do we measure that? OK Colin, pour it in, and I'll tell you when to stop."

I start pouring into the slot at the top of the machine.

"Go on, don't be shy, keep going. Go on pour it."

"But Dad, that's half the packet."

"Well, we want to make sure they get clean don't we? OK, that's enough. How much is left?"

"Just a bit in the bottom."

"Well, you might as put that in as well. OK here we go."

He puts the money in, and the cycle starts. The washing turns round in one solid lump, and in the centre of the drum, it looks as though the clothes are still bone dry.

After a few minutes, the overdose of powder starts frothing at the glass, and a few minutes after that, the first trickle of water appears at the bottom of the door. This grows into a steady flow of lather down the machine front and on to the floor. Dad tries to stop the cycle, but can't. There is by now quite a large pool of suds moving across the floor.

"Right, time for a pint, I think."

And with that, we make a quick getaway into The Travellers' Rest[1]. He has more than a pint, in fact he has four, and in that time, he talks to me again about "dealing with a nagging wife".

"You see Colin, we must be very careful now not to make her absence this week too much of a success. If we do, she'll be going away every year. I've still got a few cards up my sleeve. Take this washing for example. If, when we get back, that machine is buggered and the clothes not properly washed, that's actually a blessing in disguise. You see, if you make a cock up of the housework, she won't ask you to do it again. Make a good job of it and you'll end up doing it every week. See?   "You've got to use your head. I mean, look at poor old Stan next door. His wife's got him doing the weekly shop, the vacuuming, hanging out the washing,

---

[1] Closed and demolished in the early 2000s to give way to the Northfield bypass

and all the ironing. Before you know it, he'll be darning his own socks. Poor bugger. He's not even allowed down the pub. And is she happy? Like hell she is. She's got a face like a bag of spanners and nags him relentlessly. As I said before, do everything they tell you without question and you'll both be miserable. A woman likes a challenge, not a doormat."

With that, he orders another pint.

"Men and women, Colin, they're a completely different species."

When we get back to the laundrette, the manager has been called out and he's pushing wave after wave of soapy, frothy water out of the front door with the broom.

All the customers are sitting on the benches with their feet up.

"What's been going on here then?" asks Dad, five pints cut and assuming total innocence.

"Ah, some imbecile has overloaded one of the machines. The whole place is flooded, and the machine's overheated."

"Tut. Some people, hey?"

Dad then goes over to recover his washing from the broken machine.

"Is that your washing? Are you responsible for this mess?"

"Well, this is my washing, but why is it all sopping wet?"

"Because you buggered the machine up by overloading it, that's why."

"Well, I paid for it to be washed and spun, what am I supposed to do with this lot? I've a good mind to ask for my money back."

"Your money back? You cheeky sod, that's an eighty quid machine you've knackered."

"Well, what do you expect, if you buy inferior equipment? Spanish, is it?"

We have to wring the mess out the best we can and pile it back into the bin liners. Walking behind Dad back down the hill, I can see his trousers getting soaked with water leaking from the bag. It looks like he's wet himself. He's chattering away to himself, getting more and more worked up.

"Benidorm, my arse. That's the last time she goes jollying off like Audrey sodding Hepburn."

When he gets back in, he dumps the soapy mess in the bath.

"Another cock up. Good. At least I can say I tried."

By Friday, the week has taken its toll on him and I notice for the first time in my life that Dad looks old.

On Saturday, we hear the sound of a taxi outside, and a few minutes later, Mum bustles through the door, suntanned but exhausted, complaining, "Oh my poor feet, they're killing me!"

Before she gets the chance to start telling us everything, Dad's on his feet, "You're back are you? Right, I'm off down the club."

In sarcastic, mimicking tones, Mum says, "Welcome home dear. Had a nice time?" "Yes I did as a matter of fact. Met a Spanish millionaire, spent the week on his yacht. He wants me to go back out there and be his full-time mistress."

"I'll be back at the usual time."

"Are you even listening to me?"

"Don't wait up. …oh and there's a few wet clothes for you in the bath. I had a bit of a mishap with a washing machine. Sorry. I'll never be able to figure out how these things work. I thought it best to leave it to you. You know what you're doing."

Heartbeat. November 2004

I often think about Dad. Work for him at the factory and especially at the club in the evenings was actually a pleasure. As Mum once said, it got him out of the house of screaming kids.

For me now, it couldn't be more different. As the dark nights start to draw in, I dislike my job more and more. I never really 'enjoyed' it, but I could quite easily cope with it and there were the odd moments of triumph and satisfaction, such as with Warren.

But now the Parkinson's is just making it intolerable. Sunday evenings are even more depressing than those *Onedin Line* moments as a boy, only now it's the theme tune to *Heartbeat* that I dread and instead of worrying about homework I haven't *done*, it's now homework I haven't *marked.*

Teachers are no different to kids really. Sleep on a Sunday night was always difficult, but now it's becoming impossible. Quite often, I dread going in the next morning. There are certain kids who I pray will be away. But when I get to my desk on a Monday morning, there they are, already in their seat; coat on, no books, smiling at me as if to say, *"Right, now we're going to make your next hour hell."*

I suppose all teachers get that feeling to a certain degree. It's a tough job and you have to be at the top of your game at all times. You are like an actor in front of an audience.

If they get bored or sense a weakness, they'll go for you. The illness is making it harder and harder for me to keep this act up. Because of the Parkinson's, I sweat profusely and sometimes visibly shake, which I suppose could be misinterpreted for fear. And the last thing you mustn't appear to be, in front of a middle to low set of Year 10s, is afraid.

But I've been teaching long enough to keep on top of them. One thing I learnt as a trainee teacher: if you issue a threat, such as a detention, *always* carry it out and follow it through. Even if that means tracking the lad down all over the school to issue him with his detention slip. There's nothing that the kids will take advantage of more than a teacher who issues empty threats.

Mind you, just to walk across the playground at lunchtime or break, means a teacher 'sees' all manner of incidents that have to be tackled, then followed up, with all the paperwork that that involves. That's why some teachers 'turn a blind eye' or just stay in their rooms at break and lunch: it's just easier. They actually have time to eat or drink something. But I know that's not a healthy situation; barricading yourself into your classroom.

I've seen teachers who have done it, even at the school I attended as a boy. Those teachers never lasted. They always had a breakdown or moved to another school or even left the profession altogether. That's why I make the effort to go to the staff-room, even the departmental one, at lunchtime and breaks.

It's important to let off a little steam with other teachers, even if that does mean losing half your break as you walk across the playground, pouncing on smokers or those trying to climb the fence as you go.

Today as I enter the staff-room, Neil is in full flow about something that's irritated him.

"I mean, somebody tell me please, is it me or are we going soft on these kids?"

I ask him what's up.

"Ah, just senior management and their brilliant ideas. Have you heard the latest one Colin?"

"What?"

"Well apparently, when Shane Doolan feels like it, he can just get up out of his seat, walk to the front of my classroom, produce out of his top pocket a red card, like the ones football referees use, hold it up in front of me, then just walk out of my class."

The rest of the staff laugh.

"No, seriously, it's true. It's all part of his 'Anger Management Therapy.' Anger Management? What that boy needs is a good kick up the arse!"

Everyone laughs again. I make a suggestion.

"Tell you what Neil, go home tonight, make yourself a red card, then tomorrow, if you're having a particularly bad lesson and can't get them to shut up, *you* show *them* the red card and *you* walk out."

"Brilliant Colin! Remind me to bring it up at the next staff meeting."

When the consultant sees me again at the end of November, he asks me how I'm getting on at work.

"Well frankly, it's a nightmare. My writing just gets smaller and smaller, so that they're always complaining that they can't read what I've written on the whiteboard. I can't mark essays. I can't turn a key in my door. I can't last a lesson without having to go to the toilet, sometimes more than once in an hour, which means I have to leave the kids alone, which is strictly against the rules of health and safety. I've fallen several times, once backward off the stage. I choke on my lunch, I sweat profusely, which is very embarrassing in front of the kids. Do you want me to go on?"

"I'm sorry about all that Mr. Sparrow. You know, despite what we said about working for ten more years, now might be a good time to consider your future. It's a stressful job which obviously isn't helping your condition. There will come a time soon when you won't be able to hold that job down. If you apply for early retirement on the grounds of ill health, I'll support you and write any letters necessary."

"But I'm only forty-four, I'm less than two years in from diagnosis."

"I know, and I'm sorry but from what you've told me, I think it's just going to get worse for you."

Back at school, my classes just seem to be getting tougher. Old allies like Warren Newman have left and in a funny kind of way, I miss him. I related to him. I understood why he wanted to be in the school play: to be near to Kelly. I had done almost exactly the same thing thirty years before.

It was autumn 1975. Doreen Drysdale was a distant memory, and something totally new and exciting had replaced her. Unknown to me for all those years, swimming alongside me and all the other gudgeon, was a new species; a poor persecuted molly, skilled in the art of survival. A species totally different to the likes of Doreen Drysdale or Kelly Mulligan.

1975. Muriel

There's a girl in my class called Muriel McDonald. Everyone calls her "Farmer"' as in 'Old McDonald …'. She's always getting picked on because of the way she looks. She wears this school cardigan, which is far too small for her. It is totally frayed and worn out but her parents won't buy her a new one. There is a hole in each tatty sleeve, that she sticks her thumb through, to keep the sleeves pulled down.

She does this partly to hide her bitten fingernails, which are usually painted in cheap nail polish, partially chipped and scratched off. She's what you might call gangly, with long arms and legs. She doesn't wear tights like the rest of the girls, but long white socks that are rolled down round her ankles, a bit like Rodney Marsh.

Her knees are quite knobbly and some of the kids reckon she looks like a cross between a giraffe and Popeye's Olive Oil. Like a giraffe, she's got these big sad eyes, with huge pretty eyelashes and she blushes a deep red whenever attention is on her, such as when the teacher asks her a question.

She usually knows the answer because she's very bright, despite what everyone thinks of her. She's obviously not well off, because she never goes on any trips and comes in her uniform on non-uniform day.

Sonia Cashmore is her chief tormentor, and has driven all the other girls in the class against her. Actually, I've always thought Muriel is quite pretty in her own sort of way, but because everyone else doesn't talk to her, neither do I.

This morning in Maths, Sonia Cashmore, who looks uglier than ever, starts her daily game.

"Hey farmer, what did you do at the weekend, muck out the pigs?"

Muriel doesn't reply or even look up but just blushes a deep red. She fiddles with her pencil, trying to draw an equilateral triangle without a ruler. I look at her bitten nails and I feel sorry for her. Her eyes are like deep brown, limpid pools of water.

She stubbornly refuses to give in to the tears that are clearly welling up and her face flushes with the effort. This red-faced pride gives her a sort of handsome dignity.

Then in a moment of madness, I do something which goes against all my rules of self-preservation: I draw attention to myself. I slide my protractor across the table to her.

She looks up, and I try a sort of smile, which makes me look like a total wazzock.

"Thanks."

"It's OK."

I don't look at her again, until she slides it back.

"You'll need to get that fumigated now, Sparrow," sneers Cashmore.

Then for the second time in my life, in the space of the same minute, I truly surprise myself and hear someone else's words coming out of my mouth. "Has anyone ever told you Sonia Cashmore, you've got a face like a bosted arse!"

Everyone on our table laughs and Sonia looks fit to explode in a fury of rage. Before she can say anything, Mr. Sampson, the maths teacher shouts over saying if there's another word from our table, we'll all be staying in after school. I look up and Muriel's gaze is fixed down on her work. She is still very flushed and it occurs to me that perhaps she's angry with me for creating a scene and putting her on the spot.

Just once, I look up at her and she looks up at the same time and we both give each other the faintest smile, before quickly looking away.

When the bell goes for the end of the day, she packs her stuff away hurriedly and makes a quick exit, all the time looking at the floor with that angry red in her cheeks.

When she's gone, Cashmore makes a sarcastic comment.

"Looks like your girlfriend doesn't want to know, Sparrow."

"Girlfriend? Are you going soft in the head Cashmore?"

On the way home however, I keep thinking about her: those improvised little thumb holes, cheap looking nail polish, funny little nose and big eyes and the hint of a smile she had flashed me. I tell myself that I'm storing up trouble if I befriend her.

But forget her I can't. She's got inside my head.

At home I lie on my bed looking at the ceiling and replay my favourite scene outside the chip shop in my head, only this time, I am rescuing Muriel. Doreen Drysdale just doesn't compare. I mean everyone fancies Doreen and she certainly doesn't need rescuing.

But Muriel is different. She most definitely *does* need rescuing and no one fancies her. But the more I think about her, I realise that yes, in her own way, she really is quite pretty and no one else seems to have noticed.

Next day, in French, we have our mock O-level oral exam, for which we have to get into groups of three. No one will go with Muriel and Paula Hardcastle and I am half-pleased when Mr. Peters, the French teacher, puts me with them.

In our groups, we have to practise a short speech entitled, 'Pendant Les Grande Vacances', before going into the other room for the actual exam with Mr. Peters.

Paula Hardcastle has a support assistant to help her. Paula is a bit of a hard-knock, not to be messed with and is absolutely useless at French. She sits in the corner of the room, getting some last-minute coaching from the assistant, when suddenly she gets up in a huff and strides over to Mr. Peters who has just finished the first group.

"Sir," Paula asks, "if you say 'you really piss me off' is that classed as swearing?"

Mr. Peters, in an effort to support the teaching assistant who is hovering in the background, replies rather diplomatically, "Well, yes Paula, I'm afraid that it is."

Paula then triumphantly turns back to the ashen-looking teaching assistant, and says, "See, I told you that you shouldn't say that to me!"

I look at Muriel. She turns away, her face all red with laughter. We go in for the test. Paula is first.

Mr. Peters begins by saying, "Bonjour, comment t'appelle tu?"

Paula replies, "Err bonjour…err… je…errr …je…..then in a very thick French accent, as if to disguise the fact that she's actually speaking in English, Paula says, "My name ees Paula…"

She then proceeds to deliver her whole French exam in English with a French accent… "In thee summere 'olidaze, I went to zee beach with my familee…"

Occasionally, the accent turns into German, and sometimes borders on Pakistani. I try to look at Muriel, to make her laugh. She is a permanent shade of crimson, and gives me a gentle kick under the table to tell me to stop it.

By the end Paula is pleased with her efforts, and Mr. Peters makes some notes. "Merci, Paula, au revoir."

"Mercy, and sank yeu teu."

And off she goes, support assistant in tow.

Even Mr. Peters can't resist a little chuckle with us when she's gone.

Afterwards, outside the exam room, Muriel and I both explode into laughter and I love to see her so happy, again noticing how pretty she looks when she smiles.

At the end of the day, she's nowhere to be seen again, in a rush to avoid the bullies.

My head is filled with thoughts about her as I walk out of the school gates. Then there's a tap on my shoulder. I spin round and there she is.

"Hello," she says.

"Hello. Err, can I walk up the hill with you?"

"If you want to."

We walk up the main road laughing about the French Oral. She's very shy and keeps blushing every time she speaks. Occasionally, we run out of things to say and when we do, her face is positively on fire and she looks sideways at me and flashes just the hint of another smile.

When we get to the top, I offer to walk her all the way home, but she flies into a sort of panic and says, "No, please, … I don't want you to…sorry …bye, see you tomorrow."

With that, she runs off in her funny awkward gait. I stand there looking after her. I don't think she's gangly at all really. I'd describe her more as willowy.

In fact, more Bambi than giraffe.

Early Retirement. 2005

After dinner and Lily's been put to bed, we sit and watch an old film on video: 'Play It Again Sam', directed by and starring Woody Allen, who plays a character called Alan. I'm stretched out on the sofa and Emm is curled up in her favourite chair, her bare feet and long legs tucked under her, the way she always does.

I look at her as she watches. She smiles as Alan's wife explains why she wants a divorce. "I can't stand the marriage, I don't find you any fun, I feel you suffocate me, I don't feel any rapport with you and I don't like you physically … Oh for God's sake Alan, don't take it personally."

Emm laughs out loud. I watch her; that smile that defeats me every time. She catches me looking at her. "What are you staring at?"

"Just wondering why beautiful women are attracted to such ugly men like Woody Allen."

"Because you make us *laugh* of course!!"

During the course of 2005, I start to make arrangements to finish work on the grounds of ill health. The head tries to talk me out of it, saying I will be terribly missed and that I still have a lot to offer. He suggests I give up my role as head of department and work a reduced timetable, even part time.

But my mind is made up. I only have to look in the mirror to see what a state I'm in. Despite the massive doses of levodopa, I just keep getting worse. A typical advanced Parkinson's patient, ten or more years in from diagnosis, would be on maybe 500 mg a day I'm currently taking about 1700 mg a day.

And I continue to deteriorate. I can't walk in a straight line, or lift up my feet. I stagger as if I'm drunk, which gives the kids at school no end of jokes about, "Sir had too much to drink last night.'"

I'm on blood pressure pills to control my soaring hypertension. My left hand is useless, unable to write more than a line or two before the words become so cramped and tiny that they are illegible. What good is a teacher who can't write or walk in a straight line?

Between January and June, I am off on long term sick leave because I simply can't do the job. In this period, all letters of support are written,

138

the doctor at County Hall is in agreement, the teachers' union arrange my pension and I finally receive confirmation that I can retire at the end of the summer term.

And that was that. The end of a gloriously short teaching career and the beginning of the hardship years. Fourteen years' service doesn't give you much of a pension. It was just unfortunate that the year before I was diagnosed, after winning promotion to Head of Department, we bought a bigger house, the mortgage on which still has to be paid.

Emm stopped working in 2000 when Lily was born and eventually, I suppose, she will become more of a carer for me, for all the everyday things that I won't be able to do.

Little do I realise that all this new found leisure time on my hands and no longer needing to get up in the morning, will lead us into further financial trouble.

Emm laughs at the film. Woody Allen is trying to impress a girl on a blind date in a disco. I smile too. Men really do, do that, I think. Warren did it, trying to impress and to be near Kelly Mulligan in the school play.

Even I did it myself back in 1975, to be near to Muriel McDonald…

1975. Choir

Muriel sings in the school choir. It's the only after school club she's allowed to attend, and it's on a Monday afternoon. Miss Parker, the music teacher, is always checking that she's not going to miss it. She's her best top soprano.

Choir is 'un-cool' in everyone else's eyes, so Muriel's ability doesn't earn her any credibility points with the likes of Sonia Cashmore.

I decide to sign up for choir on a Monday.

Miss Parker is sceptical.

"Are you sure, Colin? You do realise that there aren't any other boys in the choir?"

"That's OK Miss."

"Well, have you done any singing before?"

"Oh you know, just in the bath, but I really enjoy it, I think it might be my vocation."

"Well, I won't deny that we need some boys."

They are halfway through rehearsals for a Christmas concert, and I will just have to catch up the best I can. She gives me the score. It's from *The Mikado* by Gilbert and Sullivan. The girls are singing all the male parts as well as the female. I will just be part of the 'ensemble' as Miss Parker can't trust me with a solo.

On the brighter side, the modern piece they are doing is 'I'd Like To Teach The World To Sing' by The New Seekers. At least I know that one from the Coca-Cola advert.

Muriel is also singing two solos, 'My Favourite Things' from *The Sound Of Music* and 'Silent Night.'

Monday comes round and I'm late because I had a ten-minute detention for wearing my vest under my rugby shirt.

When I walk into the music room, Miss Parker says, "Girls, this is Colin. He's volunteered to join us, perhaps the first of many boys. Where would you like to sit, Colin?"

"I'll sit over here Miss Parker, if that's OK."

As I sit down next to Muriel, she blushes pink and whispers, "What are you doing here? I didn't know you could sing!"

"Man of many talents," I whisper back.

The rehearsal is a nightmare. I haven't got a clue what I'm doing. Muriel has to keep turning my pages for me and pointing to where we are, with those sweet little fingers with the chipped nail polish. I haven't got a clue what a refrain is and think "Allegro" is a car.

A couple of times, Miss Parker stops the piano. "Colin, until you're more familiar with the piece, it would be better if you didn't sing."

At 4.45 the rehearsal is over and we walk back up the hill together. It's nearly five o'clock and there's no one else around, so I suddenly have a rush of blood to the head. I have an overwhelming feeling of affection for her.

After several aborted attempts, I clumsily take her cold little hand in mine. She blushes but she doesn't pull away and returns my grip. I am in raptures as we walk on, saying nothing. Her hand is all sweetness to hold. At the top of the lane, I again offer to walk her home, but once more she refuses, apologising, before walking off on her own.

I watch her as she goes, only this time, after a few yards, she looks back, smiles and gives a little wave.

"See you tomorrow," she shouts.

"Yes, OK."

I walk the rest of the way home in a sort of fever of euphoria. It's true. I cannot tell a lie. I am most definitely and undeniably in love with Muriel McDonald. I'll never wash my hand again. I know now.

Muriel really *is* the one.

At home, I lie in my bedroom in the dark, thinking about her. I turn on the radio just as the opening beat to Barry White's 'You're My First, My Last, My Everything' is starting up. I turn it up full blast and sing along into the hairbrush: "You're my sun, my moon, my guiding star …My kind of wonderful, that's what you are…"

Then I pause and hit the imaginary drum, in perfect time… thwack!

It's then that I realise Mum is banging on the door. "Jesus, it sounds like a cat's being strangled, will you turn that racket off and come downstairs. There's a telephone call for you. I've been calling you for ages."

In the hall, sitting on the stairs, I pick up the phone.

"Hello?"

"Hello, it's me."

"Who's me?"

"It's me, Muriel."

Thunderbolts galore! My heart takes a giant leap and the hairs stand up on the back of my neck.

"Oh hello ….. ummm …how are you?"

"Fine thanks. Was that you I could hear singing?"

"Oh no ….no … just the radio on loud. How did you get this number?"

"Oh you know, there aren't that many Sparrows in the book."

"No of course not. Stupid of me."

Silence.

She giggles.

Silence.

"Sorry, I shouldn't have rung."

"No, no, really, it's nice, I'm glad you did, really."

"Just wanted to say, see you at school tomorrow."

"Yes."

"OK."

"Yes."

"See you then."

"Yes."

"Bye."

"Bye … "

"And …"

"Yes?"

"And …sorry I wouldn't let you walk me home, it's just a bit difficult you know."

"No, that's fine really."

"And …"

"Yes?"

"And …I've been…thinking about you."

"Really?"

She giggles again. I feel a warm rush down my back, and want to scoop her up.

"Anyway …. I just wanted to tell you."

"OK, thanks."

She says, "Isn't this weird? You never talked to me before."

"I know, I'm sorry. It's funny, I'm rubbish at this sort of thing."

She giggles once more. Then the pips go and I realise she's in a call-box, not at home.

"Oh damn, gotta go, bye"

"Bye."

"You know what?"

"No, what?"

"I …"

Then the phone goes dead. I skip upstairs and fall on my mattress giving the ceiling my full, undivided attention once more. What was she going to say?

"I've been thinking about you," she'd said.

Why couldn't I tell her how I felt? *You're emotionally handicapped, Colin Sparrow*, I think to myself.

Next morning, I breeze downstairs, grab a slice of toast and put on my coat on the way to the door, when Mum stops me in my tracks.

"Where do you think you're going without any breakfast? There's no way you're going to school without anything inside you, young man."

Brian chips in, in his sarcastic, lazy tone, "Didn't you know? He's in luuuurve. I heard him on the phone last night. Nearly made me puke. And he was singing into the hairbrush to Barry White like a complete moron."

Mum butts in, "All right, all right, you don't have to tease him."

I grab another piece of toast and say, "Think what you like, I don't care."

A mocking cheer goes up around the table.

Rob says, "I can't believe it Colin, after all that I've taught you…. she's not got a mute sister by any chance has she?"

"No she hasn't."

That is all the confirmation they need.

"See, he's not denying she exists. Oh no! Pass the sick bucket, please."

"What's her name?"

"Muriel."

"Muriel? Not Muriel McDonald by any chance?"

"I'm not saying any more."

143

"It is, isn't it? It's Muriel McDonald! There are no other Muriels round here."

"Who's Muriel McDonald?"

"They're the roughest family in Northfield. Muriel's the only girl and the quiet one."

"She is *not* rough. Anyway, it's none of your business, I'm going to school."

I slam the door behind me. *Dickheads!*

I'm at school by a quarter past eight. I hang around the gate waiting for her to come in, but as the minutes tick by and the playground fills up, there's no sign of her. I go back out and look up the steep hill, trying to pick her out from the hordes walking down. I can't see her. It's ten to nine and the bell goes. I look back up the lane and there are just a few late stragglers, sprinting down.

Inside the classroom, I stare at her empty chair. I've been waiting fifteen hours and fifty-six minutes to see her and she's not turned up for school, *again.*

Mr. Crammond takes the register. "Does anyone know where Muriel McDonald is?"

"Fixing her Big End."

"Put a sock in it Cashmore."

"OK, that's enough of that please."

I spend the whole morning thoroughly miserable. In French, Mr. Peters gives us our oral mark.

"Colin Sparrow, 75%
Muriel McDonald, 90%
Paula Hardcastle, 3%."

By lunchtime, I decide I am going round to her house. Something is wrong. She definitely said, "See you tomorrow," on the phone. I walk up on to the playing fields and pretend I'm on some biology assignment, inspecting the grass, then jump the fence in the far corner, by the conker tree.

I know where she lives roughly. Her estate is fairly notorious in Northfield. There are plenty of abandoned shopping trolleys, cars propped

144

up on bricks in overgrown front gardens and roaming packs of dogs with tails curled up and over, sniffing everything that moves and marking their territory.

Muriel lives in a maisonette, in a block at the top of the hill, behind the pub. I know which landing she is on because I've seen her brothers. I walk up the unlit stairwell, stepping through puddles of I don't know what and on to the communal walk way on the first floor, where there is a dumped, rolled up carpet and a child's tricycle. I guess it's the door on the end.

The front door has got a pane of glass missing, with a piece of cardboard sellotaped over the hole. The bell doesn't work, so I push the stiff letterbox and let it bang shut. Immediately a dog goes berserk from inside. A multitude of locks and bolts are withdrawn before the door is finally opened on to the chain and I can see Muriel's face peering round the gap while trying to hold back a huge Alsatian. She looks shocked to see me.

"No Taurus, get down. Stop it, go inside."

She closes the door on the chain and I hear her pushing the dog back behind an inner door. Then the sound of the chain being withdrawn and the door finally opens and there stands Muriel in her school uniform.

"What are you doing here?"

"I was worried when you didn't turn up for school today."

"You can't come here."

"Why not?"

"You just can't, that's all."

"Sorry, but I missed you."

She flushes bright red. She looks down the walkway, then stands aside and says, "Come on then, quick, come inside before anyone sees you."

Inside, I ask, "Are you on your own?"

"Just my little brother. I've had to stay in and look after him, because my mum's had to go out."

I follow her into the kitchen. The dog is still going berserk in the front room, and she shushes at it through the closed door. There's a sink full of washing up, underwear on a makeshift line, an empty dog's bowl on the floor and children's toys scattered everywhere. There are patches of bare plaster on the walls, and the light bulb has no shade.

"I know, it's horrible isn't it? Why did you have to come here?"

"It's not horrible. Our kitchen's much worse."

She smiles, as if thanking me for that.

She sits on the edge of the table, and I sit next to her. I want to tell her all the things on my mind. She is quiet, then looks at me, as if she wants me to say something. God, I want to bang my head on the table. I screw up all my courage and say,

"I wanted to tell you something on the phone last night."

"What?"

"I think...."

"What?"

"I think you're... "

Suddenly there's the sound of a key in the lock. A look of horror crosses her face. "Oh no, it's Mum, she's back early."

"Muriel, have you been out? This door's on the latch, did you know that?"

Muriel's mum, loaded down with shopping walks into the kitchen. She drops her bags in shock when she sees me.

"Who the bleeding hell is this?"

"Mom, this is Colin, he's in my class."

"Since when have I said you can invite people round, your dad will go mad."

"Hello Mrs. McDonald, I'm just bringing her French Oral result round. She got 90%."

"Did I?"

"Yep, beat me."

"And you are Colin who?"

"I'm Colin Sparrow, Mrs. McDonald."

"Sparrow? Are you one of Eddie's boys?"

"That's right Mrs. McDonald."

"Well I never, I've worked with your father on Milk Tray for the best part of ten years. Funniest man I've ever known. Muriel, give Colin a Vimto."

My old man, the hero ... once again. I am constantly amazed at how many people he knows. He has more pull than Henry Kissinger. I'm also treated to Jammy Dodgers which I eat without my tablets, which is a big mistake.

Muriel starts tidying up, then goes into the other room to check on her brother. As soon as she opens the door, the Hound Of The Baskervilles

146

comes bounding in and goes straight for me. The shock makes me throw the jammy dodger up in the air. When it lands on the floor, the dog wolfs it down ravenously.

"It's all right, he won't hurt you, he's as daft as a brush really."

Nevertheless, my stomach starts churning and bubbling like quicksand.

"Err, can you tell me where the loo is please?"

"Up the stairs, first on the left."

The hound follows me up.

"Shoo, go on, go away!"

I close the door, and he starts whimpering and scratching outside. Oh God this is a nightmare. I survey the bathroom, and my heart sinks.

It's one of those without a window, but an extractor fan instead. That brilliant invention that doesn't remove odours, but just stirs them around a bit. Joy of joy, the toilet roll has about three squares left on it. I've got no choice but to begin. As I try to muffle the sound with a few discreet coughs, the dog outside starts howling. Oh God, I think, my relationship with Muriel is finished, she'll go right off me.

The dog gets more and more excited. To top it all, the toilet has a 'wimp' flush that uses about half a pint of water, and couldn't flush away a Malteser.

After about three flushes, I hear Mrs. McDonald shout up the stairs, "Are you all right love?"

"Yes, I'm fine, I'll be down in a minute, don't come up!"

Thankfully, I hear her call Taurus downstairs into the kitchen. When I've finished, I gingerly open the door to see if the coast is clear. The extractor is wheezing and spluttering, and no use at all. I decide to try and remove the smell by fanning the room and surrounding area with the bathroom door. This works by partially opening and shutting the door in quick succession to circulate the air.

I've been at this for a couple of minutes, face red with the exertion, when a voice on the stairs behind me makes me jump. "Colin, what on earth are you doing?"

"Oh hello, Mrs. McDonald, just checking your hinges. I think they might need a bit of oil."

Back in the kitchen, I seem to have got away with it. After making Mrs. McDonald roar with laughter by telling the story about Dad and the toilets with no doors on the campsite, I decide to quit while I am ahead, and say goodbye. Muriel shows me to the door.

"I can tell my mum really likes you."

"I'm glad."

"See you tomorrow."

"Yep."

I start to walk off, turn round, go back, give her a quick kiss on the cheek and run off. At the end of the walkway, I look back, and she is beaming at me. I bound down the stairs two at a time thinking,

Muriel McDonald, I absolutely adore you.

Secrets Will Always Out. 2006

Initially, after retiring, I positively bathe in the joy of my new found freedom. I suddenly have time on my hands. On the days when I don't feel too bad, I take Lily to school and pick her up, one of the few dads in the playground. Lily's quite proud of this and announces to the rest of the mums waiting, "My dad's on benefits and doesn't have to work."

She also tells them that my teeth aren't real.

"Underneath those white caps, he's got black teeth!"

Lily's six now and is as bright as a button. She can read and write like an eight year old. But she doesn't fully understand this adult illness. She gets frustrated when I get tired and can't play with her. She knows I've got something called Parkinson's and hopes someday I'll get better.

Just last week at school, they had to write down a wish they wanted to come true. Everyone wrote things like, "I wish we had a helicopter", or "I wish my dad won the lottery", or "I wish I could go to Disneyland in Florida" etc.

Lily wrote that she wished her daddy would get better from his Parkinson's. The teacher didn't ask her to read it out, but gave her a gold star anyway.

It's a slow illness, which I suppose is a blessing. She can get used to the changes. She's growing up with it. It's not as if I've suddenly had a road accident, or developed cancer and all my hair's fallen out. It's not a shock like that. She's being given time to get used to my decline.

My liberation from marking, planning lessons and writing reports results in a period of creativity when I paint several canvases in acrylic and start writing poetry. For the first time in ages, I feel truly relaxed and happy.

But the extra time on my hands leads me to a dark place. The catalyst for the approaching crisis is actually my medication; namely the ropinirole. One of its side effects, unknown to me, is compulsive behaviour; the most common being an addiction to gambling.

It all starts off quite innocently; a few scratch cards here and there, the odd phone call to a late-night television quiz show. I win a couple of hundred pounds, which is the worst thing that could happen. It gets me hooked.

Initially, I am ignorant about the dangers of ropinirole, or brand name Requip, the dopamine agonist. It acts on the pleasure-seeking area of the brain. In some patients - not all - this can lead to obsessive behaviour. This can manifest itself in the form of binge eating, shopping addictions, sexual addiction and gambling.

When I finally realise I have a problem, I do some reading up on it on the internet. In America, where they are considering banning the drug altogether, there was a case of some old guy, a responsible, sensible citizen (an attorney I think) who had never gambled before in his life. He was on the same drug as me, ropinirole. He blew half a million dollars in one night in a casino in Vegas.

At first Emm doesn't twig what's going on. It's three in the morning. I've got the television on low, watching a phone in quiz show and I've got the phone by my side, when Emm opens the door in her dressing gown.

"What on earth are you doing down here at this hour?"

"Oh, I can't sleep, just watching the only rubbish that's on at this time."

"Why have you got the phone with you? You're not phoning those 090 numbers are you? You know how much they cost."

"No, of course not. There was a call earlier. Wrong number."

"And what have you been eating?"

"Oh I just made myself a chip sandwich."

"At three in the morning? Colin, I'm seriously beginning to worry about you. Turn that off and come upstairs."

I listen out for the post to intercept bills before Emm sees them. When I hear the flap of the letterbox, I hurry downstairs to pick up the mail, carefully concealing those such as my bank statements and the telephone bill. The last one was for over nine hundred pounds. I'm overdrawn up to my eyeballs, have a £3000 bank loan and owe friends and family a little over £5000. I've asked them all to keep it from Emm.

That's over £10,000 in all, in little over twelve months since I retired.

I find myself sneaking out when she goes shopping to buy more scratch cards. I know it's crazy and I'm never going to win. I'm an intelligent person but I can't help myself. They say it's hardest to stop when you're winning. But in my experience, it's hardest to stop when you're *losing,* because you think, if I give up now, all the money I've 'invested' will be lost and the next person to buy a scratch card off that roll will be a winner. And I will have paid for their win.

It's like a form of madness.

Today, quite unexpectedly I am caught unawares. The washing machine has broken down and I don't have the money to repair or replace it.

Suddenly, out of the blue, Emm says, "Colin, can I ask you something? Where is all our money going?"

Her question throws me completely, I'm not ready for it, haven't a convenient excuse already prepared. I go bright red and just stumble over my words.

"Well... I've just had to pay the telephone, gas and electric all at once."

"Yes, I know, but with the amount you have saved, you shouldn't be scrabbling about struggling to pay a couple of hundred pounds in bills."

"I have got money. It's just tied up in the tax-free ISA that's all and I can't get at it."

"Yes, but where's the money like your pension that's going into your current account every month?

"It's still going in."

"Then why are you overdrawn by £1300?"

"What?"

"You heard me."

"Well...how do you know that?"

"I found the letter in your pocket from the bank listing your overdraft charges."

"You've been going through my pockets?"

"Well, I didn't intend to. I was emptying them for the wash. But it's just as well I did isn't it?"

There's an uneasy, awkward silence in which I try to avoid eye contact.

"What's going on Colin?"

Silence. She won't let go.

"This isn't your money Colin, it's *ours,* the family's. Do you understand?"

"Yes of course."

"You're not gambling it are you Colin? Please don't tell me you're gambling away our money."

"Of course not. Don't be silly."

"Then what are you spending it on? I've caught you three times now, in the middle of the night watching that quiz programme, with the phone by your side. Why haven't I seen a phone bill for the last six months?"

Each question I can't answer and my silence just condemns me all the more. She slams her hand down on the table.

"We agreed didn't we? With your lump sum and the pension, we were going to try and pay the mortgage off early, to give us a cushion."

"I know. And I have paid some of it back."

"When? How much have you paid off?"

I don't answer. She is shouting now. "WHEN? HOW MUCH? TELL ME!"

She pauses, breathing heavily, face flushed, then says in a really calm, quiet voice, "You'd better start talking Colin, because if our relationship is based on secrets and lies, then I'm out of here and I'll take Lily with me. I mean it."

My heart is pumping as I realise the seriousness of what I've done. I sigh and decide to tell her everything. When I finish, her face is white and she's crying.

"You bastard Colin! Do you know how much I scrimp and save on the money you give me? Buying clothes for Lily from charity shops. Going to the supermarket just before they close to get the reduced items. And all the time, you're blowing our money on such trash. You bastard. You stupid bastard!"

She collapses into the chair, breathing heavily. I go to her and try to put my arm round her.

"Get off me! Don't touch me!"

"Emm, I'm sorry. It's the drugs."

"Don't! Don't even think about getting out of it like that."

"But it's true. Come with me next time I go to the consultant. He'll tell you."

"I'm leaving you Colin. I'm leaving you. Or you can pack your bag right now, right this minute."

She goes upstairs and slams the bedroom door. Lily comes in from the other room. "Why is Mummy so angry Daddy?"

"Oh, it's nothing Poppet, don't you worry yourself about it. Daddy's done something silly that's all."

"What silly thing have you done?"

"It's not important darling. Come here and I'll help you with that."

"It must be important for Mummy to be so angry."

At this point the bedroom door flies open, she stamps downstairs and throws a holdall at me.

"Go on, put some things in it and go! We don't need you round here anymore."

She picks up Lily, who begins to cry.

"Come on Emm, let's talk about this, you're upsetting Lily."

"Well you should have thought about that before then, shouldn't you?"

"Just talk to me."

"What's there to talk about? You don't talk to *me*. You don't consult *me* when you spend our money on such trash! It seems to me that this isn't a proper marriage at all. We don't share things; decisions, responsibility, anything. You don't even help out with Lily any more. You just go ahead and do whatever you want and sod the rest of us."

"Now that's not fair, you know I can't…"

"Fair! Fair?! Is it fair that I am up to my eyeballs shopping, cooking, washing, ironing, cleaning, decorating, dropping off and picking up Lily from school, putting her in the bath, getting her ready for bed, getting her ready for school, and the million and one other things I have to do, while all the time, you, *you* just drain our bank account by fucking gambling! Is that fair?"

Emm never swears normally, certainly not in front of Lily, who is by now hysterical in her arms. I try to take her from her.

She screams at me, "NO!! Don't you dare touch her! You've no right. Just go. Go! We don't need you!"

And with that, she rushes upstairs with Lily and slams the bedroom door behind her.

In the silence that follows, the walls and ceiling are still ringing with the noise of her outburst. I am stunned. I just stand there and let the enormity of what I've done sink in.

The normality of half an hour ago, now seems a million years ago. And of course she's right. Every single word. How can I have been so

153

stupid? So utterly damn selfish? I mean what was I thinking of…spending all that money, on…. nothing?

Absolutely nothing. Saddled with all that debt. And for what? We have absolutely nothing to show for it. What an idiot.

Eventually, I go upstairs and look at the bedroom door. It's never closed normally. Its wooden panels facing me, barring my way just serve to remind me of her anger. I listen at the door. It's silent within. I try the handle gently. It's locked with the bolt that has never been used before. I knock softly.

"Emm, come on please, open the door."

Silence.

1975. Not Speaking

Every morning, I meet Muriel behind the huge dustbins outside the school kitchens. It's out of bounds, so we're usually undisturbed. For ten minutes before the bell, we stand close, hold hands, and she helps me rehearse my lines for the concert.

When we get to registration, we walk in separately, to avoid gossip. Mr. Crammond is handing out letters, making announcements.

"Miss Parker has asked me to say that there'll be an end of term Christmas concert by the school choir, and tickets are available from her, in her classroom, at lunchtime. I do believe that our very own Muriel McDonald will be singing a solo piece. So, I expect as many people as possible to support this venture."

Sonia Cashmore can't resist a dig.

"What, come back after school and pay to watch 'farmer'…you've got to be kidding."

I just stare at her with a face like thunder.

She retorts, "What? What did I say? Oh, I forgot, you two are an item aren't you? How sad."

Everyone laughs.

"At least she's got some talent for something, not just a bitter, twisted bitch like you Cashmore."

Muriel looks at me, horrified, as if pleading with me to stop drawing attention to her.

Afterwards, outside, on the way to Period One, I catch up with Muriel.

"Sorry, but I can't stand to let her talk to you like that."

"Go away. Just leave me alone. You just make things ten times worse. Don't talk to me anymore."

She runs off crying, to a chorus of whistles and jeers. What have I done?

She doesn't talk to me, or even look at me for the rest of the day. Last lesson is woodwork and Mr. Jones, as usual, takes ages getting us to clear away and put all the tools back, so by the time he lets us go, the bell has long gone and so have the girls from home economics. There's no sign of Muriel at the gate. Thoroughly miserable and regretting what I've done, I walk home alone.

"Don't talk to me anymore … You just make things worse!" she'd said.

It's raining and I walk the long way, via the park. Although only 4 o'clock, the early winter sky is dark, and I kick through the sodden piles of leaves in the gutter. I just happen to pass her block, and hang about outside, looking up at the windows on her balcony. The lights are on, and I can hear Taurus barking.

I desperately want to go and knock on her door but the fear of her shutting it in my face stops me. Twice, I screw up my courage and get as far as the top of the stairwell, before turning back like a coward.

I've blown everything. Trying to be a hero. What an idiot I think. Can't you see how Muriel operates? She takes the humiliation. She doesn't respond. She doesn't lower herself to their level. That way, they get bored and leave her alone. Then I go and stick my big oar in, so that the class are now talking about nothing else. Idiot…idiot, idiot, idiot. I deserve to be smashed in the face with a mallet.

I bang my head against the trunk of a tree over and over, shouting, "Idiot, idiot, idiot!"

"Are you all right, dear?"

I look round, and a couple of old ladies with their shopping trolleys, are standing looking at me in a concerned way.

"Oh yes, fine thanks, I'm fine … just rehearsing some lines for the play I'm in."

And I walk off with a big red mark on my forehead.

Back at home, I sit in my wet things and after tea at 6.30, I watch *Crossroads*. Benny still has a thing for 'Miss Diane' who is teaching him to read.

Just after seven, the phone rings. I rush to pick it up. I get there just before Brian.

"That'll be for me," I shout. "Leave it."

"Hello?"

I hear coins being inserted, and hope against all hope.

I say again, "Hello?"

"Hello."

"Is that you, Muriel?"

"Yes."

"Look, Muriel, I'm so sorry, I've been an absolute idiot, …. Muriel, …..… are you still there?"

"Yes."

"Tell me I'm an idiot. Go on, shout at me."

There's a silence, then in a quiet, barely audible voice she says, "You're an idiot."

We both let out a little laugh of relief.

"I'm a total, and utter wazzock. What am I?"

In a quiet voice again, coloured with a smile, she says, "You're a wazzock."

And she laughs again, and her laughter tells me everything is all right.

Then, with superhuman courage, I say, "You know, I do love you, Muriel McDonald."

She laughs. "You wazzock."

The Blessing Of Forgiveness. 2006

In the cold light of morning, I keep replaying in my head everything she said to me and how she had every right to say it. What a selfish pig. The last thing in the world I want to do is hurt Emm. She really deserves the best. She chose to share her life with me. She could have married anyone. But she chose me; this loser who's letting her down. I hate myself.

It's just before five and the sky is brightening. I get up off the sofa, sort and take my tablets, then begin working on a plan of how I'm going to pay it all back and how long it'll take me. But the most pressing job is to get myself off the offending drug.

Later on in the morning, I will call the hospital and try to make an emergency appointment with the consultant.

At about seven, while I'm working on some figures, the bedroom door opens and I hear Lily flush the toilet. She's chattering away about how hungry she is and can she go downstairs. I hear Emm call her back in, then close the door behind them again.

It's the holidays, so she doesn't have to go to school. It's another couple of hours, just after nine, when the door opens again and I hear feet on the stairs. I'm on the phone to the hospital, on hold, waiting for them to make an appointment for me.

Lily runs into the kitchen, straight to the fridge and takes out the four-pint container of milk that she struggles to lift. "I want Sugar Puffs!" she shouts to Emm.

Lily lays her own place at the table and gives me a quick glance. She's not sure whether she's allowed to speak to me or not. I give her a little wink and she looks sideways to see if Emm is watching her, then smiles a furtive, secretive smile back at me. Our own little 'secret conspiracy.' Then she starts to pour into her bowl.

For the first time, Emm looks at me and just says, "You still here?"

"Yes, yes I'm still here. Friday? At 11.30? That would be marvellous, thank you so much for arranging that at such short notice. OK. Friday. See you then. Bye."

I put the receiver down. "That was the hospital. I've made an appointment for Friday. I'd…like you to come with me please Emm, and we'll try to sort all this out."

She doesn't answer, but busies herself with Lily.

"Look at the mess you're making."

Lily is giggling which brings a reluctant smile from Emm. Encouraged by this, Lily says: "I want to go to the hospital on Friday as well. Can I Mummy, please?"

"I don't know. I don't even know if I'm going yet."

This is a major step forward. At least she's talking and acknowledging my existence.

Inwardly, I thank God for small mercies.

Over the next few days there are plenty more awful silences but she does finally agree to come with me to see the neurologist. Much to Lily's annoyance and sense of injustice, we arrange for her to stay with my mum in Northfield, as we don't think the hospital will be suitable for her.

In the waiting room of the Neurosciences Outpatients, I sense that Emm's shocked by some of the patients waiting. Some in wheelchairs, some having the moisture dabbed from their eyes and chins. Maybe she's visualizing her own husband, a bit further down the line.

I suppose there are no secrets anymore. My name is called and we go in together.

The neurologist is very polite and charming when I introduce Emm to him. Then I start to tell him everything that's been going on. He doesn't bat an eyelid and sounds as if he's heard this story a million times before.

"You should have told me earlier Mr. Sparrow. This is not unusual."

"But if you take me off the ropinirole, what about my restless legs? I just can't sleep without it."

"I can prescribe a sleeping tablet, clonazepam. It's an anti-convulsant, an epilepsy tablet, so works well on the jumping legs. Tell me, how much have you lost in all?"

"A little over £10,000."

He winces.

"And he didn't tell you Mrs. Sparrow?"

"No, he didn't."

"Well, I am truly sorry about this. I know how things must be financially, after giving up work, and this is the last thing you need. I'm very sorry Mrs. Sparrow. If it's any consolation at all, the secrecy is also quite common too. You know, some patients I see, keep secrets like this for years and years, despite my best advice. At least now it's all out in the open."

He looks at me, and makes me feel like a guilty schoolboy. "Mr. Sparrow, please work together with your wife. Surely she deserves better."

"I know. I'm sorry. I'm sorry."

Emm has more questions.

"So the eating in the middle of the night, that's all to do with the drug as well?"

"Yes. You know you are quite lucky. It can cause all sorts of compulsive behaviour. It's not unknown to have eating addictions, shopping addictions, even sexual addictions."

Emm tries to see the funny side. "I'd better stay off it then, or I'll be off down Harrod's with the milkman."

When we leave the hospital, we walk in silence to the car. Things have calmed down. She knows exactly how much I owe and how much I'm paying back each week. I don't think I'll ever keep anything from her again. I think, there's nothing that makes us so lonely as our secrets. As we walk on, I slip my hand into hers, which she accepts.

1975. Christmas Concert

Christmas is fast approaching, and with it, the end of term concert. I am absolutely hopeless, and Miss Parker has serious doubts about whether to let me perform. "Perhaps you should sit this one out Colin and take part in the next concert, when you will have been to all the rehearsals."

"No really, Miss Parker, I think I can do it. I've been practising."

"Well, OK, if you really want to. But whenever you're a bit unsure, don't sing, or else keep your voice very low."

She needn't worry. I've long since learnt that the secret to choral singing, if you're crap, is mime.

Posters have been put up around the school and they've actually sold nearly a hundred and fifty tickets, many of them to the parents of the choir members. Except Muriel's. She says her mum and dad won't be coming, and I think that is totally unfair, as she is the best singer by a mile and her solos are brilliant. Muriel is used to it and says she doesn't mind. But I can't sit back and do nothing.

So one morning, I wait outside her house, and watch her go to school. Then when she's gone, I put a poster through her letterbox, with the added text, in red felt pen, "featuring solo performances by soprano Muriel McDonald." Now they can't say that they didn't know anything about it.

"Did you put something through my letterbox?" she asks the next day.

"No, why?"

"Someone's playing tricks. They put a poster through the door."

"That's good. Now your parents know about it."

"Makes no difference, they still won't come."

As a sort of added dress-rehearsal, we have to perform in the assembly, the morning of the evening concert. This is actually more nerve-wracking: being watched by your peers, especially Sonia Cashmore and her cronies.

We look through a crack in the curtains and can see them in the third row, sitting slumped with their arms folded, giving off attitude, as if to say, "Go on then entertain me with your rubbish."

The curtains open, and we are introduced by the head, who commends us for all our hard work. I'm standing at the back, on the end of one of the benches arranged in a horseshoe shape, trying to hide behind Caroline Evans' huge permed hairstyle. She is more nervous than me, and tries to stand behind me, pleading for my place on the back bench.

"No you can't, I'm taller than you," I say.

"Yes, but I'm uglier than you," she replies.

Muriel is right at the front, in the middle. I know how shy she is and think this must be a real ordeal for her. I glance over at Cashmore who looks uglier than ever, with a permanent sneer on her face, staring at Muriel and whispering comments to the girl next to her.

From my position on the end, I can see Muriel's hands shaking. She has got new nail polish on. She avoids eye contact with Cashmore and looks straight ahead, dignified, her face a beautiful crimson flush.

Her hair is pinned up, and the cut of her dress reveals her swan's neck rising from her prominent collar bones and shoulder blades. My eyes adore her.

Miss Parker takes her position at the lectern in front of us and raises her baton. The orchestra at the side are really loud, one of the clarinets playing one bum note, and then we are off. The rest of the choir do Gilbert and Sullivan proud. As for me, I put all the exaggerated expression I can into my face, gesturing with my hands, my lips in perfect synch … but with no sound coming out. This is the safest bet. At least if I am miming, no one can accuse me of singing flat.

I hold the last 'note' with a contorted face, then snap my mouth shut and suck in air, as if the effort of singing has been exhausting. It's a brilliant piece of fraud, even if I say so myself and the applause is rapturous. Even Sonia Cashmore is clapping, begrudgingly.

Buoyed by the audience reaction, we tear into 'I'd Like To Teach The World To Sing' with added gusto, this time, actual sound coming from my mouth. The first solo is sung by Sophie Clarke, who sings too quietly and is drowned out by the orchestra.

Then it's Muriel's turn. She walks forward and Miss Parker introduces her. She belts through 'My Favourite Things.' With no microphone, her voice soars, competes, and completely holds its own against the raucous flutes, violins and cellos. She gets a resounding round of applause.

But the best is to follow. She sings 'Silent Night', completely unaccompanied. She really is a beautiful singer. The high notes are pitch perfect, beautifully in tune, and when she finishes, there is a split-second silence when the audience are truly taken aback at what this Little Miss-Nobody has just done.

Then Crammond thunders out his applause shouting, "Bravo!" and everyone joins in. She gets a standing ovation and I feel like bursting into tears for her. Even Sonia Cashmore is standing and the look on Muriel's face is a picture. If anyone had died and gone to heaven, it is her.

Afterwards, she's the flavour of the month with people crowding round, congratulating her.

"Well done, that was brilliant."

Even Sonia Cashmore says, "I didn't know you could sing like that."

I stay in the background and give her the broadest grin when she looks over to me, and I silently mouth, "Well Done!" and she mouths back, "Thank You."

In the evening, any seats that were spare are sold out, and we all stand nervously behind the curtains. Miss Parker chides anyone taking a peek through the crack, telling us it is "totally unprofessional."

Nevertheless, I can't resist it, and when her back is turned, I sneak the craftiest look. "Oh my God Muriel, your mum's in the audience. Did you know?"

A look of panic spreads across her face and she turns white as a sheet. "No. Are you sure it's her?"

"Absolutely positive, she's sitting on the end, in the fifth row."

Miss Parker claps her hands, "Colin, what have I just told you? Now starting positions everybody, and good luck."

I spend the whole performance looking at Muriel's mum out of the corner of my eye. When Muriel sings solo, I can see a look of genuine shock, that this is *her* daughter doing this. I really don't think she's ever heard her sing before and during the applause she blows her nose into her hankie.

She waits for her daughter in the foyer after the concert. Muriel comes out of the backstage area with me.

"Muriel, love, I don't know what to say, I'm speechless. That was the most beautiful thing I've ever heard."

She gives her a hug, and Muriel sobs into her breast.

I walk home with them. Outside her house, Muriel says, "Mum, can you just give me a minute?"

When her mum has gone in, Muriel looks at me with such a euphoric expression. "This has been the best day of my life," she says.

"You deserve it."

"Thanks for everything."

"You're welcome."

She looks at me, there is an awkward pause, I blush, then I say, "OK, well, I'll be off. Well done again."

She pulls me back.

"Oh, come here you wazzock."

She grabs me, kisses me on the lips, then runs in.

And with that I walk off down the road, swinging round every lamppost, thinking I might just stop off at the planet Mars on the way home.

A Higher Love. 2007

You know, marriage is so much more than just marrying the person you fall in love with. Who loves their husband or wife the way they did when they first met? Romantic love like that never lasts. It turns into something else. It either turns into disenchantment, bitterness, recriminations and finally separation, when one or both partners believe that the other has 'changed' and hasn't kept their part of the original contract.

Or else, if you're lucky, it turns into a different sort of love. One that will bend with the wind, that recognises and learns to accept the other's differences, and love them all the more for it. It's about respect and a willingness to sacrifice a little of your ego and personal demands. It's about overcoming hurdles together. Creating a fire from that original spark that settles down to a warm, constant glow.

This sort of love is deeper. Of course it still needs vigilance and the occasional log thrown on to it to stop it from going out, but nothing like the frantic blowing, fanning, sudden flare ups and subsequent petering out of romantic love. Romance explodes in the sky like a spectacular firework for a few seconds then disappears.

Marriage is a process, a learning process; learning to live with someone that you really didn't know at all at the outset. To sit in a room with someone and not talk, need not be because you don't get on or have nothing in common. It can simply be that you are so comfortable with one another that you don't always feel the *need* to.

Reading the paper while she reads her book, both in your slippers, is a beautiful thing and very under-rated. I have been blessed with Emm. She has been wonderful. There is so much about me now, that was not in the original contract, yet she has stuck by me, and I love her all the more deeply for it.

As my illness has developed, she has become busier, doing all those jobs around the house that I can no longer do: climbing up ladders, changing light bulbs, mowing the lawn and numerous little DIY jobs.

I'm always feeling guilty after having let her down so badly and try to do them myself when she's not there. When she finds me, she tells me off.

"You shouldn't be doing this on your own. It's dangerous. Call me next time."

She also carries out a variety of seemingly unimportant little tasks but which are a lifesaver for me. She does up the buttons on my shirt, tucks my shirt into my trousers, puts my socks on, and does up my shoelaces. She helps get my left arm into my jacket. She pulls me up out of the armchair and out of the bath. She accompanies me in the street when I walk with my stick and helps me on and off the bus.

All of these things, I can't do without her. It's alarming how much I've deteriorated. It's a good job I don't need to go to work. I'd have to start getting ready at about 3 a.m. to be on time for an 8 a.m. start. It would be like those pack-a-mack days all over again.

Then there's the medication regime. Numerous different-coloured, different-shaped tablets to be taken in the right order at different times of the day. They say that by the time you are in your seventies, you will be taking on average, around five tablets a day for all the various things that are starting to go wrong with your body.

That's a laugh, I think. I'm not yet fifty and already I'm taking 60 pills a day. Some are just to counteract the side effects of others. I have a repeat prescription account at my local chemist. They usually duck for cover when they see me coming.

This morning, when I go in, there is a new pharmacist on duty. She is young and obviously conscientious. She has a concerned look on her face as she scrolls down on the computer screen all the different tablets I'm taking.

"Mr. Sparrow, I wonder, could you spare a minute?"

She ushers me into the consultation room. Inside, we both take a seat and she goes over her notes and my huge list of prescription medications.

"Thank you for your time Mr. Sparrow. I just wanted a quick word about the large number of medications you are on and to make sure you are fully informed about what they are all for."

"Sure. No problem."

"Now, you're taking amlodipine, perindopril and bendroflumethiazide for …"

"For my high blood pressure."

"And when did you last have that checked?"

"This morning. I've got my own machine."

"Oh right, brilliant, and what was the reading?"

"About 140 over 90. Which is a massive improvement on what it was. My diastolic used to be off the scale."

"Yes, your diastolic, that's the one we're usually concerned about. Now you're taking the statin."

"Simvador, that's for my cholesterol."

"How high is that?"

"Still around six I'm afraid."

"Right, OK, so you still need to carry on with that. Now, I see here that you're taking an awful lot of Sinemet."

"Yes, that's the levodopa; dopamine substitute for my Parkinson's."

"And how come you're taking so much? When was your last review?"

"Just last month at the Queen Elizabeth, with my consultant neurologist."

"Right. Good. And how often do you see him?"

"Every four months."

"Right, right, good … erm … and why are you on this dose? It's much higher than for a regular Parkinson's patient."

"Oh, it's because they think I may have MSA, which is quite resistant to the efficacy of the L-Dopa."

"MSA? Oh dear, I really should do some reading up on Parkinson's."

"It's short for Multiple System Atrophy, a Parkinson's Plus disorder…."

At this point she starts jotting down a few notes. "Well, I'll be perfectly honest Mr. Sparrow, I've never heard of it."

"That's OK, my GP hadn't either."

"And how is this different to Parkinson's?"

She prepares to make more notes.

"Well, it's got a much worse prognosis for one thing …"

"Oh dear, I am sorry …"

"No, that's OK really. Basically, unlike Parkinson's, it attacks cells in more than one area of the brain, not just the substantia nigra. It's a bit like PSP."

"Err, PS … what?"

"Sorry. Progressive Supranuclear Palsy … you know, the thing Dudley Moore had."

"Yes … I sort of vaguely remember that … now the domperidone, you take for …"

"The nausea caused by the Sinemet."

"You've recently been prescribed clonazepam, which is a powerful sleeping tablet and treatment for epilepsy."

"Yes, that's because I was taken off the ropinirole and as a result can't sleep because of my restless legs."

"I see. Now your most recent addition to the list are the Rotigotine skin patches which are for…?

"Also for my restless legs. The withdrawal of the Ropinirole left me in an awful state."

"I see. Oh dear, what a complicated mess. And finally the Nutrizym. Now I know this one, this is for your stomach isn't it?"

"Yes, it stops me from having diarrhoea. I've had that since I was a baby I'm afraid. They thought I had cystic fibrosis. Turned out I just had a pancreatic enzyme deficiency. I think it's called entero kinase deficiency, but to be quite honest, I don't think they know themselves. And quite frankly, I'm taking so many other pills now that I don't really care anymore."

We both laugh.

"My liver probably doesn't know what's hit it!"

She laughs then begins to show me out.

"Well, thank you for the little chat Mr. Sparrow, you certainly are very knowledgeable about your condition."

"Oh it's that damn internet. I've got to stay away from it! I think my consultant wants to smash my computer."

We laugh again. She gives me my bag of medicines and we shake hands.

"See you when I come in for my next consignment."

She puffs out her cheeks, exhales and rolls her eyes. "I'll be ready."

The bell tinkles above the shop door as I exit.

There must be countless old and sick people juggling with cocktails of drugs, some just to counteract the effect of others.

This is an unknown world for the young and healthy who probably only take one multivitamin a day. When you're at that stage in your life you don't have to think about the frailty of the human condition, you just want to enjoy. That's what youth is all about. Except on those occasions when death casts its frightening shadow, just when you least expect it.

January 1976. Dad

On the way out to school this morning, I notice something unusual. Dad's bike is still in the outhouse.

"Why is Dad's bike still here?"

"He hasn't gone to work today, he's not feeling well. He's still in bed."

He's never ill. Having said that, he has seen a doctor recently, complaining of pains in his shoulder. He even had an X-ray but it didn't show anything and the GP said it was probably a touch of rheumatism. Well, he is getting on a bit I suppose.

After break, period 3 is games. I've just got changed into my rugby kit and we are walking across the courtyard to the pitches, our studs making a clattering sound on the paving stones, when Mr. Stanton calls me over.

"Colin Sparrow, come here please."

"Sir."

"Colin, you're going to have to get changed back again and go to reception, quick as you can."

"Why Sir?"

"Just do it lad, they'll explain everything when you get to reception."

On the way back, I pass the girls going out to hockey. This includes Muriel who asks, "Where are you going?"

"Dunno, they just told me to get changed."

"See you at lunch."

"Sure."

When I get to reception, Katie is there too, sitting with her bag.

"What's going on?"

"I don't know, they won't tell me anything."

Mrs. Jarvis, the secretary, comes out of her office.

"OK, a car is coming to pick you two up and take you home. It'll be here in a minute."

"What's this all about Mrs. Jarvis?"

"It's your father."

The clock on the mantelshelf ticks in the lazy way it always has, keeping time dutifully. Its raucous quarterly chimes have been turned off. The subdued budgie has got a towel over its cage and is sitting quietly on its perch in an artificial night.

The curtains are drawn against the weak winter sunlight and in the gloom, figures dressed in black with cups of tea, look at each other, saying nothing. A ticking, sipped silence.

It's Dad's funeral today. He died of a massive heart attack while I was at school. Dad has always been here, like the cherry tree and the lamp post outside our house. If either of them were to be taken away, our house would look and feel odd. Like when that row of back-to-back houses was bulldozed in Selly Oak, as part of the slum clearance scheme. Not only was there a big hole where they once were, but all the other buildings that were still standing around the open space didn't look right, they seemed out of place.

And that's what it's like with Dad gone. Not only the hole that he's left, but the rest of us, don't seem to fit any more without him.

It's funny, I didn't get upset at first. On the day he died, when Mrs. Jarvis told me at school, I didn't cry. Katie was crying, but I couldn't. I remember thinking, I should be crying but it just didn't happen.

I even thought of Muriel and how we'd arranged to meet at lunch. I mean, how cold-hearted was that? Mum came home from the hospital, her eyes red and her voice really strange.

"I'm sorry kids, your father's gone."

I just sat there in a kind of daze. Then a procession of people started turning up at the house.

"I've just heard, I wanted to just come by and say how sorry I am."

Then the telephone started ringing.

"Yes. This morning. No, in the ambulance. Thank you. That's very kind. OK, thanks for calling."

After a while, Mum took the telephone off the hook.

Aunty Vera arrived and smothered us all in her fur coat. "Oh you poor darlings, I'm so sorry."

But I felt nothing. All this sympathy, and I felt nothing.

What am I? I thought. *An emotional cripple?* Didn't I love my dad? I felt like that all afternoon, until I went out into the outhouse to use the outside toilet.

Then it hit me. It was his shoes that did it.

As usual, he'd reversed his bike in for a speedier exit the next morning. His cap was on the saddle. His gloves were on the cap. And his bicycle clips were on the gloves.

On the floor, next to the door, were his shoes, neatly pushed together, with one different coloured lace. He'd come home the evening before and done all this, in readiness for his 5.30 exit next morning, not supposing for a minute he'd never make that journey.

He'd never put on those clips again. He'd never again moan about his laces being nicked. To him, everything that previous evening was normal. And that was what pushed me over the edge. The thought that he didn't know what was coming.

Suddenly, a huge lump welled up in my throat and I started gasping. I wanted to cry but there was this obstacle. I kept looking at his shoes and the laces and the imprint of his feet on the insoles and there was a release, but not complete.

I let out a strangled, ugly sob that got stuck in my throat. I never got to see him one last time. Then I cried for him on the flagstone floor.

Mum called me from the kitchen. "Colin, love, I can't face cooking, not today. Be an angel and run to the chip shop and get us some fish and chips for our tea, there's a good lad."

So today, the day of the funeral, a man with a top hat is waiting at the bottom of the drive, keeping a look out for the cars arriving. All the houses nearby have their curtains shut, but they twitch every now and then, as they keep a look out for the right time to go out.

Suddenly, there's a collective rattle of crockery and teaspoons.

"They're here. Ruth, are you ready?"

Mum is in the kitchen, keeping herself busy, drying cups.

"Come on Ruth, put that down and get your coat on."

The huge black hearse looks unreal, parked in front of our house. Jet black, polished chrome, and a kaleidoscope of colour through the side windows, with garlands placed all over and around a coffin with gleaming brass handles.

The colours are overpowering, almost unnatural. As we all gather at the door, no one wants to go first.

Then the neighbours come out to stand on the kerb and we walk to the cars, all eyes on us. I feel as if I'm in an episode of *Crossroads*.

We are in the car directly behind the coffin. Placed at the rear window of the hearse, is a huge wreath from Aunty Vera, with just the letters **E D**, spelt out in white roses.

For the entire journey to the crematorium, we have to look at this, as it stares back at us from the leading car.

As the cortege pulls off down the road, all the neighbours bow their heads and I take a deep breath. On the way to the cemetery, strangers stop and take their hats off.

Inside the graveyard gates, there are people standing, not part of the official party, testament to Dad's popularity at the factory.

Aunty Vera told the story a couple of days ago, of how one of her old friends she'd not seen for a while had come up to her on the street and said,

"Oh, Vera, you'll never believe it. Our chocolate mixer at the factory has died. And he was ever such a nice man, so funny and not that old."

To which Vera replied, "Yes, I know, he was my brother."

A day after his death, a management representation from the factory called at the house. After expressing their condolences, they handed Mum a brown paper envelope, "There's been a whip round."

Inside was two hundred pounds.

During the service, the vicar keeps calling my dad "Eddie", as if he knew him personally, which makes me angry. I think: *you never even met my dad, so don't make out you were best buddies. In fact, for your information, my dad didn't have time for religion.* I remember how he used to tell me, "When you're dead, you're dead. After? There's just nothing, forever."

That was his religion.

Outside, after the service, we walk in single file past all the flowers and read some of the tributes. There are lots of wreaths. There was another funeral before Dad's, and this chap hasn't got any flowers at all. This tickles me.

I gesture to Rob, at this guy's lack of flowers and I say, "Billy No Mates."

I know that I shouldn't and that it's totally the wrong time, but we both have an uncontrollable urge to laugh. I think to myself, what's the worst thing I could do now? Laugh.

I have to hold my nose every time I look at Rob, as I think again, "Billy No Mates".

Back at the house, our neighbour Mrs. Perks has been busy cutting sandwiches. The front door is open to anyone who wants to come in. No one bothers to knock or ring the bell. As more and more drink is consumed, the mood gets lighter.

Aunty Vera starts to amuse the gathered throng with stories about Dad: toilets with no doors, heads on pillows outside tent flaps. The towel comes off the budgie's cage and he starts to chirrup again.

At about 4 o'clock, Mum calls me and tells me there's someone at the door to see me. I go out into the hallway and there's Muriel, in her uniform, calling in after school.

She won't come in, so I sit with her on the doorstep.

"I'm not going to stop, I've just brought this card round."

"You can stay."

"No, it's not my place here today."

"You're wrong. I don't know how to say this, and it doesn't mean I didn't love my dad any less, but I want you here more than anybody. On this day, the day of his funeral, you were the first thing I thought about when I woke up this morning. Is it wrong to say that?"

"I don't know."

She gives me the card, kisses me on the cheek and walks off up the road.

I protest, "I'll walk you."

"No you won't, you've got to stay here."

When she's out of sight, I open the card. It says:

To Mrs. Sparrow and family,
Our Condolences at this difficult time,
From the McDonalds.

There's a little folded square of paper inside that. It contains a short scrawled message:

173

To my dearest Wazzock,
I am so very sorry.
Thinking of you now with all my heart.
M.

Sports Days, Auditions. Summer 2008

My father's death is a constant reminder to me that my time with Lily is limited. She's eight now and I can see that at times my condition frustrates her, maybe even embarrasses her a little.

Last week was her school sports day. At the end of all the events were the parents' races. When the announcement went out over the loudspeaker for all the fathers in the 100 metres to line up, I could see in her eyes that she wanted me to do it, but she knew deep down that I couldn't. I felt really sorry for her. That I couldn't give her such a simple thing.

Poor old Emm had to volunteer for the mothers' race instead, even though I know she hates sports and running and stuff like that. She came last, in her bare feet. But that didn't stop Lily and me shouting and screaming like demented football fans as she crossed the line, her face flushed, gulping in air.

In early autumn I get the chance to make it up to Lily. They are holding auditions for the Christmas pantomime at the local theatre. Up to a hundred local school children try for it every year and they only ever take five or six.

At last this is a chance for me to be a real dad for her, to give her what other dads can't. Coaching for a drama audition is right up my street and I know it could be an advantage the other kids won't have.

Lily however, has other ideas. She's eight, going on eighteen. "Look, I know you went to Drama School Dad, but this is different, times have changed. It's not Shakespeare any more, this is the age of the X Factor."

I laugh. She reminds me of someone I once knew with an old pair of football boots.

"Young lady, will you just trust me? This is something I *do* know something about. I was auditioning for parts when Simon Cowell was a nobody."

She shows me her choice of audition speeches and I know instantly which one all the other kids will choose, and tell her to do the least likely. We work on it all week. I suggest little changes here and there, carefully designed to get a laugh. She is really good and she takes on board all my directions.

Then Emm works with her on her song 'Let's Go Fly A Kite'. We push her and push her all week, until Saturday morning finally arrives.

When we go into the 'holding' area for all auditionees, Lily calmly sits down in her all black outfit and puts on her jazz shoes. The other kids in their jeans and trainers look over, checking out the opposition, this one in particular.

In the waiting area, we can hear each audition through the door and I just know who will be successful and who won't.

Lily's name is called and my last words to her are, "Be big."

I listen at the door and hear the panel laughing at her speech. Then her song, really loud and clear, and I know she's done it. She comes out fairly pleased but says, "I know I won't have got in. All my friends have tried and they have singing lessons, but none of them have ever got in."

"Will you please try to be a bit more positive. Let's just wait and see shall we?"

The results will be posted on the website after 6 p.m. and we anxiously wait. At 6.10, I hear her screams from the computer in the kitchen. "Oh my God, I don't believe it! Dad, Dad, I got in!"

She runs up to me and gives me a big hug. "Thanks Dad, you're the best."

That night, before I go to bed, I sort my tablets, then have my regular 'session' at the bathroom mirror. I look at myself and reflect on my failing body. This human machine is remarkable in how it repairs and renews itself, but slowly, after a lifetime of knocks and scrapes it gradually gives up the race. It becomes rusty, its bearings become worn and its gears seize up. We can try and delay the inevitable with pills and treatments but it is always going to be a losing battle.

I look at my eye in the mirror, swivelling in its socket. I watch the pupil shrink and dilate when I move it towards and away from the light. The eye of a robot. Shutters opening and closing. Like the mechanical eye of a Dalek, or of the cyborg in the film *Terminator*.

I have a sudden realization that actually this body is indeed like a machine. The brain is sending out messages, the rest of the body is obeying. Usually this process is so fast and smooth, that we can't perceive it. Thought and action occur in the same split second. It's only when this process is damaged, through something like Parkinson's, that you begin to see how slow and clumsy the mechanics of the body are: when the actions of your body become separate from your consciousness.

The brain issues an instruction, the body doesn't respond, at least not straight away. And that's when I think, *Yes, I am not this body*.

Emm calls in, "Colin, what are you doing in there? Are you all right?"

I turn out the bathroom light. "Yes, I'm fine. Just thinking that's all."

"Lily was pleased today."

"Yeah. But I sometimes wonder are we doing the right thing by encouraging this drama streak in her?"

I get into bed.

She says to me, "So long as she's happy."

As I lie there, I think about my own dramatic aspirations thirty years ago. Back in 1978, after I'd finished my A-Levels, I made a decision. I was going to try and get into Drama School. All of the main accredited schools were in London, so I was going to have to move down there to mount my plan of action for auditions.

There was only one problem with this brilliant plan.

1978. Different Directions

"No way Colin, I can't move down there. My mum and dad wouldn't allow it."

"But you're eighteen. Surely you don't still have to do what your mum says." Her eyes become a little glassy in the smoky atmosphere of the pub.

"You don't understand. I'm the only girl. I have to help Mum with all the work. No one else can cook and wash and baby sit my little brother. I can't just get up and go."

"Well what about your brothers? As far as I can see they just sit around all day or go to the pub."

"It's not like that in our house. It's not expected of them. They wouldn't do it any way."

"Well that is so unfair. Haven't they heard of the Sex Discrimination Act?"

She chuckles and sips her drink.

"You're joking aren't you Colin? In our house it's the law of the caveman. The man goes out to hunt while the woman stays at home to cook and clean and have babies."

"But they don't go out to hunt. None of them have got a job. The only hunting they do is down the Top Rank on a Saturday night."

"I know. It's not fair, I know. But Mum's not been well and I can't just desert her. Anyway, I have another reason to stay."

She smiles with an inner pride.

"I've just been offered a place to do teacher training, here in Birmingham."

"Well you won't be able to help your mum if you do that will you?"

"Yes I will. I'll still be living at home. It won't be like I'm moving to the other side of the country."

"Yeah, but you'll have loads of work to do, essays to write."

"No different to doing A-Levels. And I did all right there."

There's an awkward silence. I finish my pint and offer to get her another. She shakes her head. I can see she's made up her mind.

I say, "Teacher training? Are you sure you're cut out for that? You have to be a certain kind of person; thick-skinned, tough, or they'll eat you alive. I mean you barely survived your own time at school."

"No I did not! Blimey Colin, you make me sound like some wilting little violet. I'm tougher than you think. Anyway, I won't be teaching older kids. I've applied to do primary."

"What! Wiping noses and putting plasters on cuts?" I regret such a smug, arrogant comment immediately. "Sorry, I didn't mean…"

"I know what you meant Colin. And yes, some of the time I'll be doing that I know. But I'm really good with younger kids. I think it'll be perfect for me."

"But what about your A-Levels? You got such good grades. Isn't it a bit of a waste?"

"No it is not Colin! Sometimes you know, you sound like my dad and brothers. It's not easy to get into teacher training. You *have* to have good grades. It's like getting into university."

She folds her arms and doesn't look at me, then sulkily says, "I'd at least thought you'd be pleased for me. Everything doesn't revolve around you, you know."

"Sorry. Congratulations."

"Huh. You could at least sound as though you mean it."

"I do, but … what about us?"

"What about us?"

"Well it means we'll have to split up."

"You don't *have* to go to London you know Colin."

"What am I going to do here in Birmingham? Work on the production line like Malcolm Pryor? Taking my washing round to my mum's on a Saturday?"

"There's loads of things you could do. You could go to college, university, anything."

"I've set my mind on giving the acting a go. If I don't at least try, I may regret it for the rest of my life."

"Well that's good. In that case, I wouldn't want you to do anything else. And I hope you're successful, I really do."

"Maybe we could still see each other at weekends and in the holidays."

She smiles at me.

"Maybe."

Somebody has put Gerry Rafferty's 'Baker Street' on the juke box. It's the sound of the summer and I know she loves it. As the saxophone bathes the whole pub in good humour, she decides to stay for another drink. She whips the glass from under my nose.

"Right" she says, "My round…and no arguing Mr. Flintstone. I do have my own money you know."

She picks up the glasses and breezes over to the bar. I think it's amazing the confidence she has now. I look at her chatting away to people at the bar and to the barman, so self-assured. So unlike the Muriel of three years ago. I'm proud of her. But there's also a sadness. It's almost like she's outgrown me. I know I'm going to lose her.

And as I sit there watching her, Gerry sings,

"…You're crying, you're crying now…"

I Meet Frank. Autumn 2009

Although a member of the Parkinson's Disease Society, I've never actually been to one of their meetings. When I suggest it to my support worker, she says I should look for a meeting for 'Young Onset' Parkinson's where there'll be more people of my own age.

"But there isn't one of those in this area, so why don't I just go to a regular meeting?"

"I don't think it'll be suitable. They'll all be much older. It may depress you."

"Nonsense. Anyway, I'm curious about people with the later stages of the illness."

"Well OK, if that's what you want but don't say I didn't warn you."

The following week, I take a slightly larger than normal dose of L-Dopa, get ready, then Emm drops me off at the residential home where the meeting is being held.

The first obstacle is the door security. Apparently many residents have a tendency to wander off.

"Yes, can I help you?"

"Yeah, I'm here for the meeting, the Parkinson's Disease Society meeting."

She gives me a look up and down as if to say, "Well, why would you want to attend that?"

Then she says, "Are you one of the speakers?"

"No, no. I have Parkinson's myself and this is the first meeting I've been to. Sorry."

I show her my Parkinson's Society membership card.

"Oh, I see, of course."

She buzzes me in.

"You're a bit early I'm afraid. It's in the Day Room, follow the signs."

"Thank you."

The first thing that hits me is the heat. Almost immediately I start to break out into a sweat. I look around to see every window tightly closed. I make my way down a corridor and after a couple of turns, realise I am lost. The corridors are identical.

A question occurs to me; why do they design buildings like this for the elderly, who are more likely to be prone to confusion? It's like putting a young child into a maze.

After asking for help. I finally arrive at the Day Room.

Many residents are sitting here after lunch. They form a sort of huge circle around the perimeter of the room. The care assistants have deliberately set up small tables with armchairs around them to encourage the residents to be more sociable but these seats have been largely ignored.

Everyone is sitting in the perimeter seats, as if they all want their backs to the wall. A good half of them are having a post lunch nap. In the corner, the television is on. Those that are awake are either staring blankly ahead or looking at the television in a vacant way.

If a chair is unoccupied, it is 'reserved' by a handbag or a newspaper, like a German would leave his towel on a poolside sun lounger. They obviously all have their own seat, their own territory, which is fiercely guarded.

At the other end of the room, a few sprightly members of the Parkinson's Society are setting out chairs for the meeting. They are in their sixties and seventies, much more independent looking and obviously don't live at the home, but are just here for the talk.

I get chatting with one who lives nearby. He's very well-turned-out in a blazer and tie with a crest on it and he has a smart, trimmed moustache, as if he were ex-RAF. He says, "Yes, we don't often get chaps of your age at these things. Of course we're not all old and decrepit like some of these old dears in the home."

He points out one gentleman in the corner.

"Except Frank of course over there. He's got Parkinson's and is a resident."

I look over to where he's indicating. A hunched old man in a smart jacket is sitting in a wheelchair shaking, wiping the moisture from his chin. The symptoms of the Parkinson's are all too clear to me; his leg bobbing up and down on his footrest.

I ask about him.

"Oh, he was a professional person in his day you know."

"Professional?"

"I think he was a professor, a professor of literature at university."

I look at Frank again and inwardly chide myself for my preconceptions about him.

"You'd be surprised how many professional guests are here in the home. There's even a High Court judge."

I look back at Frank, sitting right next to the blaring Jeremy Kyle Show. Someone called Sharon is accusing her partner Duane of sleeping with her best friend Jordan.

As the 'bouncers' hold her back, she screeches at him, "Well what about the text messages I found on your phone, you lying bastard?"

Next to this base spectacle sits Frank, dabbing the moisture from his chin and his unblinking eyes. It almost looks like he's crying. From Byron and Tennyson to this. I feel sorry for him and go over.

"Hello, it's Frank isn't it?"

I put out my hand for him to shake. He looks up, a little confusion in his eyes and tries desperately to raise his shaking arm.

Realising my mistake, I quickly take his hand in mine and give it a hearty squeeze.

Then in a quiet voice he says,

"I do beg your pardon, but your name escapes me young man."

"Oh no, sorry, we haven't been introduced. I just thought you might like some company. I'm Colin."

"Pleased to meet you Colin. Won't you take a seat?"

I sit on the edge of the armchair next to him, look around the room and smile back at him.

"And what are you doing here Colin? Visiting someone?"

"No, I've come for the Parkinson's meeting."

He strains to hear and looks up at the TV with annoyance.

"You're what? Sorry, this blasted contraption."

He looks around the day room to see if there are any members of staff about, then gives me a sort of mischievous grin and says, "Tell you what Colin, how would you like to do me a favour?"

"Sure, what?"

"Open those big French windows and wheel me out into the garden."

"Are you supposed to Frank?"

"Oh they'll never know if you're quick. The doors aren't alarmed. I've done it before. I have to get out of this place sometimes, or it drives me crazy. "

I quickly unbolt one of the big windows. The net curtains billow as I open the door and immediately there are grumblings about the draught. I manoeuvre Frank outside as quickly as possible and shut the doors before any of the staff notice. I tuck his blanket around him.

He has this naughty school boy grin on his face and whispers, "The nurses will be furious when they find out. Ha ha!!"

I wheel him down the path as fast as I can and hear him laughing away. As I push him even harder, he roars even louder. We eventually get to a bench and I put his brake on and sit down. The breeze is delicious.

I am sweating with all the exertion, and my own hand is shaking slightly now. Frank notices.

I explain. "I'm afraid I've got a less advanced version of what you've got Frank."

"What, Parkinson's? You? But you're so young."

"Makes no difference. This illness doesn't discriminate."

"Well, I'm sorry about that Colin. It is Colin isn't it?"

"Yes."

"You know, I was diagnosed in my early sixties. I was a lecturer at the time, couldn't read my own blasted notes. Your handwriting is one of the first things to go."

"Yes, I know. I used to teach as well. English as it happens."

"Really?"

"Yes."

I look around at the yellowing trees and falling leaves and say, "'Season of mists and mellow fruitfulness' … and all that."

"Ah, Keats. A fan are you?"

"We studied him for A-Level. I can still remember all the quotations I had to learn to this day. Our teacher had a passion for him. What was her name? An eccentric old girl … Mrs. Windrush, that was it. She used to talk so quickly, I couldn't write it all down fast enough. 'Close bosom-friend of the maturing sun,' she used to boom."

Frank laughs and joins in.

"'Conspiring with him how to load and bless with fruit the vines that round the thatch-eaves run…'"

"'To bend with apples …'"

"'The moss's cottage-trees, and fill all fruit with ripeness to the core …'"

Frank stops, sighs and looks around him. "Yes, autumn. A beautiful time in nature. But it makes us mindful of winter approaching."

His mind seems to wander.

I try to look on the bright side. "But there's still time to enjoy, Frank."

"Well, enjoyment is for the young Colin. Autumn in the human condition is not quite so glorious is it? I mean, just look at me."

 I say nothing and let him continue.

"You know, you become invisible when you get old Colin. Completely invisible. No more beautiful girls turning their heads to look at you. They don't even see you."

"Oh I'll bet you give the nurses in here a run for their money."

He laughs which turns into a raking cough and I wonder whether I should have brought him out. I tuck his blanket around him more tightly and his cough subsides.

"Thank you my boy, I'm all right now. Just catching my breath."

"That's OK, you take your time."

We sit for a while and look at the autumn palette.

 "So which one have you got your eye on, Frank?"

"Which one?"

"The nurses. In here."

He chuckles again. "You'd be surprised how we spend our time in here Colin. It's not like a Carry On film you know. It's almost like we're forced to revert to the life of a baby: playing childish games, watching television. All of your achievements, knowledge, they're forgotten. No one wants to know. You're just a number that has to be fed, have his bottom wiped, then stuck in a corner until it's time for bed."

"Sorry Frank. What about your family? No children to take you out for the day?"

"Never married. So wrapped up in my work. Seems pointless now. What was it all for?"

"I'm sure you made a lot of people happy, and enriched many lives."

"Maybe, maybe…let's hope so eh?"

He shivers and I know it's time to take him back. As I make a move to manoeuvre his wheelchair, he interrupts me.

"You know Colin, old age should be a time for wisdom, for reflection, a time for renunciation and preparation for what's coming."

Then he says something that takes me by surprise completely, because I've heard something like it before.

"We are not these bodies, Colin. This temporary pile of flesh; it's not really us. But no one wants to listen. They're all too busy splashing around in the shallow end. No one wants to dive into the deep water."

He shivers again and I realise my negligence. I tuck his blankets round him tighter and turn him round to go back. Halfway round the quadrangle, there is an officious-looking sign telling visitors to please keep off the grass.

"What about breaking another rule Frank?"

"Go for it my dear boy, go for it!"

On the other side, we look back and giggle at the marks his wheels have made in the grass.

After the ticking off we both receive from the supervisor when we get back inside, I realise the meeting's started and decide not to bother.

"Well, goodbye Frank. It was an absolute pleasure talking to you."

"Thank you Colin. I enjoyed it too."

That night, lying in bed, I look at my old friend, the ceiling, and think about what Frank said.

"We are not these bodies, Colin."

I think again about that scientific fact that the body renews itself after seven years. I think of myself as a boy and how I am now. Yet I still see both of them as 'me.' It's quite illogical really. How can I put it? Parkinson's has made me old before my time.

I'm like a young man inside an old man's body. Everyone's body gets old eventually, but usually at the same pace as their mind. In the case of a Parkinson's patient, particularly a young patient like me, the body ages much quicker than the mind. And this is why I'm finding it harder to identify my body with 'me.'

It's like it's someone else's body. My brain is still alert, I just can't get my arms and legs and fingers to do what I want them to do. I'm like Lewis Hamilton sitting in the driver's seat of an old, clapped out Skoda. The ultimate in frustration.

When your body doesn't do what you want it to do, then it becomes something you are working against, rather than working with. You and your desires become separate from your body, which no longer

186

satisfies you. More and more I find myself seeking answers and contentment inwardly. Like this conversation I suppose, that I'm having in my head.

I think Parkinson's patients like Frank must live much of their lives in their heads. That persistent question keeps nagging away at me: *if this body is not 'me,' then what is it that I identify with, if not my body…. My consciousness? My soul?*

"No one wants to dive into the deep water," he said. "They're all too busy splashing around in the shallows."

Emm snuggles up to me.

"Colin, stop looking at the ceiling and turn the light off, for goodness sake."

1979. London

On *Crossroads*, Benny Hawkins is in a lot of trouble. He's been accused of and arrested for the murder of a girl. There's such a groundswell of emotion about it in Birmingham. There's even a campaign to free him. At Birmingham University, the students are showing their support by hanging banners out of their windows: white bed sheets with the message, 'Benny is Innocent' and underneath, in smaller letters, the footnote, 'Sandy did it.'

My own love life is becoming complicated too. I go ahead with the move to London despite Muriel's refusal to come with me. I say I'll try to come back at weekends to see her. She says OK, but that if I meet someone else, that would be OK as well. Reading between the lines, I take that to also mean that if *she* meets someone else, then that too would be OK wouldn't it?

I get the train from New Street to Euston, and sleep on a friend's floor for a week while looking in the Evening Standard's classifieds and newsagents' windows for a place of my own. I take the number from an untidily written and dog-eared piece of paper offering a flat share in Tufnell Park in north London. At the bottom it says NO STUDENTS OR DSS.

When I get to the address, in the middle of a long, imposing, four storey terrace that stretches the length of the road, the front door is open. Builders are walking in and out to the skip outside. The flat, I am told, is on the top floor, so I just go on up. The first floor is a mess of plasterboard, dust and rubble, and when I get to the top, there's a plain white door with dirty finger marks all around the Yale lock.

On the doorstep are the biggest pair of workman's boots I've ever seen in my life. It could be the home of the Sasquatch. I knock politely and the door is opened by a giant of a man about five years older than me, with a Rockabilly haircut and ruddy complexion. When I say I've come about the flat, he grins from ear to ear, thrusts out his great shovel of a hand, squeezes all the feeling out of mine and introduces himself as Michael from Cork … "But most people know me as Mick the plasterer." He invites me in and starts to 'put me in the picture'.

"Now, Colin is it? A course I'm not the landlord, that's the Greek bhoy, but he lets me rent it to who I want cos he knows I'd bate the shite outa him otherwise. Now the only problem with this little gaff[1] is there's no toilet, so when you've been on the tear[2], and you need the wizz[3] in the middle of the night. Well, it's on the ground floor. That's four flights down. Me personally? I don't give two fucks, I just do it in the sink, here la, so if you don't mynde, then neither do I."

I agree to the arrangement but tell him that I will be a student if I get into Drama School.

"What, you wanna be an actor like? Oh that's different. That's not like a student, more like an apprentice. You'll be learning a trade. It's a noble profession, treading the boards like Peter O'Toole and Richard Harris. Not like these student types studying useless shite like Media Studies at the polytechnic. I hate 'em. You see them in the chip shop on a Saturday night, holding up the queue while they try to pay for a bag of chips with a cheque. Langers[4]. No, no Colin an actor is quite different."

He shakes me by the hand again and says I'm his man and that he'll take me up to The Boston Arms later.

"There's a lasher[5] in there Colin, I tell ya man, I been trying to flah[6] her for months."

Later on, I'm introduced to Mrs. Cable who lives in the ground floor flat. Apparently, she used to own the whole house but sold it to the Greek property developer when her husband died and she needed the money. She stayed on in the ground floor as a sitting tenant.

The Greek, Mr. Kakkas, makes her poor life a misery with all the alterations and partitioning he's carried out upstairs. I feel quite sorry for her as I see her through her net curtains, in her front parlour, rocking to and fro with her fingers in her ears, as the Kango hammer knocks down another dividing wall above her. But she is a feisty old girl, and whenever she sees Kakkas (she pronounces it 'cake arse') she goes out to give him another earful.

"No, no, no, Mr. Cake Arse, I spoke to my solicitor just this morning and he said you weren't to continue with any more alterations, without consulting me first about times that were convenient for me. And what do

---

[1] flat
[2] out drinking
[3] to urinate
[4] idiots
[5] good looking woman
[6] to have sex with

189

I find? Your workmen with their pneumatic drills starting up at 8 a.m. in the morning. It's not good enough Mr. Cake Arse."

"Mrs. Cable, with respect, I am now the owner of this property and I can do what I like with it, having acquired the necessary permissions. And my name is Kakkas."

"Well that's where you're wrong Mr. Cake Arse, my solicitor informs me that as a sitting tenant, I have rights…"

Kakkas is already halfway up the stairs, not even bothering to listen.

Mrs. Cable lived through the blitz in this house. The street was bombed and there's now a gap in the terrace on the opposite side of the road, where a stray bomb had flattened the house. She tells us stories about events back then. She's taken a liking to me, when she finds out I'm trying to get into Drama School. She says she herself went to the Royal Academy Of Music in the 1930s.

Mrs. Cable plays the piano beautifully, with her window open. I often hear Chopin drifting up on the air in the afternoon. The playing is sometimes followed by a bout of uncontrolled sobbing, as I imagine she mourns her husband, her lost way of life and the indignities heaped upon her by the money-grabbing Mr. Cake Arse. I don't think she can come to terms with sharing her house with strangers.

Once, in the middle of the night, I went down to the ground floor to use the toilet. On my way back up, on the second landing, I looked down and she was standing there at the bottom of the stairs in her night dress looking up at me. Her face was ghostly white in the gloom.

Then something scared the life out of me. Standing behind her, clear as day, was a young man in a blue uniform. I froze and stared back at them for several seconds. Mrs. Cable seemed to be unaware that the man was behind her. She shuffled off back to her room leaving the door ajar.

He kept looking at me for several seconds, then put his finger to his lips and followed her back into the room, closing the door behind him. I asked her a couple of days later, how her husband had died.

"Cancer," she said. "He died in hospital six months ago. I held his hand until the end. He was an RAF fighter pilot in the war you know? Came through the Battle of Britain unscathed, only to be beaten by something so tiny eating away at his lungs."

She knows about my auditions, and even sits and prompts for me as I recite for her my speeches from *Romeo and Juliet* and Steven Berkoff's *East*, offering small suggestions here and there.

After a couple of months, I get confirmation of my first audition which is for the Webber Douglas Academy in South Kensington. Meanwhile, I get a job in an Italian bar on fashionable Piccadilly.

Its customers are a mixed bunch. There are the gentlemen in pin stripe suits, from nearby Savile Row, Simpson's and Jermyn Street at the back, where the discerning man-about-town buys his shirt and ties, black brogues and quintessentially English umbrella. There are the arty types from the Royal Academy across the road. There are the Italians, local and tourists who drink their coffee 'ristretto' and of course there are the Japanese tourists, who've just bought their tins of Earl Grey tea from Fortnum and Mason's next door.

I'm working the Espresso machine as fast as is humanly possible for a line of customers stretching out the door. My head is a blur, as I twist one handle, knock out the grounds, refill it, twist it back on and shift the lever. The milk jug makes an angry moan as I power the steam into it. The froth rises up the sides of the jug and I flip the foam on to the coffee in its cup, to make the perfect cappuccino.

In three months, I've become quite an expert and it pays the rent.

After work in the evening, I like to walk under the neon lights of Piccadilly Circus, up Coventry Street and into Leicester Square, dodging the hordes of foreigners shrieking and shouting in every language known to man.

One evening, while still awaiting the result of the Webber Douglas audition, I decide not to take the Northern Line from Leicester Square station, but instead turn left up Wardour Street, then right into Shaftesbury Avenue.

I take a stroll through Soho, left into Frith Street, past Bar Italia and all the shady doorways with signs advertising a "New Busty Model" on the first floor. Finally I find myself in Soho Square, just before I reach Oxford Street and where I'll pick up the tube at Tottenham Court Road. I am approached by a bald man with a funny white mark on the bridge of his nose.

"Will you take one of these books, and promise me you'll read it?"

"Yeah sure. Does it cost anything?"

"Well, I'll accept a donation."

"Sorry, but I'm skint. You'd better have it back."

"No, that's OK, just so long as you read it."

"OK, I will, thanks."

I put it in my pocket, and forget all about it.

When I get home, Mrs. Cable has stayed up and is looking out for me through her net curtains. As soon as I put my key in the lock, she is on me, all of a fluster.

"Oh Colin, it's here, it's here!"

"What?"

"The letter from Webber Douglas. Open it up and tell me what it says."

I rip the envelope, trying to take in the words.

"Well, come on, come on, don't keep me in suspense."

I smile a broad grin.

"I got in."

"Oh how marvellous, how exciting, you must be so pleased!"

I kiss her on the cheek and skip up to my room. I read the letter over and over, then taking my jacket off, the book I'd been given falls to the floor. I turn on my bedside lamp and look at it. It's called *Perfect Questions, Perfect Answers* and I realise it is a Hare Krishna book. Maybe it brought me good luck.

"You are not that body," it says.

Well, I think, after the amount I've drunk this week, that most certainly is the case. I'm too excited and can't read. I put the book down, open the sash window to its limit, and lean out. The London sky is glowing with distant street lamps, but the stars are still visible. From my third floor window, London is still, but there is that unmistakable hum in the background, like the machinery of the city working.

I think of Muriel. I still do most days. I saw her a couple of weeks ago, when I went back to Birmingham to visit Mum. I spotted her in The Black Horse[1] in Northfield. She was sitting with some bloke with a beard, old enough to be her father. She came up to the bar to buy a round of drinks and smiled brightly when she saw me.

---

[1] Now a Wetherspoon's

She looked more beautiful than ever.

"Hello Colin."

"Hello, how's things? What are you up to these days?"

"Fine thanks. I've just finished my first term."

"Enjoying it? Wiped many noses yet?"

She laughed. "Let's not start that again. What about you? Steven Spielberg phoned yet?"

"Waiting on my first audition result for Drama School."

"Sounds exciting."

"Well, sort of. You should come down and visit. Can I give you my number?"

"Yes please."

My heart took a giant leap. She seemed quite keen. I wrote it on a beer mat and she looked back to her table as she popped it into her handbag.

The guy she was with was looking over. I casually asked, "Who's that you're with?"

"Oh, he's one of the lecturers at my college. He's helping me with my dissertation." I think *Yeah, I'll bet he is.*

"Do you want to come over and meet him?"

"Thanks, but I can't really, I'm already late."

She raised her eyebrows with a knowing, cheeky look and said, "Oh really, on a date?"

"No such luck."

She gave me a smile then squeezed my hand. That same cold little hand of hers.

"Lovely to see you Colin. I'll call you."

I stopped breathing. And with that, she took her drinks back to her table, glancing back at me as she sat down. I knew then in my heart that she was, is, and always will be 'the one.'

I finished my drink and went out, giving her a little wave as I did so. I wasn't late. I'd just said that. Like Porphyro in Keats' poem 'The Eve of St. Agnes', I was 'buttress'd from moonlight', in the doorway of Barry Brookes' fishing tackle shop. The pub door opened and I heard their voices. She was laughing at something he said as she got into his Citroen 2CV.

Bearded toss-pot.

That was two weeks ago. She never called.

Slow Lane. Spring 2010

I hate not being able to keep my promises. I said I'd go and see Frank as often as I could, bringing him a few books to read. But I was ill over the winter and didn't want to take my stubborn cough into the old people's home.

I'm still pale and drawn on the day I finally choose to go. It's a beautiful March morning and he's not in the day room. I look out of the window and there he is, sitting by our old bench, engrossed in a book.

"Hello Frank. Not too cold for you?"

"Colin my boy, welcome, come and take a seat."

"Sorry I haven't been for a while, but I've not been well and I didn't want to come spreading my germs around."

"That's all right Colin. You're looking well now."

I smile a sort of wry smile. "Am I? You know I don't mind *you* saying that to me Frank. But I get it all the time."

"What?"

"People telling me how well I look. I don't know whether they say it because they think it'll make me feel better or whether it makes them feel better, so that they don't have to talk about it. No one actually says, 'How are you?' They just say, 'You're looking well,' because it's easy."

"So, how *are* you Colin?"

"Well, if you really want to know Frank, I'm a bit down actually."

"What's brought this on?"

"The winter doesn't help. But there just doesn't seem to be any light at the end of the tunnel. I just seem to be getting worse and worse. And it makes me think of how I'm going to end up."

I realise what an insensitive thing this is to say, Frank being the way he is. "No offence Frank."

"None taken Colin."

He sits and looks at the garden for a while then says, "Shall I tell you what I used to do, when I was just a few years in from diagnosis and still mobile?"

"What?"

"I used to meditate on my immediate and long-term future, trying to foresee what would become of me. I accepted the stage where I was at, then tried to picture all of the stages that were still to come and tried to accept them too. It went something like this:

"Already, I can no longer do my job. I'm not a University lecturer anymore. I accept it.
Already, I have given up driving my car. That part of my life is over. I accept it.
Already, I receive a pension and state benefits. I am no longer able to independently provide for myself. I accept it.
Soon I will be too immobile to walk around the shops. I will no longer buy clothes for myself. My time as a 'fashionable' person is over. Accept it and move on.
Soon I will no longer go out with friends on social occasions to the pub or the cinema or to a restaurant. Accept it.
My time as a member of the opposite sex is over. No one looks at me in that way anymore. Accept it and let it go.
Eventually, the time will come when I can no longer dress myself. Someone will have to do it for me. Accept it.
Then will come the time when I can't walk at all, I am in a wheelchair. Accept it.

"Then I got to the really difficult stages.

"There will come a time when I can't feed myself and am fed through a tube. Accept it.
There will be a time when I can't go to the toilet by myself. I will need someone else to wipe my bottom for me. Accept it."

He stops and catches his breath from the effort of such a long speech, then looks at me. "It's just about letting go, Colin. We're never going to be the same people we were. Accept it and move on."

"Yes I know, you're right Frank and I feel so bad feeling sorry for myself when you are the way you are. But I sometimes ask myself would I want to live like that? Am I able to live like that?"

"What's the alternative? Are you going to kill yourself?"

I raise my eyebrows and say, "Well the news is full of stories these days about our rights. Our right to a dignified death if we want it. Why can't we choose when to go? Why do we have to wait until the bitter end,

195

when things get messy and dying is an ugly, frightening business? Not to speak of the burden of care and the distress caused to loved ones."

He says, "So what are we all going to do? Get on a plane and book ourselves into that clinic in Switzerland? You know I read an article on it Colin. You drink poison in that Dignitas place. It takes a couple of minutes to work. What if you drink it and suddenly change your mind? If you have a sudden desire to get up tomorrow and go and visit that snow-topped mountain you can see out of your window. 'Hold on a minute, I think I've made a mistake. I've just realised I've never been skiing. Quick, give me a sick bag.'"

We both burst out laughing, he carries on, having tickled himself. "Those bastards. They probably give you Cheerios for breakfast!"

I laugh out loud and Frank starts to cough. So we are quiet for a while.

Then Frank continues. "You know Colin, we're quite lucky. Our condition on the whole is pain-free, which is a blessing. Some people suffer pain, minute by minute, hour by hour. There are such things as 'pain clinics.' That must be terrible; pain with you at every waking moment. I can understand someone like that wanting to end it all."

"Yes, I know. But I think about my wife and daughter. Can they bear to see me living like that? I don't know. I wouldn't wish it on them if they didn't want to."

"If they love you, they'll accept you however you are. You just have to detach yourself from all those vanities that in the past you thought were so important: appearance, reputation, fame, wealth, popularity. They are impostors Colin.

"You know, I was walking down the street with an academic colleague a few years in from my diagnosis. I could see he was getting frustrated at how slowly we were walking. He knew I was ill, but he also knew me from our university days when we played rugby together.

"He said to me, 'Doesn't it frustrate you that you have to walk that slowly?'

"I replied, 'It's all relative. To a snail I am moving at the speed of sound.'"

Frank looks at me with a twinkle in his eye. "Colin, I have accepted that I just live in a slower universe now than everyone else. I am permanently in the slow lane of the motorway. People can roar past me at

100 m.p.h. in the fast lane, in their inadequacy-compensating cars, if they want. I just smile at them and think, 'Yes, you go ahead…. wanker.'"

We both laugh at this until my head aches.

It starts to spit with rain. I get up and say, "Right, I'd better be getting you back or we'll catch our deaths."

When we get back inside, I wheel him to a position as far away from the television as possible.

"Whoa, where are you putting me? Closer to the set please, it's my favourite show: *Countdown*."

He winks at me and says, "You can get used to anything if you really have to."

1979-1982. Drama School

The newly opened Pineapple Studios are packed with Sloaney mums buying their little darlings ballet, tap and jazz shoes, tights, leotards and tutus.

The assistant, who looks and sounds like Mr. Humphries from *Are You Being Served?* repeats the price. "Jazz shoes, size 9. They're £10, would you like me to wrap them up?"

"Have you got anything cheaper?"

"These are your standard, black, drama school jazz shoes."

"Sorry, but I'll have to leave it then."

He gives me a sympathetic look. "Which drama school did you say you were going to?"

"Webber Douglas."

"Oh, you're very lucky, such a good reputation. I know the head of dance very well."

I smile and turn to go, when he calls me back. "Hang on a second, I've got an idea. Just wait here for a minute."

He disappears round the back, then returns with an enormous pair of bright yellow shoes.

"Now I know they're not your size, a bit big for you and they're not the regulation black, because they were used in the last show I was in, but you're welcome to them if you want them, for free."

"Thanks, that's very kind of you. I'll take them."

As for the tights and dance belt, I'll just have to improvise.

In the changing rooms on the first day, it's like PE again, only for adults. Like those football boots years ago, my footwear is again the focus of attention. Jazz shoes, size eleven, two sizes too big for me, and bright yellow.

Also, I couldn't afford the proper thick dance tights, so I'm wearing a normal pair of ladies' tights. They are wrinkled over my thin legs and I've already laddered them at the crotch because I am constantly hoisting them up.

I don't have one of those dance belts, designed to keep your wedding tackle in one smooth lump. Instead I'm wearing just an ordinary pair of Y-fronts, which are clearly visible through the sheer tights and which in turn, are revealing the meat and two veg underneath. A pot-belly and the absence of any kind of upper body muscle is covered with a tight T-shirt.

All the other boys look like John Travolta or Patrick Swayzee, with muscular legs, vest revealing pecs and biceps and Rudolph Nureyev bulge contained in dance belt. In contrast, I look like Max Wall.

This first dance lesson is on the stage of the main theatre, so that the dance teachers can assess us and put us into appropriate ability groups. But I get the feeling that it's a bit like those games lessons, when the two captains pick who they want and that I'll end up in the duffers' group.

First exercise is 'spotting.' I've never had a ballet lesson in my life. Everyone else seems familiar with it. Individually, we have to sort of pirouette diagonally across the stage. Eyes must be fixed, or 'spotted' on a set point. The body turns first, then the head is quickly whipped round to catch up, and eyes spot the same fixed point again. Body turns, head follows, body turns, head follows, etc; pretty easy if you are grade six at ballet.

Pretty damn impossible, if the only dance move you know is 'Tiger Feet' by Mud.

My turn arrives. I take the stance, arms outstretched. There's a ripple of giggling from the girls at my outfit.

The teacher stops proceedings. "Err, you there, what's your name please?"

"Colin Sparrow."

"Well, Colin, did you not receive a kit list for the required items needed for a dance lesson?"

"Yes, I did."

"Then would you mind explaining why your shoes are yellow, and why you're not wearing a dance belt?"

"The shoes were a gift and I couldn't afford a dance belt."

Drama training usually being the preserve of the rich, I don't think he's ever heard that excuse before. He looks at me with incredulity, along with the class of students. There's a silence and then he says, "OK, proceed with the exercise please."

If everyone wasn't looking at me before, they certainly are now. I pirouette like ... well, like a cyberman, all stiff with arms held out. The swivelling of the head is making me giddy. As a result, after several revolutions, I start to veer off course.

Next thing I know, I've fallen off the front of the stage, into the orchestra pit, taking all the skin off my right elbow and laddering my tights even further. There are gasps of horror.

"Are you all right in there, Mr. Sparrow?"

My voice is heard from within the hole. "Yes, yes, I'm fine, sorry."

There's the clash of a cymbal, then I start to climb out.

"Go to the changing room and clean that wound please. Then, when you're ready, you can re-join the class."

As I limp past him, I hear him mutter under his breath,

"Dear God, where do they find these people? Whatever happened to our standards?"

I'm back in time for the 'routine.' We learn a set routine of steps to the tune of 'All That Jazz' from *Chicago*. We learn it in stages, then put them all together, and finally perform it in groups of three. My group is last to go, which is a blessing, because it gives me extra time to memorise the moves, while watching the other groups.

When I take to the stage, he puts me in front, presumably so I can't copy the others. Everything is going brilliantly and I grow in confidence, so that at the end, to the strains of "All ... that ... jazz ..." I deliver my kicks with particular gusto and on the last kick, my size eleven flies off into row D in the auditorium.

The teacher is not amused. "Mr. Sparrow, it's incredible how well I feel I know you after just one hour. Go and retrieve your shoe please. First thing tomorrow, I'm making an appointment for you with the osteopath. Your body is a knot of tension."

I end up in the group for the rhythmically challenged, in other words, the two left feet group. Well, I console myself, this is supposed to be an 'acting' school. No one ever said anything about becoming a dancer.

Back in my flat after that first day, I flop down on my bed. OK, so not the best start imaginable, but at least I'm in. Colin Sparrow, a student at drama school. Half the battle won. I'm finally on the right road, on 'their' side of the fence.

I think of the line from Sweet Charity; "If my friends could see me now ..." Everyone back home thinks I'm living the most glamorous life. If only they knew.

Mick shouts in to me from the kitchen:

"Jeesus Colin, yer a dirty fecker. Don't you ever do any washing up? How am I supposed to have a piss with all these crocks in the sink?"

Quality Time. June 2011

Despite Frank's best advice, I get more and more depressed about my remorseless decline. My consultant confirms that I'm clearly not following the usual Parkinson's path. He concludes that although I probably don't have MSA, I do seem to have a variant of Parkinson's that is very drug-resistant.

This means that I'll never fully reap the benefits of the dopamine medications, that most sufferers enjoy, and any benefits I *do* get, will be very short lived. So instead of my L-Dopa giving me five hours of fluid movement, I'll maybe get two hours at the most. And to cap it all, I'm now beginning to get the long-term side effects of substitute dopamine use, namely Dyskenesias, or uncontrollable body movements, such as twisting and jerking. Which can be quite frightening to an outside observer. So, in short, I get the side effects without the benefits. I'm paying for something that I never fully received.

This depresses me and I begin to lose motivation. Through sheer will power though, I force myself to go swimming once a week. I deliberately choose the quietest time of the quietest day in the week at the swimming baths: Tuesday at 11.30 am, squeezed between the mothers' and toddlers' group and the lunchtime keep fit zealots who cram a hundred lengths into half an hour.

Yet still I can't get the slow lane to myself. Ever since I was a kid, banned from going swimming, I've never been able to swim well. So every week, this same bald-headed arsehole insists on swimming in my lane, nearly capsizing me every time he overtakes me.

After the tenth mouthful of chlorine, I've had enough. As soon as I get out, baldy switches to the fast lane. Bastard. He does it on purpose. A sort of superiority thing. OK, so he can swim front crawl without coming up to breathe for a whole length, and I can only manage a stuttering breast stroke without getting my face wet. But he probably has a penis the size of a peanut.

Now I just feel so tired all of the time. I get up, have breakfast, then crawl back up the stairs to lie on my bed and, in the foetal position, stare at the pattern on the wallpaper. It's the only time I feel comfortable. This is becoming the structure of my day. It's almost like I'm a thing. A jelly fish. A grounded seal.

Just to roll over on my bed is an incredible effort. I even need Emm to help me turn over in bed at night to lie on my side. I feel like I'm losing it. I can see where I'm heading and it's a bit scary.

Soon I won't be able to do anything for myself. Only when I take a large dose of L-Dopa, do I have any independence and can go out, potter in the garden or walk fifty yards to the post office or local shop. But the window of opportunity that the drug buys me is getting shorter and shorter, until I return to the slug lying on my bed.

I don't really know how to explain the discomfort of Parkinson's to someone who's never experienced it. It's not exactly painful - although I do get arthritic pain in my feet and knees, but is more like living in a constant state of extreme tension.

You can *never* relax. Picture yourself clinging to a cliff face by your fingertips. Imagine how tense your whole body would be in that situation. Well, that's how I feel as I sit at the dinner table trying to eat my dinner. Every movement of the fork to my mouth is an incredible balancing act.

That tension in all my muscles is with me every minute of the day, twenty-four hours a day, three hundred and sixty-five days a year. It's like a Chinese water torture. There's never any release. So much so, that some days I just want to let go of that cliff face and fall to my death.

I'm starting to have vivid dreams when I sleep in the afternoon. I know it's to do with taking too much dopamine. Although not yet causing waking hallucinations (which some elderly patients experience), these dreams can nevertheless be quite disturbing and frightening.

I regularly dream of Dad. He's back from the dead and has been allowed to live with us again, but any amount of stress could trigger another heart attack. So we all try to be good and well behaved and tiptoe around him.

I wake up from such dreams drenched in sweat and my body paralysed with stiffness, waiting for my next fix of dopamine. As I open my eyes and gradually come to my senses at five in the afternoon, it does indeed feel like re-entry for a drug addict. Returning to the real world.

The late afternoon sunlight is pouring into the bedroom, striking the angles of the windows and the folds of the curtains with the sharpness, and brilliance of a Vermeer painting. Particles of dust floating in shafts of light. It's like reality drawn in super focus.

I lie there with such an over-riding, all-encompassing sense of dread, fear and doom. I'm losing my sanity.

Night times are the worst. No more than three or four hours sleep are possible before the electric jolts start in my legs. So I'll get up and wander round the house in the dark at 3 a.m. I look out of the attic window at the twinkling lights in the valley below, like some sort of insomniac super-hero: *the silent vigil; keeping a watchful eye over the slumbering metropolis!*

My consultant, when I tell him all this, tries to encourage me. "Mr. Sparrow, I can see you are becoming a little depressed. You shouldn't dwell on this diagnosis. As I have said many times before, you have a lot of things going in your favour, not least your age.

"With proper exercise and a positive outlook you can slow the decline. The more sitting and lying down you do, the more your muscles will waste, until one day, you'll find you can't use them anymore.

"Every day you should get up and make an effort. Go for a walk, no matter how short. Get out into the fresh air. Soon you'll find you can walk a little further. Then as you get fitter, you may be able to dust off the cobwebs from your bicycle and go for a little ride. That's an exercise that won't put too much pressure on your painful feet.

"If all you have to look forward to every day is lying on your bed, you'll just get stuck on a downward cycle. You feel bad, so you don't exercise and the more you don't exercise the worse you'll feel and so on.

"Tell me, what sort of hobbies did you used to enjoy? Gardening perhaps?"

"Well actually, I used to enjoy a spot of fishing."

"That's it. Perfect. Nothing too strenuous but something to get you out of the house and get some sun on your face. Anything else?"

"I also used to enjoy the theatre."

"There, you see? So much for you to do. Now please, when you come back to see me, let me see you with a smile on your face and some colour in your cheeks."

He's right, I think, as I manoeuvre my way round the elderly patients in the waiting room outside on my way out. I'm not ready for my wheelchair just yet.

I am sent a Parkinson's Disease Newsletter and the PD Magazine every three months or so. There's often a feature article written by a well-known, not quite 'celebrity' sufferer, sharing their experiences and how they are getting on with their life. I usually read them. On the whole, they are optimistic and looking forward to the future. They're nearly always much older than me and I think, *Well, if they can still get about and remain so upbeat, then so should I.*

My mobility problems are largely caused by my lack of balance, stiffness in my legs and pain in my feet when I put any weight on them. But taking the neurologist's advice, I resolve to walk outside at least once a day. I look a bit of a sight hobbling and staggering down the street, much to the consternation of one particular person.

Yes, I fear I am becoming an embarrassment to Lily. She's eleven now and getting to that self-conscious stage when she has to impress her peers. She hates me going out with my stick.

"Dad, you're not going out with that are you? People will think you're disabled."

"Well that's because I *am* disabled I'm afraid Lil, so people will just have to get used to it."

Yesterday, I was walking to the post-office when I spotted her walking home from school towards me on the other side of the road. She had all her friends in tow. Even from a distance it was clear that she was the centre of attention, making everyone laugh.

Then she spotted me coming towards them, hobbling with my stick. I could see her face drop. As they drew level she smiled a sort of pained smile. One of her friends recognised me from across the road.

"Look Lily, it's your dad. Hello Mr. Sparrow."

"Hello you lot. Behaving yourselves I hope?"

"Course!" They all chorused, except Lily who was bright red.

When she got home later she said, "Dad, will you do me a favour? *Please* don't walk around when school has just finished. People can see you."

"Well I'm sorry but I do have to go out occasionally you know."

"Yes I know but just not at the time when everyone's coming out of school."

"What's the matter? Do I embarrass you or something?"

"Yes, you *do* as a matter of fact."

"Well, I'm sorry you're ashamed of your own dad."

"No it's not like that. I mean everyone's dad is a bit of an embarrassment aren't they? The way they dress, how they dance, their taste in music and all that. That's all it is."

But I knew that it was more than that. She was ashamed of my disability. I can't blame her. She's only eleven. These are the most important things in the world to an eleven year old. But she's going to have to get used to it. I wish she didn't have to but what can I do? I actually think her friends accept it more than she thinks.

They are always fine with me. Maybe we should spend more time together.

As the summer moves on, Lily just happens to mention one day that all the boys at school were boasting about how they go fishing and how, according to them, "Girls don't know how to fish".

I see an opportunity and tease Lily. "Well of course they're perfectly correct. Girls can't cast, they can't put a worm on a hook without crying and they certainly couldn't land a proper big fish."

"How sexist can you get Dad? OK, show me how to do it and I'll prove you and all them wrong!"

She takes the bait, hook, line and sinker, as they say. So one Sunday morning we go fishing at one of the local lakes. I take two extra lots of medication with me so that I'll be able to get through the day, even though we'll be sitting for most of it. Emm makes us a packed-lunch, only this one is a bit more substantial than the brown sauce sandwiches of forty years ago. She also gives me the digital camera, just on the off chance that we hook some monster. Then she drops us off in the car.

It's still early and the mist is just hanging above the water.

"Tight lines!" Emm shouts, then drives off.

I show Lily how to tackle up; how to put on her float, with lead shot and how to tie her hook with half-blood knot. Then I show her how to bait the hook (she's not in the slightest bit squeamish) and how to cast.

We sit there, staring at our floats, waiting for the slightest knock or shudder. I look over at Lily, her face a picture of concentration, gripping the handle of the rod in expectation and I am fascinated by her profile.

Her forehead is undoubtedly mine - large and high. Her nose and her eyes are her mother's, yet her chin and slightly protruding top lip are also clearly mine.

After an hour, she furrows her brow and lets out a rasping wobble of her lips in frustration.

"Dad, this is a waste of time. I know we're not going to catch anything."

"What is it with kids your age? So pessimistic. You don't know how lucky you are. Do you know, when I was your age, I fished in a dirty old polluted reservoir next to a chemical factory that you'd think nothing could ever survive in. And do you know what? On my first cast, I caught a goldfish!"

She laughs. "In a reservoir?"

"Yes, in a filthy reservoir in Stirchley near Nanny's house."

At that very moment, her float goes down and I shout, "Strike!"

She jerks her rod upwards and it bends at a crazy angle. Her line sings and the clutch on her reel screams.

She shouts, "Dad, Dad, help me, I don't know what to do, it's pulling me in!!"

She falls over on her bottom into the mud and is literally being dragged down the bank towards the water. I grab hold of her and pull her up.

Standing behind her, with her own hands on the rod, which I tell her to keep up, I take charge of the reel and start winding in the line, pausing every time the fish objects and tugs.

After several minutes we get it close to the bank. When it breaks the surface of the water with a loud angry splash, Lily shrieks, "Oh my God, it's enormous!"

I get the landing net and with one hand on the reel, gently get the fish's head up and coax it over the rim of the net. As I lift it clear of the water, the pole bends under the weight.

"That's a beauty!"

We both admire it as it lies there on the grass, opening and closing its mouth for air. We weigh it. It's an eight pound carp. I take a photo of her holding it. It takes a couple of attempts as the fish is slippery and keeps wriggling, flapping water into her face which makes her squeal. Finally, I get the perfect shot. She's beaming with pride into the lens. She'll take the photo to school on Monday, to show all the boys. Then I let it go while she's busy wiping the slime off her hands.

When we've calmed down, we start on our packed lunch. Lily says, "You know I'm really enjoying today Dad."

"Any time Lil. I've forgotten how much fun it is."

"We should do more stuff together, shouldn't we?"

"Absolutely."

"When I show them the photograph at school, I'm going to tell everyone how *you* took me fishing.

"What, your disabled old Dad?"

"Oh don't say that Dad. I didn't mean it you know, about being ashamed of you."

"Really?"

"Of course, you're my dad."

We carry on watching our floats and Lily throws a bit of her sandwich in for the ducks.

After a while, she says, "What happened to my other grandad? I mean I've only got one and everyone at school has two."

"My dad?"

"Yes."

"Well, he died from a heart attack."

"When?"

"I was still at school."

"What, like me?"

"No, I was a bit older than you."

"And were you sad?"

"Well, yes of course. So was your gran. We all were."

"What was he like, your dad?"

"Well, there's a question. It's funny you know. I used to get embarrassed about my dad too. He was a bit older than all my friends' dads and he used to wear clothes that were a little old fashioned. It seems silly now when I think about it. Now it's too late."

"Too late for what?"

"Oh you know, to tell him how much I liked him. Some of the things he did make me laugh, even now. On Sundays, we used to go up the Lickey Hills. He used to tell us if we looked real hard, we could see our house from up there.

"Once, he decided to test how steep the hill was by having a little 'controlled' jog. Of course it was so steep that once he started, he couldn't stop. There were dozens of people watching, screaming with laughter as his legs were going like the clappers before he went head over heels, skidding along the grass on his backside and doing forward rolls.

"It was like that cheese rolling festival in Gloucestershire that we saw on TV, when all those people chase a rolling cheese down a very steep hill. He broke his glasses and lost his wallet. Mum didn't half tell him off when he got back up. His suit was ruined with the grass stains. We were all laughing, saying 'Dad, what were you thinking of?'

"Then he said, 'I only started a little jog like this....' He started to show us what he had done and before he knew it, he started to pick up speed again, and the whole spectacle started to repeat itself all over. Faster and faster he went, again so fast his legs just couldn't keep pace until he somersaulted into the air then rolled all the way to the golf course at the bottom.

He got a round of applause when he came back up again for the second time. He had grass burns all on his elbows and knees."

Lily is killing herself laughing.

"Sounds like a right nut case, but a brilliant dad to have."

"Yes...I suppose he was. Some things you don't miss until they're gone."

We carry on watching our floats. Then she says, "I'll miss you, you know, when you're gone."

"Oh, don't be so morbid Poppet."

"It's not morbid Dad, it's just the truth isn't it? Everyone has to die." She stares at her float. I watch her. Sometimes she says the most grown up things.

Later Emm arrives to pick us up, pulling the car to a halt in a cloud of dust. "Hello you two, had a good time?"

"You'll never believe the fish I caught Mum. I've got a photo to prove it and everything."

"Well, let's see then. What about your dad?"

"He caught nothing."

It's true. But I honestly couldn't care less. Today was all about Lily.

When we're packing all the gear into the back of the car, Lily says to me quietly, "Thanks for today Dad. I really loved it."

"I'm glad Lil. Let's not wait too long before we do it again."

209

I am totally knackered. The last of my extra medication wore off an hour ago and I literally fall into the passenger seat. Emm has to fasten my seatbelt for me. On the drive home, I close my eyes and hang on to my arm which is shaking quite badly by now. But I feel a sense of peace. After the crisis of diagnosis and all those problems with the medication and the gambling, I feel happy for the first time in ages.

I feel I'm actually doing some good. I made someone happy today. I also feel I'm beginning to 'let go' and accept that I'm never going to be the person I once was, ever again. But so what? I honestly wouldn't want those days back again when I was consumed by myself, my career, my future etc. Me, me, me, me.

Muriel was right; the world didn't revolve around me. Drama School. Who did I think I was kidding?

1982. Thespian

Events at the Crossroads Motel have been overtaking me since I've been away. In January 1980, David Hunter was shot by his ex-wife Rosemary. And last year, fire gutted the motel and Meg was feared dead in the ashes. Life is more exciting in the sleepy village of King's Oak than the great metropolis that is London.

Despite the traumatic start, my skinny frame and Brummie accent slowly become accepted in that bastion of tradition, standing straight and received pronunciation that is Webber Douglas. They actually take quite a liking to me, offering me a scholarship when I fail to win a local authority grant for the second year and it looks like I'll be forced to leave.

The principal tells me, "Don't let us down Colin, we think you can go far."

Despite them paying my fees (nearly £3000 for the year) I'm given a pittance to live on, just £25 a week. This doesn't go far in central London, so I'm forced to work at weekends in the café to get me by. I also persuade the principal to let me be the school cleaner in the evenings when everyone has gone home, mopping the common room floor and refilling the vending machine, which gives me a few more pounds a week.

After a few months I've become quite resourceful. There's a nightclub near Goodge Street. It plays Latin dance music and once you've paid to get in, there's a free Mexican style buffet. I've become quite friendly with the girl on the door who works the till.

After a few weeks she starts to let me in for free. Well, that's my evening meal paid for every night, even though all those chillies and spices play havoc with my poor old stomach problem. So I get free food, become quite good at the Lambada, and by about ten p.m., I walk all the way from Goodge Street to Tufnell Park (quite a way, if you've ever tried it), to save on my bus fare, which means I'm also a whole lot fitter.

If I can afford it, I stop off at Camden Town for a pint in the Devonshire Arms. And if I'm really lucky, someone I know in there will buy me a second or even a third.

In 1982, I am cast as Father Mullarkey in *Once A Catholic*. Mick thinks my attempt at an Irish accent is hilarious. When I give him a line or two, he howls with laughter and exclaims, "Jeesus Colin, you langer, that accent is worse than Dick Van Dyke's cockney in Mary Poppins!"

Saturday night and the final performance is attended by some of my family who have travelled down from Birmingham, including Aunty Vera.

She wants to come and see how "my favourite nephew is getting on in the acting business in London".

As we wait in the wings on our beginners' call, I can hear Vera's voice out front. "Ooh, it's quite a big theatre isn't it. Look, there's his name in the programme. Is he on from the beginning do you think?"

All of this in the broadest Weoley Castle, Brummie accent imaginable. I'm dreading her reaction when I walk out on stage.

When I do, my worst fears are confirmed.

"Ooh look, there he is, there's our Colin."

She bellows one of her drain-like laughs when she sees me in priest's costume and I first speak with the stereotype Irish accent. Backstage, word begins to spread that there's some nutter in the audience and the whole cast come down from the dressing rooms and gather in the wings for a good laugh.

I can see them all looking at me from behind the black drapes, as I listen to Mary Mooney's confession while eating a plate of sausages and drinking a pint of Guinness.

Mary says, "Father, I think I'm going to die."

And I reply, "Not at all Mary Mooney, a fine strapping girl lyke yerself, in the best a health! Now help me out with one o' these sausages will yer?"

Vera finds it hysterical and her infectious laugh gets the rest of the audience going. It's definitely our best night to date, with huge roars of laughter at even the smallest of jokes.

Mary's confession continues, "But I've committed a mortal sin father."

"What did he make you do Mary?"

"I think he called it a twentieth century fox."

"What the devil?"

"No it wasn't that, it was a J. Arthur Rank."

I wait a second for the joke to register. Cue Vera's drain laugh. She shouts out, "Jesus wept, I'm gonna wet myself."

It brings the House down.

In the pub afterwards, Aunty Vera is the toast of everyone. Sitting at the head of the table, all of the actors, during the course of the hour, go up to her and say, "Thank you Aunty Vera, you really got them going. You're a star."

"Ooooh think nothing of it, you were all absolutely brilliant."

Vera asks one of the actresses,

"And is this what you want to do for a living when you leave college?"

The girl replies, "Of course, I'm a confirmed thespian."

"Really dear? Don't you like boys then?"

We take the tube back to their hotel in Camden. Vera is agog at all around her. On the escalator, I have to tell her to stand on the right, to keep the left-hand lane free for those in a hurry.

"What are they all in such a rush for? Standing on the right on an escalator, I've never heard of anything so daft in all my life."

On the platform, I point down to the little black mice that live and scurry around in the litter under the electrified track.

She is fascinated. "Poor little darlings. Don't they get electrocuted when the train passes over them?"

In the train compartment, we are all squashed in, and there's a commuter who's been working late, who doesn't look very happy.

Vera says, "Jesus wept, look at him, he's got a face as lung as Livery Street[1]."

She must think she's on another planet.

When I get home, I ask Mick the usual question. I get the usual answer.

"No, no calls. Nothing."

---

[1] long street in Birmingham city centre

Eternal. 2012

I've started watching daytime television. It's not good for my sanity. I watch all that macho 70s and 80s stuff on ITV4: *The Sweeney*, *Minder* and *The Professionals*, with Ford Granadas and Capris crashing through piles of cardboard boxes while the cockney geezer who's driving shouts at his passenger in the back, "Shat it, you slag!"

The 90s version of the TV detective is a little more sedate. On ITV3, in *Midsomer Murders*, John Nettles investigates macabre and ever more unlikely deaths in sleepy villages.

George, the pathologist, played by the Birmingham-born actor Barry Jackson, always greets the Chief Inspector with the line, "Got an unusual one for you here Tom…"

"Really?"

"Yes, this poor chap's had his balls cut off with a guillotine, which fell when this rope was burnt through by this candle, while this tape of Europe's 'It's The Final Countdown' was playing on this tape recorder by his side."

On Saturday afternoons, when Emm and Lily are usually out shopping, I watch endless reruns of *Grand Designs* on More 4. It's a programme designed to undermine the masculinity of the average British male, who has difficulty assembling an IKEA flat-pack set of shelves.

On the screen, these 'supermen' self-builders project manage the build themselves, while holding down a full-time job at the same time, and *still* from somewhere summon the energy to impregnate their wife with their umpteenth child.

After the show, there must be millions of men, nagged by their wives, "Why can't *you* do that? You're bloody useless you are. I've been waiting six months for you to fix that dripping tap."

Yes, on behalf of all those poor emasculated men, I'd like to wipe that smug, self-satisfied grin off the face of that smarmy hippy Ben Law and his frigging cruck-framed house in the woods.

Still, Gordon Ramsay never fails to cheer me up on Channel Four with his *Kitchen Nightmares* show. In one particular episode, Gordon visits a failing gastro pub run by a married couple who are always arguing.

On the first night Gordon observes the couple's normal routine. She's serving at tables, he's cooking. It's not long before they are shouting at each other.

She bellows through the kitchen hatch, "Where the fuck is order 42? They've been waiting an hour!"

The camera pans to the kitchen where the sweating husband is battling with a frying pan with flames shooting out of it up to the ceiling.

He shouts back, "I'm doing my best you fucking bitch!!"

Hilarious.

On Monday, I go and see a good friend. He is sitting at our favourite bench again.

"Hello Frank. How are you?"

"Colin, how nice to see you. You're not looking at all well"

I laugh. "Thank you for noticing. What are you reading?"

"Oh, revisiting James Joyce. *A Portrait Of The Artist As A Young Man*. Have you read it Colin?"

"Years ago."

"Remember the passage about eternity?"

"Erm, sort of, you'll have to remind me."

"Well, why don't you read it to me now. I've just got to that part."

"Are you sure?"

"Yes. Go on, humour me. There is a point to all this."

He hands me the book, smiles, then closes his eyes in anticipation.

I start the passage where the priest asks Stephen to contemplate a beach and how tiny its individual grains of sand are. We are asked to imagine how many millions make up a small child's handful. Then imagine a huge mountain of that sand millions of miles high, wide and deep.

We are then asked to picture a small bird arriving just once every million years to carry away just one grain of sand in its beak. The priest asks how many millions and billions and trillions of years would pass before just a square foot of that mountain would be carried away.

Imagine the ages and eons, the incalculable amount of time needed to carry away the whole mountain! He says to the reader, after such an immense, uncountable amount of time, eternity still wouldn't even have started.

Then he says, once that whole mountain has been carried away, it rises up again, and the little bird gets to work once more, one grain every million years. He says, imagine that with the little bird's efforts, the mountain rises and falls by as many times as there are feathers on all birds, hairs on all animals, scales on all fish, drops of water in all the oceans, atoms in the air and stars in the sky.

After that amount of time that we can't even imagine, that makes us dizzy, that is greater than the lives of planets and galaxies many times over, **still** after all that time, eternity will not even have started .... and it never will. The priest then asks us to reflect soberly on the awful truth of eternity.

As I finish, I look up at Frank and he is staring hard at me.

He asks, "What do you think?"

"I think it frightens me."

"Why?"

"It's the idea of something never ending. It's actually really scary. The thought that after I'm dead, that's what faces me. Nothing. And it will *never* end.

"My dad said something similar before he died, 'When you're dead you're dead, and after, there's nothing, forever.' But I've often thought, did he really understand what he was saying? Did he understand what 'nothing forever' means? Because if he did, he would have been frightened to death."

"Yes," says Frank, "it scares me too, and I've thought long and hard about this and I've come to the conclusion that you can't measure eternity with time. It just doesn't make sense. And that's why it's so scary. One of them; either time or eternity has to be false. The two cannot co-exist side by side, as James Joyce so eloquently illustrated.

"And eternity scares me because I think of it in terms of time. But, if I flip it on its head, and think *time* doesn't exist, then eternity all of a sudden becomes so much more friendly. Oh, I know that sounds an absurd thing to say: time doesn't exist. *Of course it does,* we think. *We are not living in the same moment as prehistoric man was a million years ago.*

"But are we sure about that? If we try to see time as just a tool that we use to help us order and make sense of material nature decaying then renewing over and over, then I begin to see. Time applies to these material bodies, not to spirit or consciousness or whatever you call it. For spirit, time isn't real and it is always just the present, eternally. I have always been here and I will always be here. I was here when prehistoric man was walking the earth."

He stops, exhausted and out of breath by so much talk but with a serene look of satisfaction and excitement on his face. "Don't you see? Isn't it wonderful? And so simple."

I sit and think about what he's just said. I know it makes sense because someone once told me something very similar. I make an observation.

"But maybe eternity is not that scary. I mean, if you're dead and not conscious then you won't be aware of not existing for all that time anyway, so why worry about it?"

"Well, think about what you just said Colin. To have no sense, not even of ourselves EVER again. Isn't that just as terrifying? No, the only way to allay this terror is to recognise that by nature, I am permanent not temporary. I can't conceive of a time when I will *not* be conscious. The thought of life ending or not existing at all, is totally alien to me. I will always be here in some form or another.

"That's why 'nothing forever' is so unfathomable. We think of time as 'passing' because of our cycle of birth and death: things getting older over time, material decaying then renewing, the seasons passing. But this cycle is merely a distraction for us from the bigger picture. We think of ourselves as bodies, being born, getting older, getting sick, then dying.

"But what if I am not this body? What a thought that is to try and get my head around. I am not this person called Frank, I am a spirit soul living in the body of Frank. When poor old Frank is dead and gone, the real 'me' will still be here, or somewhere, outwardly manifest differently, but inside, spiritually still me. Then all of a sudden, I'm not frightened anymore. Because there's no such thing as the end of life, I just continue on my journey towards my goal; via a sort of spiritual evolution

I reply, "Well, some people will say that that sort of endless 'reincarnation' is in itself quite hellish. Life is suffering, so to live eternally is just as scary as to not exist at all eternally."

"Of course," he says. "Life in this material world, in this material body is miserable. But this body and this planet are not the be all and end all. There is a better place. And when we're 'ready', in whatever capacity that means, we won't have to take on another of these gross bodies, on this material planet. We'll go to that better place as pure spirit. We will have attained bliss, and it will last forever."

"Like heaven, you mean?"

"Yes. It's hard for us to imagine the spiritual world from our position of darkness in the material world. It's a bit like trying to explain 3D to someone who lives in and has only ever known 2D. In the spiritual world, or heaven, call it what you will, there is no need for time because nothing gets old or dies. So there's no more mourning, no more tears. I also believe it is always light there. There is no need for artificial lights because there is no darkness to dispel. We are just eternally 'in the light'. No loss, no pain, no distress, no fear. Just 'enlightened'".

"You'll be telling me next that you believe in ghosts."

"Actually Colin, I do."

"Well, how can a spirit live in the material world without a material body?"

"Well, I believe some restless spirits don't take on another body immediately. For example, if you have had a particularly shocking or traumatic death, you need a period of recovery. Indeed, some may not even realise they've passed on. They may need a time of healing, or reflection or even a review of their whole life before they can move on. Some may have unfinished business of the heart, and so they may return fleetingly, to visit old friends and places to reassure or be reassured. I don't know. I don't have all the answers."

"But eventually we all move on? The death of this body is not the end?"

"Yes. We either go back to the spirit world, or we get another opportunity to qualify ourselves to go back." He looks at his shaking hands. "And that's what I've learned after seventy-nine years in his body called Frank. There are cynical people who will deny all this, clinging to the concept that everything begins and ends with this body. But every great thinker, all the wise and spiritually enlightened people from the past, have all come to the same conclusion.

"One of the greatest philosophers of them all, Plato, in the Phaedrus, said: 'We are pure ourselves, not buried in this thing we are carrying around now, which we call a body, locked in like an oyster in its shell.'

"And on the subject of time, even the greatest modern scientist of them all, Einstein, in his theory of relativity, showed that time passes at different rates for observers travelling at different speeds; it can slow down or even stop entirely. Time is not an absolute Truth. It is a creation of our mind to make sense of the ever-changing material world."

His face is so animated, positively glowing. One of the nurses calls over to our bench. "Frank, I really do think you should come back inside now. It's far too chilly out here for you."

The excitement has exaggerated his tremor and he is now shaking quite violently in his chair.

She walks swiftly over. "There, see, what did I tell you? You're shaking. No arguments, you're coming straight back in."

She wheels him back to the day room, giving me a disapproving look. "Really, you should know better, keeping him out for this long."

"Sorry, we were talking and I just lost track of the time."

He's in quite a state by the time we get him back and he is immediately given his medication then taken to his room to lie down.

I follow behind as he's trundled away, trying to talk to him and encourage him, "Bye Frank. I'll try and visit again soon."

As he's being wheeled, he is writing frantically, then he raises a shaky arm, and I see he's holding a piece of paper that he clearly wants me to take. I catch up with him and take it from his grasp just as the nurse disappears round the corner with him and I hear him descend into a fit of coughing.

When he's gone, I start to make my way back to the exit, and realise once more that I'm lost in the labyrinth of identical corridors.

An old guy in his pyjamas approaches me with a look of distress - almost horror - on his face. He pleads with me, "Excuse me," he says, "but where am I?"

I smile in an attempt to calm him.

"Don't worry, I'm lost too."

His haunted face stares at me as he repeats, "But where *am* I? What is this place? Where's my house?"

He starts to cry and a nurse arrives to lead him away. His look and words leave me shaken.

I'm still in wonder at all that Frank said, the same words of wisdom that were first shared with me nearly twenty-five years ago, in another country.

1988. Italy

It's the end of an era. *Crossroads* finished this year. In the final scene, Jill was riding off with her lover John Maddingham, to open a new hotel.

When asked what name did she think they should give it, she replied, with a tear in her eye, "I always thought *Crossroads* was an awfully good name."

Cue the electric guitar twang of the theme tune.

I don't think the producers realise just how popular a programme it was, especially in Birmingham. Everyone watched it. It regularly drew in 18 million viewers at its peak.

I suppose the trial of Benny was its greatest moment, but similarly, in March 1975, when Meg Richardson got married to Hugh Mortimer, they filmed the wedding at Birmingham Registry Offices on Broad Street, just round the corner from the old ATV studios.

A crowd of thousands turned up, blocking all the traffic. My Aunty Vera was among them. She said people were surging forward to get to the car.

If they managed it, they were sticking their heads in through the windows, saying "Good Luck Meg!" as though it was a real wedding. *Crossroads* was the foundation for the latest Australian success, *Neighbours*. Its theme tune and lyrics are even written by the same couple who wrote the *Crossroads* theme; Tony Hatch and Jackie Trent. But now it's all over. I can now safely say that I'm never going to be on *Crossroads*. I'll never hand back the keys to Chalet 43.

I think about my career. Six years since I graduated from drama school, and the big break never arrived. Endless Theatre-in-Education tours around the country, one tiny part in a film, a few 'blink and you'll miss me' moments on TV, such as playing an armed robber on *Crimewatch*, and a couple of adverts. That was it.

According to Dr Johnson, I must be tired of life, because the more I look, the more I am beginning to despise London. The area around Camden Town tube station on a Saturday night is pitiful and scandalous: people walking past bundles huddled in blankets in doorways. The food, vomit, blood and urine all over the pavement. The wine drinkers with plastic bags on their feet, their hands and faces black with the soot of the street and the underground; the same black that you blow out of your nostrils into your handkerchief when you get home.

I taste the unpleasantness of London first hand one night in Camden Lock. I walk under the railway bridge and a voice from the shadows asks me, "Excuse me mate, you got a light?"

"Sorry, I don't smoke."

They follow me out from under the bridge and I know I'm in trouble. I start to run and feel a blow to my back. I don't remember anything else. I must have hit my head on the kerb when I went down, because when I wake up there is blood all around the back of my collar. People are just walking past me, to go into the Hawley Arms. No one stops to ask if I'm OK. I've got blood all over me and no one seems to care. Do they think I'm drunk and have fallen asleep on the pavement? English people are so cold at times.

When I get in, Mick is shocked at the state of me and says I need to go to Casualty. "Jeesus Colin, you've had the shite bate outa ya. Head injuries always need to be checked, especially if you were unconscious."

"No, I'll be fine. I'll just take some paracetamol."

"I'm serious. You get yerself to hospital man, you don't know what's been done in there. You could have a bleed on the brain like a boxer. You could end up like a vegetable. Look at poor Mohammed Ali."

I decide to go to bed anyway. I wake up late, with a terrific headache and dried blood all around my ear. What's the time? They even took my watch. I roll over. Sod going to work at the café. What am I doing in this city? Kidding myself I'm going to become an actor or that Muriel is going to call.

Stick London, with all the dirt and ugliness and violence. I want to go somewhere better. I go to the travel agents to book a flight to Italy. I pay Mick to the end of the month on the flat and hand in my notice at the Café.

Two weeks later, I'm walking across the tarmac at Cagliari airport in Sardinia. The heat of the October sun is a comfort on my shoulders and back. I apply for a job teaching English at the Big Red Bus School Of English.

At the interview the husband and wife team who run the school ask me what my Italian is like.

"It's basic but I can get by."

I'm lying of course. I've only been in the country two weeks.

"OK," he asks, to test me. "So how do you say, 'Come here please' in Italian?"

I know this. "Vieni qui, per favore."

Then *she* says, "And how do you say 'Go over there, please' in Italian?"

This throws me. *'Over there', how do you say 'over there'?*

I go bright red for a few seconds, then say, "Well, *I* would go over there, and then *I* would say 'Vieni qui, per favore,'" which makes them laugh, and incredibly, I get the job.

I'll teach a few hours in the school, to adults in the evening. But my main income will be made up of private visits to expensive apartments on the rich side of the city, to children of the wealthy who want a bit of extra one-to-one tuition.

I rent a room in the beach area of Poetto, and buy a cheap Piaggio Vespa scooter to get around on.

One of my private pupils is Roberto, twelve, who lives in the plushest apartment block in Cagliari. His mother owns her own flower business, and has gone to work long before I arrive for our lesson on a Saturday morning at 10 a.m. I ring the bell and wait for the same routine. I ring it again, then several times, before little Roberto opens the door in his pyjamas, pretending to yawn.

"Oh insegnante, mi dispiace di aver dimenticato di nuovo."[1] By the time he's dressed, has cleaned his teeth and brushed his hair, and we are ready to start the lesson, it's 10.20 and we've lost a third of our time. This happens every week.

Eventually, his mother phones me up at my flat in the evening.

"Oh hello Colin, I am calling to say we won't be requiring your services any more. I'm going to cancel the lessons."

"Why? Is there a problem?"

"Well, to be perfectly honest Colin, I'm a little disappointed in you. I thought Roberto would be much further advanced by now."

"Yes, but….."

"And Roberto tells me you're late every morning."

---

[1] Oh teacher, I'm sorry, I forgot again.

My jaw hits the floor and before I get a chance to respond, she says that it's not open for discussion and hangs up. Spoilt little brat. Good riddance.

As October moves into November, the lido is padlocked, and the beach is generally deserted. Poetto out of season is a bit like Barry Island or Whitley Bay in winter, if you know those places. Summer attractions boarded up.

Every morning, when I walk for my morning paper and ciabatta and prosciutto di Parma, I step over the countless syringes left there from the night before. The beach is a magnet for the heroin addicts in winter.

I live a solitary life, teaching middle class Italian children by day, and in the evening watching RAI Uno and Canale Cinque light entertainment TV shows like *Drive In* and *Indietro Tutto*[1]. I can't understand what's going on most of the time, but find myself laughing along at the slapstick humour of the presenters.

One week they ask all the viewers in the north of Italy to flush their toilets simultaneously. Then they ask all the viewers in the south to do the same. There are two huge tanks of water in the studio, labelled "nord" and "sud" (north and south). So they calculate if more people are watching in the north than the south of the country, by how much the water has gone down in each tank. Italian TV seems so much more innocent and childish. But it makes me laugh.

The city's children's hospital is, unbelievably, on the beach. I often go for a walk in front of the surf and see little faces at the windows watching me. At least they have a view of the sea, not the Post Office Tower in Birmingham. Little Italian versions of Gary, having their blood washed.

Christmas arrives and I buy a cheap little tinsel tree with flashing lights. I cook a chicken and some vegetables and wrap up a present for myself; a tape recording of some songs by the Italian singer Mina in her seventies heyday. My favourite tracks are 'L'importante é Finire' and 'Parole Parole'[2]. It's a sort of 'euro pop' sound that I have grown to love and which is totally unappreciated in England.

---

[1] *Everything Backwards*
[2] 'It's Important To Finish' and 'Words, Words'

While the chicken is cooking on Christmas morning, I go for a swim in the sea. There isn't a soul about. Again the little faces at the window of the hospital are watching me. The sea is cold but not as freezing as at Withernsea near the Humber Estuary in high summer. I shiver my way back up the beach, in just a towel, before I eat Christmas dinner alone.

On Sundays, on my day off, I venture out on my scooter and explore the island around Cagliari. One Sunday in January, I pass a sign on the roadside inviting any passers-by to a free lunch. Curious, I take up the offer and turn off.

A mile up a dirt track I hit a clearing and suddenly I find myself in the middle of a sort of religious community. People are wearing orange robes and have shaven heads. Then it dawns on me: I've stumbled on an Italian Hare Krishna commune. I didn't even know they existed in Italy.

In a slight panic, I turn my Vespa round to get the hell out of there. One of the orange-sheeted monks hurries over to me, before I get a chance to speed off back up the dirt track.

"Per favore, si prega di rimanere per un po! Hai fame? Presto serviremo il pranzo."[1]

Well, what harm could there be in it? They are hardly going to cut off my head, and put me in the pot.

I have Sunday lunch, which is delicious. The food is all vegetarian, with a spicy Indian flavour and I can't get enough of it. I sit and watch them chanting, and singing and dancing in their makeshift temple. There are lots of ordinary Italian families sitting around, chatting with them. It all seems perfectly normal.

Not like the stigma associated with Hare Krishna in England, where people are suspicious and use the word 'cult.' Here, families are happily eating, discussing subjects like reincarnation with the monks, while their children play with the Hare Krishna children. Then, at the end of a Sunday afternoon, they go back home to their lives and their jobs, and maybe to the Italian version of *The Golden Shot*.

"Bernardo, thee bolt, per favore."

I stay behind and get chatting with some of the monks, or devotees, as they are called. They sleep on mats on the floor and they all look very thin

---

[1] Please, stay a while. Are you hungry? We will be serving lunch soon.

and tired, with bags under their eyes, but eyes that seem to have an inner happiness. Their temple smells of sweet incense.

When I tell them I am an English teacher, they can't believe their luck. None of them can speak a word of English and are desperate to learn, so that they can go and preach to the tourists on the mainland in Florence where they have their main temple.

I offer to teach them one night a week in exchange for an evening meal. The first week when I arrive, they are all ready with pencils and notebooks. We go through the basics, I speak and they all repeat:

"I am, You are. He is, She is, It is. We are, They are..."

It occurs to me that they are copying me exactly, even my Birmingham accent.

Within a couple of weeks, they are all greeting each other, in role play, in their best Brummie accents:

"Alrite? My nayme's Franco, how are yoo today?"

"Fyne thank yoo.."

"I am Bruno and this is Domenico.."

"Oh hallo, pleesed to meet yoo."

It's completely unintentional, but they copy me exactly. For them, it is the Queen's English and they take it all deadly seriously, marvelling at the sound of the words coming from their mouths. I smile to myself when I hear them, and wonder what would happen if they bump into a real Brummie tourist in Florence.

Sometimes on a Saturday night, with no work in the morning, I spend the night at the temple and talk into the evening around the fire, about the soul and reincarnation. I lie on a mat under the window to sleep and look up at the stars; the same stars I used to look at when I dreamed of Doreen Drysdale in the fields at the back of our house.

It's a magical time for me. So when some of the devotees say they are moving to the main temple in Florence to do some preaching, I secretly plan to follow them over there.

In March, I pay up the rent on my flat, hand in my notice at the school and get the ferry from Cagliari to Civitavecchia.

Standing on the dock, waiting to board, with my one bag, I think to myself, *What the hell am I doing?*

The sea is stormy, the voyage many hours and I am sick several times. I feel so poorly when I get to Rome, I don't even bother to explore while I wait for my connection but just sit in a huddle in the smoke-blackened station.

As the train heads north into Tuscany, the sky clears and the sun breaks through. When we arrive in Florence, the city is bathed in sunshine and I'm taken aback by the beauty of the red-tiled Renaissance city.

I get a taxi and show him the address of the temple in San Casciano. Does he know where that is?

He nods and says it's right up in the hills. On the way out of the city, he asks, "Vuoi vedere la vista piu bella del mondo?"[1] I say yes, and he pulls the taxi in on to the car park of the Piazza Michelangelo, which from its raised position, overlooks the whole of Florence. I get out and the view is breath-taking. The red Duomo and the Ponte Vecchio across the River Arno, which glitters in the late afternoon sun. My goodness. Is there a better view anywhere in the world?

We drive past field after field of Chianti vineyards, planted in gently rolling hills for as far as the eye can see. He stops outside a grand entrance to what was previously a huge country home. I tell him I'll walk the rest of the way. The taxi driver looks at me after I pay him.

He knows what this place is, gives me a concerned look, offers me his card, then says, "Chiamami se cambi idea." [2]

We both laugh and he does a U-turn, then drives off and I'm left standing there in the dust, with my bag, looking down the tree-lined driveway. It is dead straight and disappears into the horizon, like a Michelangelo exercise in perspective. It could be the set of *Brideshead Revisited*. No turning back, I set off down the avenue of poplars to who knows what awaits me.

By the time I reach the main buildings, I'm sweating. There are peacocks crying out in the dappled shade of the avenue of trees. Again, when I see the orange robes, I slightly panic and wonder what I've done but this passes in a minute when one of those that I know from Sardinia, rushes up to greet me.

---

[1] Do you want to see the most beautiful view in the world?

[2] If you change your mind, you can always call me.

They find me a bed in the guest dormitory and tell me that I'm just in time for supper, which will be served on the main veranda. I unpack my things and look out of the small window down to the valley below, which is shrouded in mist and low cloud.

They sure picked a nice spot.

I sit crossed-legged on a mat on the veranda. I'm all alone and wonder if I've got the right place, when slowly, out of every doorway, alleyway and buttressed corner, across the lawns, down the stairwells, hundreds of people slowly start to appear. Old, young, children, some dressed in orange, some in white, all taking their places before the huge stainless-steel pots that are brought up, steaming, from the kitchens below.

I am surprised by the sheer number living here and the organisation of the place. There must be two hundred devotees living on the estate, many of them married with children. There's a school, a temple, vineyards, a working farm with a herd of cattle, a farm shop and even a Pizzeria in the gardens.

They also broadcast live from their own purpose-built radio station to the outside community around Florence. Everyone works to make the place a going concern. There's even a resident Hare Krishna dentist.

I spend my mornings washing pots in the huge kitchens and sometimes, I help the chef make the bread: dough rolled out in huge quantities, before being baked in enormous wood burning ovens. But I'm the only English person here and news of my arrival soon spreads, so that I also land the job in the evenings of teaching English to anyone who wants to attend.

I end up with a thriving class of over thirty, all keen to learn English (with a Birmingham accent).

One evening, the senior devotee and president of the community comes over to chat with me during supper. He speaks very good English.

"So, Colin, how are they all getting on with their English?"

"Oh fine. We're still only at the basics, you know, 'I am, he is. etc.'"

"Oh right. So now they can all say, 'I am fried, I want to leave.'"

He bursts out laughing at his own joke. "Seriously though Colin, what brings you here? We don't see many English people."

"Well, I got to know your devotees in Sardinia."

"So what attracted you to them?"

"Well, my first meeting was just by accident, then I got chatting, read a bit of the *Bhagavad Gita* and sort of liked it. It felt as though I belonged."

He smiles at me. "You know Colin, the spirit soul can live many, many lifetimes, before it reaches the stage to question, who am I, why am I here? You are a 'grande anima,' a great soul, to have arrived here."

"Well, I'm not thinking of shaving my head just yet."

He bursts out laughing again. "You don't have to do that. We have plenty of 'plain clothes' devotees living in the outside world. Look at George Harrison, he does so much for us."

"Well, I'm hardly George Harrison."

"You'd be surprised who you really are Colin, and how much Krishna really cares about you, for him to have arranged all this for you. It was not an accident that you met the devotees you know. Everything has a cause and a consequence. It's called your karma.

"And if you stay long enough, you'll begin to understand something about yourself, that you are not that body. You are a spirit soul who has experienced birth, death and rebirth in countless bodies before the one you are sitting in now. We take our accumulated karma, both good and bad, from one body to the next. The conquest of karma lies in intelligent action and dispassionate response.

"Our ultimate goal should be to escape this endless Samsāra in the material world, this wandering from one body to the next, suffering reaction after reaction, and to finally return to the supreme spirit, Krishna, in the spirit world, free from karma and material suffering. You are eternal and you live forever, and when you know that, you will be happy. You will have nothing to fear from sickness, old age and death because all of these things are Maya. They are mere illusion."

He looks at my blank face and laughs. "Yes Colin, even time itself does not really exist. Can you imagine that? There is no such thing as time.

"Let me tell you the story of Narada and Vishnu. Narada was a holy man who was seeking knowledge. One day, he meets Vishnu and asks him to show him the powers of Maya (illusion). Vishnu asks him to walk with him. After some time, the two find themselves in an arid region, and Vishnu asks Narada to bring him some water from the village nearby.

"Narada leaves and calls at a house in the village. The door is opened by the most beautiful girl Narada has ever seen, and he immediately falls in love with her. They spend a long time together, and Narada decides he'd like to marry her. Her parents agree and Narada decides to give up his search for truth and settle down.

"They are married and the girl soon becomes pregnant. They have a beautiful baby daughter who enchants Narada and his wife. So much so, that they have two more children, another girl and a boy. The children grow strong, their farm prospers and they are very happy.

"Then one night, a terrible storm comes. There is a great flood and Narada watches helplessly as his wife and three beautiful children are taken by the torrent. He has to swim for his life and clings to a rock. He drifts into unconsciousness and hears a voice asking him, 'Where is the water you promised me? I have been waiting for more than an hour.' The voice is Vishnu's. Narada opens his eyes and sees the flood has gone.

"Vishnu smiles and bows his head and says, 'Now do you understand the secret of Maya?'"

After telling this story, the devotee looks at me, laughs and says, "Yes Colin, even time is illusion. And when you free yourself from all of these misconceptions, you will be truly liberated and happy, as though a whole universe of weight and worry has been lifted off your back."

When he stops laughing, and swallows his next mouthful, he chuckles again and says to me quietly, with a smile in his eye, "Krishna always sends someone to help you to continue on your spiritual journey, from where you left off."

When I go to bed, I think about the chain of events that led me here, right down to the chance sighting of the invitation to Sunday lunch at the roadside. What made me see it and made me stop? Then I remember the brief meeting in London with the guy who'd given me the book in Soho Square years before. I'd forgotten all about that.

And how much of a coincidence can it have been for me to meet the devotees in Sardinia? They were desperate to learn English, and I was an English teacher. It seems almost as if it had been prearranged.

The windows of the dormitory are open and the hot dry air is full of the sound of cicadas. I can see straight up to the stars. I think again about the devotee's words at dinner. "Krishna always sends someone to help you continue on your spiritual journey from where you left off."

More and more, I am beginning to see that all of these 'chance' events and meetings were not just coincidence, but part of God's bigger plan for me. He seems to be actively intervening, guiding and taking a personal interest in my case. He's going to all of this trouble just for me. Am I really worth that much to him? As I have this thought, I realise that he is actually talking to me and I suddenly burst into tears.

I make a resolution.

I get up at 3.30 a.m. the next morning, to go to the 4.30 a.m. service in the temple for the first time. Outside the main entrance, there are hundreds of discarded shoes, some stacked neatly, some kicked off in a rush. There are enormous 'Jesus sandals', which have clearly clocked up some miles in the service of the Lord. Sling backs, flip flops and lace ups with the backs all trodden down. But these shoes are different to the ones in our outhouse when I was a boy. These are the shoes of saints and pilgrims, all respectfully taken off before they go in barefoot to worship God.

It is a humbling sight. I take my own shoes off, and to my horror, see that my socks have got a big hole in the toe. So I quickly take my socks off too. I'm late and last in.

The service is just about to start and every eye is on me as I enter, surprised that I've managed to wake up so early and taken a shower in time for Mangala Arati, morning worship. I try to remain as low key as possible and so walk up the steps to the back of the temple where I can be anonymous and watch proceedings from a distance. It has the opposite effect. A female devotee walks quickly towards me shaking her head and wagging her finger at me, gently scolding me in Italian before ushering me back down the steps to the front section. It seems I have been standing with the women!

When he hears about it later, The president of the temple roars with laughter.

I try to explain. "Well, I didn't know you had to stand separately. And why do the women have to stand at the back? A bit sexist isn't it?"

Again he laughs. "Colin, we are not these bodies. We shouldn't think of ourselves as men and women. But if it bothers you, think of it like this; they may be at the back, but their part of the temple is higher up. They are closer to God!" And he laughs again.

Over the next few days I start chanting the Hare Krishna mantra regularly. It's only three words; Hare, Krishna and Rama repeated in a certain order over and over:

Hare Krishna, Hare Krishna,
Krishna Krishna, Hare Hare,
Hare Rama, Hare Rama,
Rama Rama, Hare Hare.

I sit on the marble floor of the temple and chant, looking at the deities of Krishna and Radha. The whole temple hums with the sound of the devotees chanting.

After about an hour, the sound becomes so sweet that I can't explain it. The words just sound so beautiful, that I want to keep saying them over and over. I look at Krishna's smiling face and feel a connection, as if he's smiling at *me*. There is a spirituality about this place that I can't explain. I look around at the other devotees, a whole room of people addicted to chanting this name. I feel a sense of belonging and of the enormity of what's taking place all around me. I am swimming in deep water.

Later, I ask the President about this and he smiles warmly at me.

"Of course Colin. You are getting a taste of spiritual life, which is so sweet compared to material life. You can never find this sort of sweetness in the material world. You are chanting and becoming attached to *God's* name. Of course it is beautiful."

I read passages from the *Bhagavad Gita*, a sort of bible in India, and the more I read and the more I chant, the more beautiful everything looks around me. It's weird, and it makes me laugh. I look at the grass and the flowers and the sky and feel a sense of euphoria, as I watch the tiny cars on the autostrada in the valley below, like ants, following one another in a long line from Florence to Sienna.

One day, I make a telephone call home. I haven't been in contact for a while now and know that they might be worried about me. Mum answers the phone, and her accent takes me by surprise. It's been several months since I've heard an English voice.

She asks where I'm staying, and I just say, "With friends". She asks how I'm getting on for money and I say I'm OK, teaching English here and there. She sounds concerned and asks me when I'm coming home, so I reassure her that I'll be home for Christmas.

After putting the phone down, I feel a sense of guilt, for not telling her everything, but I know she'll only worry herself. I try to imagine what my family and friends will think when I go home, when they find out who I've been living with. I can just picture their reaction; that I've been 'brainwashed' into a cult.

This evening at dinner, I sit with the president of the temple again. He is such a jovial fellow, with a glint in his eye. Awkwardly, I bring up the subject of religious cults and accusations of brainwashing.

He smiles at me. "And do you think *you've* been brainwashed Colin?"

"No, of course not, it's just that I worry what my friends at home will think."

He looks at me quite intently and with a seriousness in his voice,

"Well let me tell you Colin, yes, you *have* been brainwashed!"

"I have?"

His face breaks into that enormous grin of his. "Yes Colin, and about time too. Your mind, which was so full of Maya, illusion and attachment for things not worth having, like money, appearance, etc, has had a good wash. Now you are seeing clearly for the first time. Just like that song, Amazing ….?"

"Grace?"

"Yes, yes, that's the one, how does it go now? 'I was blind, but now I see.' Sums it up perfectly. We're not Buddhists Colin, but do you know what the word 'Buddha' means? It literally translates as 'awake'. The Buddha is he who is awake while everyone else is sleeping. That's true, but unlike Buddhists *we* believe that God, Krishna, can wake us up and open our spiritual eyes (after, of course, our brains and our hearts have had a good wash!).

"Tell me Colin, what do your friends at home think about God?"

"They don't. They're either atheist or agnostic."

"Ah my English! What do you mean by agnostic?"

"They say they'll believe him when they see him. But they need proof to believe. The proof of their own eyes and senses. They can't just believe blindly what someone else tells them."

"Ah I see."

He smiles at me. "You know Colin, one of the conditions of enlightenment has always been a willingness to let go of what we thought we knew, in order to appreciate truths we had never dreamed of."

A look of sadness crosses his face. "They will never understand God their way. It's no good just standing there, saying: 'Show yourself to me

232

and I will believe in you.' No, it doesn't work like that. First we have to become qualified. We have to behave in such a way that he is pleased with us, then *he* will reveal himself to *us*.

"It's not our place to give him instructions and ultimatums: 'Show me, then I'll believe …' No. It should be, 'believe first, then you will be shown.' And by belief, we don't mean just blindly accepting.

"Belief is a skill that you develop by practical routine and service. Belief is a physical activity. It's a discipline. You have to become good at it through practice. We get up early, we bathe, we go to the temple, we pray, we worship, we meditate, we chant, we sing, we dance, we discuss during the lesson, we offer our food to him before we eat, and sometimes we fast.

"Then in the day, we give service by our work. We live a lifestyle where we put others first, before ourselves always, and there must be no conceit or pride about this. We must do it willingly and humbly. Didn't Jesus say something similar?

"And we do all this activity as a group, in a community, to support one another. If you live your life in this way, God will reveal himself to you eventually. And you will understand him in your *heart*, not through your blunt senses. God is unknowable if we try to intellectualise about him and just read books. Belief comes from practical activity.

"It's like learning to drive a car. You will never learn if you just read the manual and a copy of the highway code. You have to actually physically engage with the car to fully understand it and drive it. You have to open the doors, get in, turn the ignition, press the pedals and turn the steering wheel.

"Gradually, from physical practice you will become more skilled. This is how religion and belief work. You have to do the practical work as well as just the reading. Doesn't it say in the bible, 'Faith without works is dead'? The two go hand in hand.

"And that is why these so called 'atheists' and 'agnostics' will never understand, because they have never tried to engage. They just read and talk and intellectualise, pleased with their own opinions. They will never come to God that way.

"Stay with us Colin, and see what happens."

As the summer moves on and it gets hotter, I also lend a hand on the farm, helping to coral the wild cattle. I'm up at four every morning, chanting

Hare Krishna on my beads, washing pots, herding cattle, teaching English and before I go up to the dormitory, I read my little *Bhagavad Gita.*

Then I collapse into my bed at about nine p.m.,, suntanned and absolutely exhausted, sleeping the best night's sleep I've ever had in my life. It is blissful, and I seriously think about staying for good.

But Mum's anxious voice keeps going round in my head. I don't want to worry her unnecessarily. Thinking of her, starts me thinking again of London and my old way of life.

I suppose it's human nature, that whenever we find contentment, the little demon within us plants seeds of longing for something else. When you have to wake up at 3.30 a.m., it's easy to roll over and go back to sleep. I've always been a lazy bugger and these early mornings are beginning to get to me.

The no sex or alcohol rule is also difficult and more and more, my old way of life begins to seem attractive again. Deep down, I know that this is like a relapse into illusion. Anyone trying to walk the spiritual path needs to be disciplined. The draw of the material world and all its attendant pleasures is very strong.

I deceive myself by thinking that I do actually have some business in London that I need to sort out. I resolve to go back to England. I rationalize it to myself thus: the experience I've had is never going to leave me and I think, well, maybe like George Harrison, I too can still follow, as a sort of 'plain clothes devotee'.

So one Sunday morning in late August, without telling anyone, I pack my bag, walk back up the dappled avenue of trees, and catch the bus from San Casciano to Florence and, from there, the sleeper train to London. I move back into my old flat.

I've only been back a week when the phone rings.

Epiphany

I receive news that Frank has passed away. Wracked with guilt for keeping him out too long in the cold, I'm determined to go to his funeral. It turns out to be a fairly wretched affair. No relatives, just a couple of colleagues from the university and one or two from the care home.

We stand in driving rain, and I feel the chill go through me. I was unfamiliar with the book reference that he'd passed me that day. It said, "Dostoevsky ... *The Possessed* ... Stavrogin talks with Kirilov about time ..."

Well, I'm nowhere near as well read as Frank, so I had to look it up. I went to the library, and after about an hour of poring over the text, I think I found the passage he was referring to.

When I read it, it was like a light bulb being switched on. Stavrogin is asking Kirilov whether he believes in a future eternal life:

> *"No, not in a future eternal life, but in this present eternal life. There are moments – you can reach moments – when time suddenly stops and becomes eternal."*
> *"And you hope to reach such a moment?"*
> *"I do."*
> *"It is hardly likely in our time. In the Apocalypse, the angel promises that there will be no more time."*
> *"I know. There is a lot of truth in it; it is clear and precise. When man attains bliss, there will be no more time because there will be no more need for it. It's a very true thought."*
> *"Where will they hide time?"*
> *"Nowhere. Time is not a thing, it's an idea. It will vanish from the mind."*

Wow, I think to myself. "Time is not a thing, it's an idea." That is mind blowing. Now I know that Dostoevsky, apart from being one of the greatest visionary writers, was also a famous epileptic. And epileptics, immediately prior to a seizure, experience what has been termed as 'the ecstatic aura'. Epileptics themselves describe it as a feeling of familiarity, as if everything has happened before. Time seems to slow down, things seem really big or small and in this 'slow time' they can have complex hallucinations. Almost as if the epileptic sees a higher reality than the rest of us for a few seconds, then his brain is overloaded with information and shuts down for its own safety. Kirilov's "moments when time suddenly stops and becomes eternal" could be Dostoevsky trying to describe his aura. That fleeting moment when he can 'see' beyond this illusory material world. The list of great artists, philosophers and those with unusual leadership abilities who were apparently epileptic is compelling: Socrates, Plato, Napoleon, Lenin, Dostoevsky, Van Gogh, Charles Dickens. Even as recently as Ian Curtis of Joy Division. All were visionary thinkers.

"Time is not a thing but an idea." This fascinates me. Is time just an idea to help us make sense of the material world around us? As James Joyce - and Frank - concluded, time is illogical. Many modern scientists tend to agree.

If we plot time on a line from left to right, the past being to the left, the future to the right and the present in the middle, I ask myself when does the past become the present or the present become the future? How 'thick' is the present? A second? A billionth of a second?

The past turns into the future instantaneously. In this linear timeline model, there is no room for the present. Yet I am here, now, inhabiting the present. How can that be? Is it because the past and the future don't actually exist, that there is only just a continuous present?

Just as time can't coexist with eternity, the present can't coexist with the past and the future. As Frank said, the present only makes sense if it is eternal. The same 'eternal present' that Dostoevsky experienced during his 'aura' before a seizure.

Suddenly, everything is clear to me. Time isn't rushing by, *we are.* Our changing bodies and faces are growing, blossoming, blooming, maturing, ageing, shrinking, shrivelling and dying. The changing hues and textures of material life in metamorphosis, are painted in quick, bold brushstrokes on the blank canvas of time.

In the same eternal moment that is now, our hearts take a beat, an hour ticks by, night turns to day, winter melts into spring, mighty oaks rise and fall, planets and galaxies are born and die. The whole universe is in flux, but its backdrop, time, is still.

After the soaking I got at the funeral, I catch a cold. All fairly commonplace. I develop a dry, irritating cough, a headache, muscle pain and a little temperature, nothing to worry about.

After a few days I feel it's getting worse and retire to my bed. Just like the old days again. My meals brought up on a tray. Poor old Emm, as if she hasn't got enough to do.

My condition worsens. I have a temperature of a hundred and two. The cough has moved to my chest and I'm starting to bring up some pretty horrible stuff.

Emm calls the doctor. He sits on the edge of my bed and listens to my chest with his stethoscope. I have a slight infection in there, he says and he prescribes a five-day course of Amoxicillin, a mild antibiotic.

The medication works for a while but the cough doesn't fully go away. When the course of tablets finish, the chesty cough comes back with a vengeance. As if strengthened and emboldened by the failure of the penicillin, it gets its claws into me.

It's now painful to cough. I can barely eat anything with the coughing and sometimes, bits of food and drink go down the wrong way. I choke and try to cough them back up but they stay down, making me wheeze even more.

This time a different doctor arrives after Emm calls the surgery.

He wears a very serious expression when he hears my cough. He listens to my chest then says, "Mr. Sparrow, I'm afraid you have a very bad infection on your lungs. I'm not going to prescribe the same tablets, because they would now be useless. I'm going to put you on a two week course of a more powerful antibiotic called Doxycycline, which hopefully should see off the infection. However, I'm going to call back in 48 hours to see if there's any improvement, just to be on the safe side."

I try to answer but the coughing makes conversation impossible. Emm speaks for me. "On the safe side? What do you mean?"

"I'll be frank with you both. This is a particularly nasty infection. There's a possibility that it could develop into pneumonia if we don't halt it in the next few days. If we can't, I'm afraid he's going to have to come in on to the ward.

"Now, if he gets much worse or his temperature rises by more than a couple of degrees over the next twenty-four hours, I want you to phone me. If it's out of hours and you are concerned, dial 999."

Emm's face is white.

Noticing her alarm, he tries to calm her. "Hopefully, it won't come to that. This drug I've prescribed is powerful, and we should start to see the effects pretty quickly. I'll go to the pharmacy now and bring them back for you. He can start them straight away."

At around midnight, I am lying awake, drenched with sweat and burning up with a fever. I am sleeping in the spare room to try and give Emm a break as she has to get Lily up for school in the morning. I pop the thermometer into my mouth and wait a couple of minutes.

My pillow is soaked and I put a towel over it and mop my brow. The mercury is just nudging 105. This alarms me. Is it possible to die from overheating? I throw all my covers off the bed with the exception of the sheet and try to cool myself down.

I drink a whole glass of water which makes me cough. I spit bright red blood into my handkerchief, which alarms me even more. I lie there, propped up with extra pillows and stare into the dimly-lit gloom. I feel a little delirious with the fever.

For some reason, I've got that line from the Lord's Prayer stuck in my head: *"Give us this day our daily bread, and forgive us our trespasses, as we forgive those who trespass against us."* I think I've finally worked out what it actually means. Behind all those Ss, it's about
just taking what we need, and no more. The birds in the trees are provided for, and so are we. But we're all so busy in our lives, accumulating more and more, taking more than we need, more than our daily bread, often at the expense of others.

At the end of the day, it's totally pointless. So long as you have enough to live on. The rest?

Well, you can't take it with you. All our wealth and property, as Johnny Cash sang just before he died, it's just, "my empire of dirt".

I know death is not a subject most people want to talk about, but why not? It is the one thing we know for sure that is going to happen to us, so why not prepare for it? Instead, we deliberately shut it from our minds till it's too late and then we have to stare into the full horror of the abyss. It's not morbid to think about it. It's part of life.

Over a million people worldwide die every week. That's about 150,000 a day, equivalent to Old Trafford stadium filled two times over. Every day, all of those people have to confront reality and stare death in the face. Lying on his death bed, Srila Prabhupada, the founder of the Hare Krishna movement, said to his assembled devotees just before he left his body; *"Don't think this isn't going to happen to you."*

I know it's going to happen to me sooner rather than later. I am in the early winter of my life already, when I should still be in the late summer. Old before my time. But actually, we're all dying from the moment we are born. As soon as we let out that new born wail, our death date in the future is set and inevitable.

Mine is approaching a little faster than everyone else's, that's all. What's twenty years in the life of the universe? A fraction of the blink of an eye. Emm's time will eventually come and so will Lily's.

Dear, sweet Lily, how will you get on without me? I try to see your future life unfold and all that I won't share with you. Your eighteenth birthday. Celebrating your 'A' levels. Driving you down to your hall of residence on the first day of uni. Noticing how much you've changed when you come back to visit at Christmas. Introducing you to Keats and arguing with you that Great Expectations really *is* the greatest novel ever written. Picking out a little hatchback for you from the classifieds, checking the colour of the oil on the dipstick, and the tread on the tyres before knocking him down by fifty quid.

Then the day that all fathers of daughters, particularly only daughters, dread most of all; the day you introduce me to the ungainly young man with the bad complexion who shakes my hand as I size him up, asking him questions about his prospects, while you interrupt, saying, "Dad, don't be so rude."

Then, when you get your heart broken, I won't be there to pick you up in the rain and lend you my shoulder to cry on. Or my arm to lean on as you walk down the aisle. I won't be there to fuss over and marvel at the wrinkled little alien with an oversized, misshapen head in the maternity ward, declaring what a handsome chap he is and that he takes after your mother!

I'll miss the Christmases you'll all spend together at our house, the walks over the Malvern Hills on Boxing Day. Up past St. Anne's Well and on to the top of the Worcestershire Beacon where you'll sit, sheltering your children from the wind that is howling up from across the plains of Herefordshire and the Black Mountains of Wales beyond.

You'll point down to little Malvern Link below, and, like my own father before you from the top of the Lickey Hills, tell them that if they squint their eyes and look very hard, they can just see our house from up there.

Like mine, your father will be just a memory by the time you have children of your own. Be happy in the security of your childhood. It won't last long. The time for childish pleasures will soon pass. For youth, all is vanity. But enjoyment will give way to work and responsibility and then to resignation and hard truths and finally pain and letting go.

From birthday parties, to wedding invitations, to funeral announcements. The natural direction of life. In the same song, Johnny Cash went on to say: *"Everyone I know, goes away in the end."*

The Dalai Lama was once asked what he was meditating on. He said he was preparing to leave his body. He was actually *practising* it, so that when that moment came, it would be familiar and he wouldn't be frightened.

Why is it only in the West that death is such a taboo subject? Why can't we look at it, study it, prepare for it? Why do we wait until the frightening stage, until we look over the edge? The endgame for a human being can be an agonising, messy and ugly business.

I think the *process* of death is more frightening than death itself. Lying in a hospital bed, being subjected to painful, futile attempts to prolong life for a few more hours. It's terminal illness, life support machines, and punishing medication regimes that we should be afraid of, not the relief and blessing of death.

So why does death hold so much fear for us? We are frightened of it because we think it's the end and there is nothing more. We see our body as us, and therefore, when *it* dies, we think *we* die. *That's* why we don't want to think about death. All our lives, we have invested in the temporary: our youth, our appearance, our health, our possessions, our loved ones, and ultimately, our own life.

We spend billions on insurance and health and beauty products to try and protect this transient happiness. And it's because we are so attached to this temporary body that we are frightened. But really, death itself is no scarier than being born.

In fact, the two are inseparable. The seed or fruit has to die and fall from the main plant or tree into the ground before it can germinate and start up a whole lot of new life. As the leaves drop dead from the trees in autumn, it's just as certain that new ones will grow back in spring.

Indeed, sometimes the whole tree has to die and fall, which creates new light on the forest floor, to allow the new trees to come up. The one thing cannot happen without the other. Birth follows death just as certainly as death follows birth. Some cultures refer to this as 'the circle of life'. Material decay is a necessary part of this circle. But the life force that animates this matter, does not decay. It is eternal and ageless.

But this prompts an important question: if I am a spiritual being who belongs in the spiritual world, what am I doing *here* in the material world, inhabiting this material body that is causing me so much distress and pain?

Well, I think the answer is, we are put on this earth to teach us an important lesson. We try to enjoy, apart from our spiritual source, but ultimately learn that we can't. We'll never be happy like this because in this world, nothing lasts. This body of matter will die.

And when those that we love are taken away, it is distressing and breaks our hearts. We have a great capacity for love. We feel it naturally. It's our instinct. As if we are programmed to love. Our love for each other, it seems to me, is just a manifestation of the innate love we have for God, which we no longer know how to express.

We have been trying for so long to enjoy separately from him. We find it hard to ask him to accept us back.

Sophisticated western people particularly, have a problem with pride. They find it hard to get down on their knees. You see it in church. Half the congregation are uncomfortable with it, not knowing what to do. They just remain sitting during the prayer. Some find it hard even to just bow their heads.

I've done it myself at family weddings and funerals, crippled with self-consciousness and pride. We have lost the art of humility and opening ourselves up to something greater and more 'unknowable' than ourselves. 'Surrender' for us has connotations of 'losing' and 'defeat', and we don't like it.

Hindus and Muslims find it so easy to prostrate themselves on the floor before God. For them, surrender is to *win.* They recognise how small and insignificant they are and how little they know, and willingly surrender to the truly supreme, the creator of all things, and to know their place before him.

And they can do this because they *practise.* They get down on their knees and pray several times a day. They fast for long periods, during

Ramadam for example or Janmashtami. Where is the 'practice' of religion in the West? It has almost died out.

Do most people even realise why breakfast is called breakfast? It was the first meal you ate after a period of fasting, such as Lent. You would 'break your fast' with that first meal of the day. We have lost all knowledge of these things. That is why we don't know how to believe any more, and our lives are poorer for it.

As anyone who sincerely engages in religious practice will testify, it introduces them to a transcendence that gives meaning to their lives. We will never understand this unless we actually *try* engaging ourselves; unless we actually get in the car and try to drive it. It's an *experiential* thing, not an *intellectual* one. You understand it by *doing it*. Non-believers may offer very clever, intellectual arguments, but have they ever actually tried engaging with God themselves? What have they got to lose? What have any of us got to lose?

Just more of the same. Existence is suffering. All religions say that. All of us will come to realise that eventually. No matter how happy and content our life may seem at the moment, we will all eventually suffer, and these material bodies are our chief source of suffering.

You will get old and you will get sick and you will lose the ones you love.

So how do we begin? How do *we*, the unpractised, find a starting point? Well, just by improving our behaviour is a start. Trying to live a more compassionate life, finding time for some loving kindness and charity for those less fortunate than ourselves, can often be the spark that re-ignites our spiritual flame.

There's a line at the end of the final song of the musical 'Bugsy'. It goes something like this: "*You give a little love, and it all comes back to you.*"

That is so true. Just try it for yourself. Do something good for someone else today. And do it unconditionally, not for your own selfish reasons, but sincerely and humbly, purely for the benefit of the other person, with nothing to gain from it yourself.

You will be amazed at how that love comes back to you, often in ways you just didn't expect. Read *A Christmas Carol* and share in Ebenezer Scrooge's joy at the end. The giver always gets more pleasure than the receiver. Giving is a Godly quality and when we do it, we feel his pleasure in our hearts. This is the beginning of our understanding.

He communicates with us through our *hearts*, not through our intellect or our dumb senses. Just read the words to that beautiful hymn, 'Dear Lord And Father Of Mankind' to see that truth so eloquently expressed: *"Let sense be dumb, let flesh retire.... O still, small voice of calm."*

Lying on my back, still drenched in sweat, I try to manoeuvre myself to lie on my side for more comfort. It's a mistake as I am consumed by that awful crackly cough which feels like flames in my chest. An unbearable pain which frightens me into lying still, together with a wish not to disturb Emm.

I glance at the clock, it's twenty minutes to four. What a state I'm in. Why has it come to this? What wrongs have I committed to deserve this? I really wouldn't wish this on my worst enemy. In my desperation I say out loud a clumsy attempt at a prayer.

"Dear God, if you are there, if you exist, please hear me. I am in pain and I admit I am afraid. Please give me the strength and courage to fight this. If you are there, please stay near, please protect me, please don't leave me, I need you now. Amen."

I lie still to let the urge to cough abate. I do believe he spoke to me twice before, once in my dream in the children's hospital, and once in the dormitory in the temple in Florence. The same God. There is only one, despite the different names different people of the world have for him.

I wait for a sign. For anything. A thought comes into my head. What would my life be like now, if I wasn't sick? I'd be down the pub every night, wasting my life away like I had done for the twenty or so years before the sickness took that pleasure away from me. Yes I'd still be trying to enjoy, or forget, by drinking until that little switch in my brain clicked off, and I no longer cared about anything. The sort of oblivion sought by millions every day. My end of life would seem so remote and far off, that I wouldn't give it a moment's thought, I'd just carry on trying to enjoy ... fruitlessly. What would I have achieved from a life like that? My time on this earth would have been a complete waste. I would have learnt nothing.

Is that what I want? At least through my suffering, I am being *forced* to face up to the truth. The illness has slowly taken away all of those material pleasures, one by one. Pleasures that would never have satisfied me but would have distracted me from my purpose in life.

Then suddenly, in this moment of clarity, he speaks to me: Of course! This Parkinson's is not a curse, it's a *blessing!*

How could I have ever doubted him? He has always been there for me when I needed him, he is here for me now. He answers my prayers. He is so good to me. Sometimes, his taking away is more loving than his giving. The tears of gratitude for what he's done to me, or rather *for* me start to fill my eyes.

I see how my distress has made me call out to him. It's made me realise I need him. Sometimes God has to crush us with his mercy, to bring us to him, otherwise, we resolutely ignore him and continue to try to enjoy independently.

Sometimes, for the particularly stubborn, he has to take away *everything*, until there is nothing left but him.

God makes us suffer, to help us cry out to him. He doesn't do it out of cruelty but out of pure love and compassion. He knows what's good for us, what we need, and as the loving father that he is, he administers to our needs, cruel as it may seem sometimes. The fire of hardship is often the process by which God purifies the gold of our faith.

Yes, his *taking* can often be kinder than his *giving.*

I make a vow here and now that if I get through this night, I will go to church the first Sunday I feel strong enough. I will work for him. I will give myself to him completely. I am his.

I whisper, "Thank you for this gift of suffering."

The room is silent and still but I feel his presence. I think, "You are so good to me, thank you."

Once again I find that the more I thank him, the more he smiles down on me. Gratitude seems to be the key to my communicating with him. It's as if my gratefulness opens my spiritual eyes.

The tears are now running freely down my cheeks. The sweetest surrender. This time, he totally conquers me with his love. My cup overflows with joy. I open my heart, let him in, then pray to him: "Forgive my foolish ways and my forgetfulness. Please don't let me neglect you ever again."

With him by my side, all my fears for the future just melt away. I know we'll face it together. He won't leave me. I am not alone. I'll never have to be afraid of the dark again or cling to this failing, unreliable body for security. Never again will it enslave me and chain me to fear.

What did the vicar say at my dad's funeral? "Even in the midst of life, we are in death." I never understood those words until now.

Dad, I wish I'd been there when you died. There was something I needed to tell you.

Father's Day

Mum's bath tap used to drip when I was a boy. It still drips now. *Tick ... tick ... tick ...* like the sound of the second hand on an expensive Swiss watch. The drip has created a brown stain in the bath where it has worn away the enamel. Like a river cuts out a canyon, or a glacier grinds out a valley. *Tick ... tick ... tick ...*, marking out time.

Counting seconds and the passing of ages.

Outside, the garden has grown in my absence; the weeds as well as the flowers. Jeremy Potts didn't live up to his mother's expectations. He didn't become a doctor. In fact, he never even made it to university. He got expelled from the grammar school for smoking marijuana and ended up working on the production line at Longbridge for thirty years, until he was made redundant ten years ago.

Wayne Brooks' life of petty crime has seen him in and out of Winson Green prison.

As for Doreen Drysdale, she's huge. I was going to say she looks like Pat Butcher out of Eastenders. But on second thoughts, she looks more like *Frank* Butcher. As they say up north, "She must have flattened some grass in her time."

Graham hasn't turned out too bad. He still smokes sixty fags a day and looks like a shadow of his former hearty self, with the most terrible hacking cough, but he has a steady job and stayed out of trouble.

He works for a tool hire company, hiring out anything from cement mixers to chainsaws and belt sanders. He counts the tools out and he counts them back in. They all have their place in the tool shop. He's even painted their outline on the wall where they hang, so if something is missing, he'll notice.

Still counting and organising, as if to compensate for the chaos and lack of order in his childhood home life.

Mum still lives in the same Bournville Village Trust house. She appreciates her little rented home now. She waters and feeds her lawn every day, so that it is now the greenest on the road and she doesn't need to covet from over the fence any more.

Rob never found his good looking, rich mute and is the only one of us who never married.

The molly lived to the ripe old age of eighteen, about a hundred and eight in goldfish years and in all that time was perfectly happy swimming round and round.

After the demise of *Crossroads* in 1988, they tried to revive the show between 2001-3. But it wasn't the same. It was a mistake to kill off Jill, murdered by the treacherous Adam Chance, after only a few months into the run. The viewers never forgave them for it and the show was finally laid to rest on Friday 30th May, 2003.

Vera's husband died shortly after Dad. Then twelve years ago, she developed Alzheimer's. She had to go into a home when she couldn't cope on her own at her old gnome-flanked house. She would run away from the care home in the middle of the night and find her way back to Weoley Castle.

Friends often found her wandering around the parade of shops in The Square in the early hours of the morning in her night dress, slippers and mink coat.

"That's funny," she'd say, "Where's the wet-fish shop gone?"

One of those snippets of useless information that I like so much, claims that about ninety percent of the world's population live their entire lives within a twenty-mile radius of where they were born. Like house sparrows that seldom fly far from their birthplace, often making their own adult nests in the same or the neighbouring garden.

I see no reason to doubt it. Vera died two years ago and was buried in Lodge Hill Cemetery, a stone's throw from her beloved Weoley Castle.

This particular sparrow also flew home. When the acting career didn't work out, wearing shoes that were too big for me, it seemed to be fate that I should return to the Midlands and do a job more my own size. That's when I retrained as a teacher and I became thoroughly normal, unaware at the time, of the beautiful truth that was still to come.

Today, Mum's got some unexpected visitors. As soon as Emm's parked, Lily jumps out and lets herself in quietly by the back door. Emm follows her and through into the kitchen. I linger in the outhouse.

There are shouts of "Surprise!!!" from within followed by laughter. I look through the kitchen door and smile at the three of them enjoying themselves. Lily asks if she can go out into the garden.

"Of course you can," I say.

She waits for an answer. "Can I Gran?"

"Of course you can darling."

She brushes past me on her way out.

Mum pours herself and Emm a cup of tea, then asks how things have been.

"Oh you know. Today is particularly hard for Lily. Some days I think it's getting easier, then suddenly out of the blue, I'll find something of his, something quite insignificant that brings it all back. And then I can't stop crying."

She stares into her cup.

"It's silly I know."

Mum puts her hand on Emm's.

"Not at all. I remember how it was with Ed."

The conversation turns to Dad. I learn something about him today that I never knew. Mum tells Emm that he was part of the Allied Landings in southern Italy in 1943. I had no idea. It's something I could have boasted to Jeremy Potts about. But he never spoke about it. Why? I'm learning more about the old man every day.

They carry on chatting, getting on fine without me, so I go back into the outhouse. Most of the family's shoes on the shelves have gone now but Mum still keeps and polishes Dad's size eleven work shoes. The imprints of his feet on the insoles are still clearly visible after all this time.

I look around. The outside toilet door remains pock-marked with dart holes around a perfect circle of unblemished wood where the dartboard used to hang and here and there, are a few surviving scribbled messages in biro and chalk on the brick walls:

> BCFC Trevor Francis
> CS4MM (TLND)
> [true love never dies.]

So what became of Muriel?

Well, I was right. That awkward, willowy frame and self-conscious, unhappy face grew into a beautiful swan. To me, she was always the one. However, she acquired many admirers along the way. She blossomed out of my league and received propositions from the clever, the handsome and those more qualified than myself.

But in the end, she turned her back on them all to marry some total wazzer she'd known since she was fifteen.

In a drawer at home, Emm keeps a little faded square of paper that she found at the back of my wallet.

On it is written:

> To my dearest wazzock,
> I am so very sorry.
> Thinking of you now with all my heart.
> M.

She never liked her name: Muriel. She said she thought it was old-fashioned, and so from the day of my dad's funeral, in the same way she anonymously signed her note, I always called her 'M' or Emm.

Barry White was right, she was "my first, my last, my everything".

While she and Mum drink tea and Lily plays in the garden, I drift upstairs for a look in my old room. I lie on my bed and look up at the familiar cracks in the ceiling. I feel such a sense of well-being. I close my eyes and feel like I'm floating in that halfway zone between two worlds. I hear voices, I travel through time......

"I hate you! I hope you die and your eyes pop out, and I wouldn't save you!"

I smile into my pillow as I remember. The bed linen has that familiar scent from my childhood. Smells, more than anything, transport me back. The smell of the chocolate in the air, of the grass on my knees as I get into bed without a bath. The smell of beer and tobacco, as I watch the glow from the end of Dad's cigarette in the darkness while he sits on the end of the bed, watching over me until I fall asleep after a bad dream.

There's a burst of laughter from below. I can hear more voices: Mum and Emm. They are watching Lily from the kitchen while she sings Lady Gaga in the back garden.

Mum says, "She's getting over it already. The young are very resilient aren't they?"

Emm replies, "Yes, but she's thinking of him. You know, she still made a card for him for today and put it on the mantelshelf."

Unaware they are talking about her, Lily continues to sing, *"I can't believe how you looked at me with your Johnnie Walker eyes..."*

Songs about fathers. Grown up words in the mouth of a child. Thinking thoughts beyond her years.

Before they leave, Lily clomps upstairs in her shoes. The bedroom is empty and her footsteps echo on the floorboards. She stands, looking at my old bed for a moment and shivers despite the summer month.

She opens the curtains and the room is bathed in warm sunshine. Emm's voice can be heard from downstairs in the hallway, "Lily! Come on darling, time to go!"

She looks at my bed for one last time, thinking the same thought that broke my own heart a lifetime before: Dad, you left without saying goodbye. I didn't get the chance to tell you I love you. And isn't that what Father's Day is for?

When she's gone, the bathroom tap continues to drip.